The
Woman
in my
Home

BOOKS BY KERRY FISHER

The
Woman
in my
Home

Kerry Fisher

bookouture

Published by Bookouture in 2022

An imprint of Storyfire Ltd.
Carmelite House
50 Victoria Embankment
London EC4Y 0DZ

www.bookouture.com

ISBN: 978-1-80314-170-1
eBook ISBN: 978-1-80314-169-5

To all the women doing their best, everywhere

PROLOGUE

It's a mystery to me how families survive. I reckon most of us get by with an odd and unpredictable mixture of ferocious love and forgiveness. That, and sweeping uncomfortable truths about each other under the carpet. Even the people who post pictures of kittens and puppies on social media to brighten everyone's day have their own secret set of unpleasant character traits.

Among my relatives, I can always sense trouble brewing at the first ripple in the water, long before an outsider has any inkling that a tempest is on its way. I'm far too kind to provoke the tempest myself, tempting though it sometimes is. But if I wanted to, I know the weak spots, the shady corners, the soft underbelly where I could land an easy strike.

I defy anyone not to sit on the sidelines at a large gathering without wondering about the peculiarities of shared DNA. How we can be so alike, yet also so different, so alien. At the average birthday party/Christmas Day/wedding reception, a couple of people will get into an argument about *what really happened* at an event well over two decades ago, a cross section will roll out a few booze-fuelled home truths and someone will cry because the day hasn't lived up to expectations. And that's just scratching the surface.

There's also the gift that keeps on giving – the fact that a family knows which buttons to press. The 'funny' story trundled out on every occasion that makes one person in the room look a complete idiot, leaving them seething for the rest of the day about the smart retort they failed to deliver. There's also the perennial 'joke' about weight, relationship failures, lack of skills or whatever particular insecurity pokes the bear.

And, most infuriating of all, the assumption that you are still the same person at thirty, forty or fifty as you were at fifteen. The second anyone starts down the road of 'You've always been.../Ever since you were young, you've...' I'm on the alert as, without a doubt, no good is going to come from that conversation. My answer, if only I were brave enough to confront them all, is 'You have no idea who I am now.'

With anyone else, these mean little jabs designed to undermine would be a deal-breaker. No friend of mine would get away with this kind of surreptitious sabotage. But somehow, we learn to push our rage down, smother it with the blanket of the need to keep the family ship on course. I'm the worst offender. I stumble on, clinging to an illusion of unity and hoping to God that I never have to address the landscape of cracks and crevasses that divide my nearest and dearest.

I had assumed that a common enemy would be our silver lining and unite us all. But, actually, I think it's forced us into opposing factions. Not that it's a topic of discussion, of course. God forbid we should voice our feelings out loud and confront the elephant in the room. I've discovered in these situations, there's always one person in the tribe who feels more outraged than the rest, who remembers the details with a fresh fury, as though it all happened yesterday. One standout relative, who, unlike all the others shrugging and waving the water under the bridge, just can't let it go. In my book, the simple rule of families is – or should be – that those bonded by blood can have their 'moments', their faults, their unfathomable ways; they can hurt us, wind us up, often without even saying a word, but when push comes to shove, we should all be on the same team.

Except sometimes, that's harder than it sounds. Now and again, a look, a sigh or a gesture is enough to make me feel like I need to stomp over a few hills in a howling wind before I can be civil again. But I'd like to think we've got each other's backs. That anyone who does us wrong will need to keep their wits about them because they might fall victim to a vengeful side-swipe when they least expect it.

Society makes a big song and dance out of forgiveness. And on the surface, yes, I suppose it's a good thing – accepting that humans make mistakes, do their best and sometimes it doesn't work out. But some people are idiots and take everyone else down with them. I don't find that particularly forgivable. Others hide under an umbrella of false love, pretending they've got your best interests at heart, but all the time they're smoothing and fine-tuning what's best for them.

And that, my friends, deserves retribution.

1

CATH

I wasn't sure why my thirty-two-year-old son, Sandy, suddenly considered himself so much smarter than I was at fifty-seven, but he wasn't making any secret of the fact that he clearly thought my marbles were well and truly on the loose.

'A man you've been seeing for six weeks is moving in? I mean, what do you actually know about him?' A flash of disgust passed over his face as he considered that I might know more about what he was like in bed than anything else.

I wanted to say, 'I haven't been in a serious relationship for twenty-one years, I've worked my fingers to the bone to create a successful business, I never brought men home when you were living here and now I want to have some fun and enjoy myself before it's too late.' There was a huge temptation to add, 'And guess what, I'd even like some sex.'

Instead, I said, 'What do you think I should know? I mean, how is it any different to you meeting Chloe in a nightclub and her practically spending every night here within weeks?'

Sandy picked at some mud on his sleeve. 'But she had her own place. She could always go back home if things didn't work out.'

'Robin has got his own place, it's that his soon-to-be ex-wife is in it at the moment. It's only temporary until she sells it and he gets his half of the money. It's ridiculous him living in a hotel when I'm rattling around here alone.'

As I said the word 'temporary', I felt the weight of a lie. Despite being on this earth long enough to know that my foot was unlikely ever to fit into a glass slipper, I couldn't deny that my stubborn and pragmatic heart flipped every time Robin texted or walked through the door. I'd spent so long thinking about what was right for Sandy, determined that his dad finding just about anyone other than me attractive wouldn't impact on his life in any way, that I'd stuffed my own needs into the deep freezer. And now, I had Robin. He understood me, and had the kindness to think about what I needed. I craved his company.

I hadn't been unhappy in the slightest, perfectly content working all hours and pottering about my home in the evenings, curling up on the sofa with a book or catching up on the business news in *Money Week*. I was never lonely. Or at least, I never allowed myself to consider that it would be nice to come home to a dinner that someone else had prepared, to unload some of the day's small frustrations and share the victories. Now, however, it was as though a door had been opened onto another world, the one that so many people inhabited, where women, even at my age, laughed about their husbands' inability to sort the recycling or complained about their snoring, but always finished off with 'I wouldn't be without him though.'

Sandy was shaking his head. 'What if he moves in and won't move out?'

I was so tempted to start criticising Sandy's wife, who, beyond her ability to make a fabulous beef stroganoff and fold a napkin into a flower shape, fell into the category of people whose talents and charm I'd need a magnifying glass to locate. I wanted Sandy to think beyond himself for a moment, to be pleased for me, in the same way I'd tried to be delighted for him when he announced he was marrying Chloe. I'd repeated to myself, 'If she makes him happy' ad nauseam and smiled my way through many evenings when it felt as though she'd been criticising Sandy under the guise of 'having a bit of a joke'.

I hated being at odds with Sandy, so I stifled that train of thought and said, 'He's just coming to stay here for a bit, no big drama – I'm not signing over half the house or getting him to contribute to the mortgage. I know it's a big adjustment because you haven't been used to me being in a relationship, but give him a chance.'

'Don't you find all that Billy Big Bollocks talk about his property "empire" a bit over the top?'

I laughed. Now we were getting to the crux of the matter. Sandy hated any overt discussion of wealth, detested people talking about cars, holidays and work in all but the broadest sense.

'It's different for him, darling. Apart from the first few years after your dad left me, you've never really wanted for anything – having a pool and a gym at home and being able to go on skiing holidays was the norm for you. You see things differently if you've had to struggle. And as far as I can make out, Robin started with nothing and has pulled himself up by his bootstraps, so I also understand why he is so proud of that.'

'Yeah, I get that, but he's so snobby in the way he talks about people on a "budget" as not being his target clientele.'

I agreed with Sandy on that front. I'd always been absolutely rigid about him being grateful for what he had and never looking down on other people. 'Perhaps he didn't have the benefit of a mum endlessly saying, "It's not what you've got, it's who you are." You'll like him when you get to know him a bit better. Trust my judgement. Please.'

Sandy gave me a hug. 'I don't want to see you get hurt.'

I wasn't sure whether to read that as a genuine concern for my welfare or to interpret it as 'I don't want another man to become more important than me.' I tried to see it as a compliment that Sandy was so interested in my life, but it felt more like proof that equality between the sexes was still several centuries away. His dad seemed to work his way through a series of women closer to Sandy's age than mine and Sandy regularly dismissed that with a casual 'You know what Dad's like.'

Before I could dig any further, the landline rang and, with barely a hello, Mum launched into how she was sure that the neighbours converting their attic into a sitting room for their teenagers had led to mice, rats or squirrels getting into her roof. I gave Sandy a silent kiss on his cheek and mouthed, 'See you soon, love you,' as I waved him out of the door.

As Mum rattled on about the dirty vermin she was convinced had been attracted by the crisps and cake that she had no evidence of lying about next door, I made a promise to myself that my family were going to have to adapt to a new chapter in life. In between organising Rentokil and helping Sandy adjust to the idea that his mother hadn't yet resigned herself to living in a convent, I was going to enjoy every minute of getting to know Robin and no one was going to spoil it for me.

2

REBECCA

I thought the bitterness might choke me. Graham's mum and dad, my in-laws, Marge and Pete, were shivering at the end of the drive, ready to load his suitcases into the boot of their Volvo estate. Lucky Graham off to lick his wounds at their bungalow in Shoreham-by-Sea, a few minutes' walk from the beach, while Marge bustled about bringing him tea and slated his fickle, unforgiving wife.

The kids rushing out to hug them carried a sting of both exclusion and treachery. Maybe one day I'd find some generosity of spirit again, but until then I wouldn't be in a hurry to forget that Marge and Pete had dared to suggest that if I'd been a better wife, we would have ridden the storm of my husband's reckless behaviour. His mum had finished me off with her conviction that having the house repossessed was nothing to do with Graham offering personal guarantees for the loans on the fleet of catering vans he'd bought – 'Make a fortune at festivals during summer'. She'd decided to overlook the reality that for two summers in a row, there hadn't been any festivals and focused instead on the fact that, in her view, I didn't run the household as a tight ship. Then again, she was a woman who considered using a teabag just the once as really pushing the boat out.

They should have been grovelling around in the gravel, ashamed that my children's father had put us in a situation where we could be out on the streets without so much as a discussion. Since it had become apparent we would lose the house, I was the one creeping through to Megan in the night when she was crying about leaving her best mate, Tilly, who lived next door, while Graham snored away like a rhino on happy pills. If I heard Marge say, 'Poor Graham' one more time, there was every chance that I might treat the neighbours to a showdown that they'd still be talking about in ten years' time.

I stopped myself asking Eddie and Megan to come back inside. I wouldn't give Marge and Pete the satisfaction. Instead, I wandered out into our tiny garden where Megan's Wendy house had stood till recently. I loved that little patch of paradise. Graham had laughed at me, chucking seeds in willy-nilly and getting proper excited when something that cost a couple of quid blossomed into a fat display of lupins, marigolds and corn-flowers in the summer. There wasn't much to see yet, apart from a few snowdrops signalling the approach of spring. I'd always associated them with hope before. Not this year.

I sat on the low wall, listening to Graham's footsteps echoing on the stairs inside. I didn't even want to say goodbye. This man that I'd had two children with. The man whose BMW, then Escort, then burger van I'd listened out for, waiting for it to draw up on the drive every evening, the slam of the door to signify my brood was safe under one roof again. And now, because of his stupidity, that roof was being taken away from us. Every last drop of love had drained from our marriage, seeping away gradually, then at an alarming rate over the last few years.

It wasn't – as Marge kept saying – that I expected married

life to be 'a bed of roses'. It was that this man, the person I relied on, had risked everything we had to keep his business afloat without saying a word to me. I could have coped with his business going down the pan, with selling up and renting somewhere. I would have worked evenings, got a bar job, washed up in a pub, anything to hang on to our house. But he didn't tell me, and I didn't get a choice about the next steps for our family.

I turned as he came out of the back door. He stuck his hands in his pockets. 'I'm off now.'

I nodded.

'I know you don't want to hear this, but I'm so sorry.' He stood, waiting for a response.

I wasn't interested in hearing how sorry he was. It was a word that no longer meant anything to me. Sorry used to be something that we said to each other when we really cared about each other's happiness, not the 'I've said sorry, so stop going on about it' that it had become. I didn't care that he regretted what he'd done, I wanted him not to have done it in the first place. Sorry was not a get-out-of-jail-free card.

He shuffled about, coming close to stepping on a little patch where I'd planted poppy seeds. I shouldn't care. I wouldn't see it myself after today. 'Don't tread on my seeds.'

He moved to one side. 'Let me know how the kids are. And if you need anything. I'll come up and see them in the next week or so.'

'And what if I do need anything? Are you going to raid your mum's coin jar?'

Hurt flashed across his face. I couldn't think about him as the defeated dad, who'd sobbed into Eddie's blonde curls as he'd explained that he'd made some 'silly decisions' that meant that we couldn't afford to live in our house any more. I'd wavered then. Wondered if I could concentrate on appreciating the man who'd kicked a football about with Eddie, who'd loved getting back from work early enough to fetch Meg from school. But I couldn't. The years of supporting Graham's latest get-rich-quick scheme, cheerleading when he lost interest as inevitably it was more difficult than he expected, had slowly killed off my ability to love him, to make allowances. That carefree, adventurous side that I'd been attracted to before we had children had forced me to take the dull and dependable role afterwards, to make sure we had something to fall back on when Graham's attention switched to the next glittering opportunity. I'd always put a bit aside to give us some breathing space, money we could use as a cushion to pay the bills and keep the car on the road until he started earning again. But even I had never envisaged that things would get so desperate.

'You know I never meant for it to turn out like this.'

'I don't think you did. But it doesn't take away from the fact that you didn't bother to consider where we'd actually live if you put the house up as a guarantee and you lied to me about how you were getting your hands on the money to buy the vans.'

He hung his head. 'I wanted more for us, Rebecca. I wanted to be a success for you. Buy somewhere bigger, take you on fancy holidays.'

I didn't have the energy to explain again that it wasn't the financial disaster that had finished me off, it was not involving me in the decision-making that had been the last straw. I would have loved a bigger garden and I liked my two weeks on a sunny beach as much as the next person but as long as my family were safe and healthy, I didn't need a lot to be happy.

His shoulders slumped as he walked outside. I didn't want to witness him say goodbye to the kids. Couldn't bear to see Megan dig her little fingers into his back as she clung on for one last hug before our marriage slid into the swamp of decaying dreams. Or Eddie scuffing at the kerb, trying to look like he wasn't about to cry and telling Megan not to be such a baby in a wavering voice. I certainly wasn't going anywhere near his parents, especially not Marge, with her furrowed brow and hand-wringing. I bet she was delighted that her precious son was going to be under her control again. From my point of view, if there was a sliver of a silver lining, it was not having to drive down to theirs for Sunday lunch every other weekend. No more tinned carrots and potatoes ever again.

With a determined step, I locked the back door for the last time and walked through my empty house, ignoring the bright white spaces where the collages of our family photos used to hang. They were cluttering up my sister's garage now, along with some of our furniture, which meant she had to park her car on the road. I stepped outside and slammed the front door. There was a hollow sound as though all our hopes, all the things we'd counted on, had emptied out along with the boxes of our belongings.

I forced myself to call calmly to the kids. 'Eddie, Megan, come on. Time we got over to Auntie Debs.'

Graham walked over with Megan in his arms. 'Bye, bye, darling.' He kissed her head and put her down, then ruffled Eddie's hair. 'See you soon, champ. Love you.'

He got into his parents' Volvo.

I was afraid to examine my feelings in case the fragile bravery I was forcing out for the children collapsed. Right now, it seemed so much safer to be numb. I'd find a way to start again, I had to. I shuffled the kids into the car, posted the keys through the letter box and drove to my sister's.

Her husband, Jason, was watching out for us. He ran to open the car doors and swung Eddie high. 'Hello! How are you doing? Who wants some ice cream?'

As Eddie seemed to forget that life had changed completely and even Megan found a spring in her step as she followed him in, I had the urge to lean against the bonnet and drift to the floor, murmuring, 'This is all too hard.'

My sister appeared at the door and flung out her arms.

'Don't. Be. Nice. To. Me.' The tears welled anyway.

She hugged me, arching her back so we didn't squash her bump. 'I won't be. Wine? I'll join you with a liquorice tea.'

'Just tea for me too, but proper tea, none of that herbal nonsense. Wine might turn me into a snivelling wreck.'

She whispered, 'Did you see Graham? What about his parents?'

'Yep. I've probably ground my teeth down a good millimetre gritting them.'

'At least you won't have to have her for Christmas any more.'

She led me through to the kitchen and filled the kettle while Jason scooped out ice cream for the kids.

'So how's the babe coming along? Are you knackered?' I said, eager to focus on someone else's news, to stop the panic racing through my veins about the mountain I had to climb before I'd have a half-decent life again.

Debs pulled a face. 'Not too bad. Nearly halfway through at least. Twenty-three weeks to go.'

'It'll go quicker than you think,' I said.

Jason looked up. 'I painted the nursery at the weekend, so it would be good if the kids try not to bang into the door or mark the walls.'

I watched Eddie jiggling about on the stool and managing to flick ice cream over the work surfaces. 'Eddie! Eat that properly. Did you hear what Uncle Jason said about not banging into the walls and doors in your bedroom?'

Eddie looked blank.

Debs frowned at Jason and stepped in. 'Anyway, it's lovely to have you here. Mum lent me some cushions to make a bed up for one of them on the floor and I've got a blow-up mattress for the other. You're on the settee, I'm afraid.'

I slumped onto the bar stool. 'I'm sorry we're crowding in on you when you've got so much going on yourself. I'm not sure what we would have done otherwise. Hopefully it won't be for too long.'

Jason gave Debs what could only be called a 'meaningful' look and judging by her shrug of annoyance reflected a discussion about how long we'd be staying.

A surge of self-pity threatened to overwhelm me. I hated being a burden, detested the thought that at thirty-six, the best I could offer my kids was a makeshift bed on a floor. I excused myself and ran upstairs to the bathroom. I peered into the nursery and my eyes prickled. It looked so lovely. The vision of a couple right at the beginning of parenthood, thinking that a baby would complete them rather than act like a tiny hand grenade to keep them exhausted, scratchy, broke and resentful. I'd probably best keep those uplifting thoughts to myself if I didn't want to find us demoted to a tent on the drive.

I picked up the photo on the landing of Debs and me when we were still at primary school, all tombstone teeth and bunches. Mum had an arm around each of us and looked quite glam. Again, I felt that lurch of fury that Mum wasn't in a position to help me, to be a safety net for us all. I'd have given anything for her to say, 'Move in with me, stay as long as you like.' Somewhere I could find a temporary haven with Megan and Eddie, without watching every week of my sister's pregnancy tick away, wondering where we'd end up in five months' time once the baby arrived and we had to sling our hook.

I stroked the primrose-yellow walls, my fingers tracing the shape of the sailing ships stencilled below some hooks. I didn't want to consider how many grubby fingerprints might complete the décor in a couple of months' time. I tried not to imagine the thousands of other ways Eddie might exhaust their goodwill: throwing a tennis ball against the kitchen wall, knocking over his squash at nearly every meal and failing ever to have a bath without a serious mop-up session.

Thank goodness my dad wasn't alive to see my mum living

in her rented room with all the joy sucked out of her. Though when I dared to pick over ancient history, she'd get quite animated, belligerent even. I wanted to be sympathetic, but every time I walked into her bedsit, crowded with too much furniture from our old house and Mum all long-faced on a settee that we had to squeeze past to get in the door, I almost despised her for her helplessness. Now and again, I'd try to talk to Debs about it, but she'd either change the subject or walk away.

Both of them, Debs and Mum, were so defeatist. I'd said as much to Debs one evening before she was pregnant but just after I'd realised that it was highly likely that Graham's 'investments' were going to go belly up. We'd been experimenting with cocktails and on the back of a few tequila slammers and the dregs of a bottle of Christmas Cointreau, she'd told me that my expectations of life were too high.

Her words had cut deep with the stab of injustice. I didn't see anything wrong with expecting a lot from life. It wasn't as though I wanted to live in a mansion or race about in a Ferrari. I simply wanted to wake up without the gnawing fear about how we'd pay the mortgage if Graham's brilliant ideas hit the buffers again. It didn't make me a bad person, though it probably increased my impatience with Mum sitting in her grotty little room, lacking in the oomph to find a place to live that didn't have takeaway rice littered up the stairs. 'I know Mum's had some bad luck,' I'd said, translating that into 'made some bad choices' in my head. 'But she's only fifty-nine. She turned that promotion down at the garage because she "didn't want the responsibility" at her age. I reckon she's pinning all her hopes on finding love among the screen wash rather than pulling her finger out and making it happen for herself.'

Debs always took Mum's side. 'But what's the point in going on about it? That's just the way she is. It's generational. She doesn't feel right without a man around.'

That one sentence summed up the undoing of so many women. I'd never again put myself in the position where a man could pull the rug from under my feet and reduce me to throwing myself on other people's mercy to keep my kids safe.

3

REBECCA

Once I'd got the children off to school on the following Monday, I went straight into town, walking into shops and offices and asking about vacancies, trudging through the drizzle and becoming more and more despondent as the day went on – 'anything at all... cleaning, office work, general dogsbody'. I received one of two responses – a blank and offhand 'there's nothing going at the moment' as though being desperate for a job would somehow make me less good at it, or the head tilt of pity – 'I'm so sorry, we don't have any vacancies at the moment, but if you'd like to leave your details...' The result was the same though. I was no further forward. My flimsy financial planning relied on the bank getting a better price than expected for our house when it was auctioned off and there being something left over once all the debts had been paid.

It was the first day of March, but spring still seemed worlds away. I pulled my hood up, but nothing was a barrier to the persistent damp. The trouble with losing everything was that the day-to-day worries didn't evaporate, they were still scrabbling away in the background, biding their time to spurt to the surface if there was ever a dull moment. Eddie was falling

behind at school. It was hard to make learning to spell 'accommodation' top of my priority list when actually finding some
accommodation was so pressing. Being penniless didn't mean
that Megan didn't care when her best friend wouldn't sit with
her at lunch. It just meant that I had to work doubly hard to give
her a big hug rather than snapping, 'Go and find someone else
to sit with!'

I couldn't face going into another reception where someone
young, someone whose roots didn't need doing, someone who
could afford to go out for a drink after work would barely
manage to glance up from their phone to tell me that today
wasn't my lucky day. I had a bit of time to kill before I picked up
the kids, so I drove away from the big industrial units of the
town centre, into the avenues on the outskirts. The roads gradually became more tree-lined, and the terraced houses gave way
to detached homes with huge gardens and oak-framed garages.

I parked up and wandered into Hetherington Close, one of
my favourite streets for peering through the fences at the luxury
houses, outdoor sculpture and flower beds that wouldn't have
looked out of place on *Gardeners' World*. I particularly loved
the area at night when the lights were on and you could see into
some of the kitchens with families gathered around a big central
table. So many people had benches rather than chairs. If I had
their sort of money, I wouldn't be spending it sitting on a hard
wooden bench that relied on everyone agreeing how close to the
table they wanted to be. Eddie and Megan could argue about
who'd seen a fly first.

I stopped by the house with the elaborate metal fencing,
tracing the insets of flowers with my fingers. It must be
wonderful to be so wealthy that you could afford to splash out
on designer gates that were really pretty rather than just func-
tional enough to stop the dog and kids running onto the road. As
I was putting my eye up to the dandelion cut-out to see if there
were any new sculptures in the garden, the gates started to slide

back. An elderly lady was hauling a wheelie bin down the
sloping drive. She didn't look too steady on her feet, tentative, as
though she might slip in the wet. She ground to a halt halfway.

'Do you want a hand with that?' I asked. She did that thing
that rich people do, the split-second pause to weigh up if you're
a threat. I must have passed 'the nearly-middle-aged woman
with a friendly face and her own handbag therefore not looking
to steal one' test.

In a voice that was less calling for the butler and more
shouting about the latest cleaning products on the Friday
market than I expected, she pulled her hat down firmly over her
ears and said, 'Oh bless you, duck. I've come over a bit dizzy.
I'm getting too old for dragging these bins about. Turning into a
right old crock.'

I walked up to the woman and took hold of the recycling
bin. 'Let me help you.'

She waved her hand. 'I don't usually do the bins, but my
daughter asked me to put them out as she won't be back till late.
She works ever so hard.'

'I bet she's really grateful for the help.'

'I do all her cleaning. Truth be told, it's too much for me
now. Don't have so much energy and it's a big old place. Lord
knows why she needs so much space. Till the last few months,
she's been rattling around all by herself. I can hardly keep up
with my own house, but I don't want to let her down. And now
she's got this fella on the scene... she's even busier than normal.'
She tucked her scarf further into her coat. 'Bit miserable today,
isn't it?'

I squashed down the flash of envy that this woman's
daughter had a whole house to herself. And someone on tap to
clean it for her. I stepped forward. 'Can I help you back inside?'

She shook her head. 'No, I'm off home shortly. I'll have a sit
down in the bus shelter.'

'Is it a long journey?'

'No, just down by the park, but I'm not keen on walking in this weather and I don't drive.'

'I've got my car round the corner. I could drop you if you like, save you getting soaked through?' I wasn't quite sure why I felt the need to add, 'I'm not a weirdo or anything.' Probably because I'd think twice about hopping into a car with any old bod that crossed my path.

The woman didn't acknowledge what I'd said, but she did glance up at the darkening sky, hovering between accepting, not wanting to be a nuisance and not trusting me. 'Do you live near here?' she asked.

'I'm living with my sister at the moment, long story. She's got a house on that little estate they've built down by the railway, but my kids are at school on this side of town. St John's.'

At the mention of children, she perked up. 'How old are they?'

'My youngest, Eddie, is seven, and my oldest, Megan, is nine. Chalk and cheese they are.'

'I never had a boy. I'd have liked one, but it never happened for me. I only had the one, Cath. She was a good girl, loved her schooling. Always had her nose in a book. She's done ever so well. Got her own business.'

'That's brilliant. You must be very proud of her.' I tried to keep my voice steady, to stop the hurt creeping in that my mother, who had always sung the praises of my 'lovely little family', had more or less rocked in a corner and said she 'simply couldn't bear it' when I'd told her that Graham and I were bankrupt and splitting up. Luckily for her, she had Debs and Jason ready to slip into the slot of the 'lovely little family' when their baby was born.

'I am proud of her. She slogged away – single mum she was – her husband was one of those, always off with other women, never had any money to give her for Sandy, her boy. But she wouldn't accept any help from me, though she did live with me for a bit. Such a stubborn girl. She worked all hours, and finally set up on her own. Recruitment. I don't know how she finds the people... they're these important boss types, you know, the top ones, and as far as I understand, she gets them new jobs and somehow gets paid for that.'

'I could do with someone like that to help me find a job. Though not as high level as that.'

'What do you do?'

'I've done a bit of everything really. Shop assistant, garden centre work, carer in an old people's home. I can't afford after-school care for the kids, so I'm tied to a school day. Cleaning work probably, preferably in a private house where it doesn't matter if I'm a bit late starting as long as I do the right hours,' I said.

'What about their dad? Can he help? Surely he should be taking some responsibility?'

I smiled to myself. I couldn't wait to be old so I could be really nosey and ask whatever questions I wanted without even realising the other person might think I was rude. 'We've recently split up, unfortunately, and he's gone to live in Shoreham-by-Sea with his parents.'

The old lady frowned and clicked her tongue. I had enough with my mother's disapproval without inviting a stranger to pile in.

'Anyway, if you don't want a lift, I'd better let you get out of the rain.' I didn't want to leave her there, but I couldn't be late for the children.

She put out a hand and patted my arm, her skin mottled and paper-thin against mine. 'It's kind of you, but my daughter would be so furious. She says I'm far too trusting and that I'll end up in a ditch with my throat slit, gets cross with me talking to anyone and everyone. But that's what makes the world go round, doesn't it?'

I smiled. 'It's been nice meeting you. I'm Rebecca, by the way.'

'Dolly. Well, Doris, but everyone calls me Dolly.'

'Like the musical?'

And it was as though I'd flicked a switch. She sang a few lines of 'Hello, Dolly!', her bony hands swaying, then stopped abruptly. 'I'm amazed a whippersnapper like you has even heard of it.'

'You're kidding! My nan's favourite film. Must have seen it ten times. Never was a Christmas without *Hello, Dolly!*'

Dolly looked at her watch. 'Don't suppose you could still drop me home, could you? I've just missed the two-forty-five bus and the next one's not for another forty minutes. My little dog, Alfie, will be crossing his legs.'

I stifled the irritation that I was now going to be tight for time. 'You'd better call your daughter on the way and let her know I'm taking you.'

'I forgot to charge my mobile. Cath gets so annoyed with me.' Dolly looked as though she was having second thoughts.

'That's okay. You can use mine.' And I shot off to fetch the car before she could faff about any more.

I insisted Dolly rang her daughter. 'I'll put it on speaker for you so that she can talk to me and reassure herself I haven't kidnapped you.'

Dolly stared at the phone. 'Can you put the numbers in for me? I haven't got my glasses.'

I stabbed at the numbers and set off. A posh-sounding assistant answered and sighed slightly as Dolly asked to be put through.

Cath came on the phone – 'Mum? Are you all right?' – as though the only reason Dolly ever made contact was to report a problem.

Dolly said, 'I wanted to tell you that a nice lady helped me with the bins. She's driving me home because I came over a bit dizzy, and it's tipping it down.'

'Are you okay though? Is it someone you know?' Cath sounded a mixture of concerned and impatient.

'She's called Rebecca. I only met her today, but she's very kind. She's here right next to me. She's put the telephone on that microphone thing so you can hear her.'

'Loudspeaker. Hello? Rebecca? Thank you for taking Mum home. Was there a problem?'

'No, not really, I just saw your mum struggling. I didn't want her to have a fall in the wet. I'll see she gets in all right.'

'Thank you, that's very kind.' Despite her words, she sounded a bit harassed, as though we'd interrupted her in the middle of something or – I suspected – Dolly was in the habit of calling her at work over trivial things. Cath said, 'If you're sure you're all right, Mum, I'll call you a bit later.'

Dolly ignored the get-off-the-line signals from Cath and said, 'Do you want to come round for your tea? I've got some nice ham that wants eating up.'

'I can't tonight, Mum. Sorry.'

Cath sounded tetchy in the way I recognised that I was with my own mother, always feeling as though I was never doing enough, stretched too thinly for all the people who wanted a chunk of me and, at the same time, cross with myself for not living up to other people's expectations.

She rang off with Dolly muttering about how Cath ate all the wrong things, needed to watch her weight now she was on the wrong side of the menopause, followed by a diatribe about how young people never even take a packed lunch to work any more and waste a fortune on buying sandwiches and coffee. 'And the size of the coffees! Everywhere you go, they give you a bucket. If I drank that, I'd be rushing to the loo all day.'

I drew up outside a little terraced house with a front garden jam-packed with hellebores, crocuses and an overgrown tangle of rosebushes. 'I bet this is absolutely stunning in summer.'

'Ah, it's only tiny, but it runs away with me. I can't get on my steps any more to clip everything back. That new fella of Cath's said he'd get it sorted for me, but he's another one who works all hours.'

'What is it he does?'

'Something in a foreign country, you know, those places where they have one pool where all the houses share. Always flying off to Spain. I've only met him once or twice.'

'Would you like me to come over one day and help you? I love gardening.'

The relief on Dolly's face made my heart leap. 'Would you? I can pay you.'

'We'll talk about that another time,' I said, though I couldn't afford to do anything for free. I pulled out a pen to write down her phone number.

She paused at her front door. 'I can manage now, thank you so much.'

I hovered, aware of my promise to Cath to see her in. I didn't want her to think I couldn't be trusted. Dolly hesitated, then unlocked the door with fumbling slowness before slipping inside, but not before I'd seen the chaos of newspapers piled up in the hallway.

Time was ticking on, so I brushed off Dolly's thanks with a promise to call and sped off to pick up the children, feeling better than I had in ages. I didn't want to milk the old lady for money, but if I could do a bit of gardening, it would earn me a few quid and do her a favour into the bargain. Perhaps my luck was turning.

An image of my dad flashed into my mind, the day we moved into our house and my mum showed us into the garden with a little tree house and a slide. 'Aren't we lucky?' she'd said.

My dad had swung me high onto his shoulders and laughed. 'You make your own luck.'

I remembered having some vague idea of a luck-making machine and wondering out loud how to get one.

Dad had kissed me on the nose. 'Hard work can make you lucky.'

I went for weeks without thinking about him now. But then a memory would fly in and my longing for him would cause a physical ache in my chest. I was so glad he wasn't around to see what had happened to my 'lovely little family'.

4

CATH

Six weeks after he'd first moved in, the novelty of watching Robin sleep while I crept about getting ready for work hadn't worn off. I wished Sandy could see what I saw. He either didn't mention Robin at all, as though he hoped by ignoring him, he'd fade away, or he'd ask questions such as 'What exactly does he do in Spain? Why doesn't he invite you out there?'

Slowly, his questions got to me. Like the insidious earworm of a cheesy song you never wanted to hear again, I started to wonder why Robin hadn't suggested that I accompanied him on a trip, given that he said he missed me so much when he was away. When I finally broached it, his face lit up. 'Let me know when you can get some holiday and we'll make it happen. Though you might have to amuse yourself while I have some boring meetings with the engineers and the council planning department.'

Just like that, the doubts Sandy had sown in my mind dissipated. When he rang one dinnertime, I couldn't keep the smugness out of my voice when I told him that I was intending to join Robin in Spain in late May.

'Can I house-sit while you're away?' he asked.

'That would be great – would you and Chloe water my houseplants? Mum often forgets. And if I could show you how to top up the chemicals in the pool, that would save me having to arrange a key for the maintenance guy.'

'It would only be me, Mum. Staying at yours would make the commute to work too long for Chloe.'

'Won't she mind?'

Sandy did the laugh that made him sound like his father, a brittle guttural noise that had nothing to do with fun or enjoyment. 'I think she'd be quite pleased.'

'Is everything all right?' I crossed my fingers for a yes because, selfishly, I was hoping to have some evenings with nothing more pressing than sitting outside in the sunshine with Robin. I never thought that life would hold this for me again, but I felt an urge to touch him all the time, to understand every little detail about him. It was a totally different feeling from when I'd fallen in love at twenty-two with Sandy's dad, Andrew. Then, I'd gone with the flow, not bothering about whether we had the same attitudes to money, to work, to children. But so many things about Robin – how driven he was, his beautiful manners, his generous attitude to money – were huge ticks on my life's checklist.

Sandy paused. The words came out in a rush of sadness. 'We're splitting up. She's got someone else.'

'Oh sweetheart. How long have you known?'

While my poor boy spilled out his humiliation, I watched the salmon in watercress sauce that Robin had cooked for me as a special treat congeal on the plate. I tried to catch his eye and apologise, but he took his dinner through to the sun lounge.

After I'd got the worst of the detail, Sandy said, 'Actually, Mum, can I come back to live at home until we sell our house? I can't bear hearing her get in at one in the morning, knowing that she's been with lover boy. Or not coming back at all.'

To my shame, I hesitated for a moment while I wondered

how Robin would react, before saying, 'Of course, you're always welcome,' trying to imagine supporting Sandy and continuing to forge a relationship with Robin under the same roof. 'Obviously, Robin is living here at the moment.'

'But that's just until he gets the money through from his divorce, isn't it?'

I already felt the dread of being piggy in the middle.

'I'm taking it one day at a time, darling. Seeing what happens.'

Sandy grunted. I wasn't sure whether his irritation that I was in a relationship was a hangover from growing up with me always available and not having to compete for my attention, an innate rejection of his mother as a sexual being or simply an assumption that I'd be overjoyed to have my son back at home.

The truth was, I'd slipped into the rhythm of Robin working in my study when he was in the country. When I could, I'd snatch half an hour at home with him on my way back from meetings, a half an hour that sometimes involved me arriving back at work red-cheeked and flustered and unable to concentrate on contracts for the rest of the day. I had a lightness in my step, a place my mind could take me that felt free and full of promise. The future looked less like a slog through finding opportunities for men whose entire self-worth appeared to centre around company car policy and more like one of possibility, a stepping out into a bright dawn after a long winter.

I rang off, praying that the two people I loved most in the world wouldn't pit themselves against each other. Judging by the way in which Robin said, 'Since when did everyone expect to be happy all the time? If another person who works for me says they're not feeling that great "mentally", I'm going to give up property development and buy shares in the Priory' – he would expect Sandy to brush off a failed marriage and bounce back. I also suspected Sandy's laid-back attitude might be anathema to a man who often got up in the middle of the night to make notes about a business idea or to send emails to his site managers in Spain.

I wandered into the next room, stunned that Sandy's life had imploded. Robin sat scrolling on his phone. He didn't look up immediately.

'So sorry about dinner. I'll go and get mine now. It was just—'

He didn't quite slam his phone down, but there was no mistaking his irritation. 'Why didn't you say you'd call him back?'

A little sting of anxiety flared, alongside something resentful at being told what I could do in my own home. Maybe I'd had too many years as a boss and had become used to deference or perhaps I'd forgotten about the compromise required in a relationship.

I prided myself on being a woman who didn't immediately back down because someone else thought they had the monopoly on a bad temper. I said, 'Sorry, I know you made the effort to cook for me and usually I would have called Sandy back, but he was in a bit of a state as he's splitting up with his wife. I didn't want to say, "Sorry your life is going up the spout, but can it wait until I've eaten my salmon?".'

Robin jumped up. 'Oh, that's terrible. Poor Sandy. And poor you.' He hugged me. 'Sorry for being grumpy. You sit down and I'll fetch your dinner and you can fill me in. Wine?'

I nodded, relieved that we'd got our first spat out of the way without a big drama.

He came back with a tray and a heart drawn on a Post-it note next to my plate. If anyone else had done it, I'd have found it corny. But it made me smile despite myself.

He filled up his glass. 'So, what's the story with Sandy?'

I explained what I knew and then said, 'There's a slight fly in the ointment that he wants to move back here until he sorts himself out.'

Robin sat very still. 'What did you say?'

'I said yes, of course.' I laughed. 'Didn't expect to have to keep the noise down from the bedroom at our age, but I'm sure we'll manage.'

'He won't mind me living here?' He sounded defensive, as though I was about to ask him to leave.

'Not at all. There's plenty of room for us all.' I tested the waters, wondering whether I'd ever stop being on my guard. 'I mean, presumably you'll want to buy a place when your house is eventually sold?'

Robin leaned forwards. 'Of course. Maybe you can help me look? I'm hoping the divorce proceedings will gather a bit of momentum soon. Ideally, the house will be on the market by the end of July. I'd like to move in somewhere by November, or Christmas, worst case.'

I felt an odd mixture of relief that he hadn't taken it for granted that he could live in my home indefinitely, coupled with a recognition that I didn't want him to move out. It wasn't like me to get carried away like this. At least Robin intended to include me in his house-hunting plans. I indulged myself in a brief fantasy of choosing a Christmas tree with him. 'I'd really enjoy helping you look. I'm so nosey, I love snooping round people's houses.'

'Nothing too big and I need an easily maintained garden – no lawn to get all overgrown when I'm abroad for a few weeks. And we could have some privacy.'

My fantasies screeched back into reality. 'I know it's not ideal Sandy coming back, but he might patch it up with Chloe, or he might go and rent somewhere. He'll be out at work during the day anyway.'

Robin's face relaxed. 'As long as it won't be too much for you having to deal with him as well as all your other commitments.'

I accepted that his words came from a place of concern,

rather than defaulting to the snarky attitude I'd honed over many years of doing business with alpha men: that I wasn't some delicate flower that would be flattened at the first sign of a storm. 'I'll be fine. Don't worry.'

He squeezed my hand. 'We'll be fine.'

I squeezed back. I was so lucky that fate had brought him to me.

5

CATH

I'd put aside the whole of Tuesday morning to double-check that I had all the printouts I needed before I left that evening for a three-day conference in Amsterdam. At 10.30 a.m., my assistant buzzed through to say Mum was on the line. 'Tell her I'm in a meeting,' I said. 'I'll call her from the cab later on.' I needed to concentrate for a moment without getting diverted by a complaint that her bins hadn't been emptied or she hadn't had a newspaper delivered today. But when she rang my mobile – something she never did for fear of running up a huge phone bill – I resigned myself to losing the next twenty minutes and answered.

'Cath, no need to worry, but I'm on the way to the hospital with Rebecca.'

'What? Are you okay?'

'Sort of. Rebecca was here cutting my lawn; thank goodness she was. I was coming outside and Alfie saw next door's cat and dashed in front of me and I tripped over him. I'm hoping I've just twisted my ankle, but Rebecca thought I'd better get it checked out at A&E.'

'Mum! That dog. He'll be the death of you. Does it hurt?' Fear that she was really injured made me snappy.

'I can't seem to put much weight on it. I'm sure it's nothing. I wouldn't trouble the doctors, but Rebecca says it might be broken.'

'I'm supposed to be leaving for Amsterdam tonight.' My mind was racing. I was speaking at ten o'clock tomorrow morning. It would be cutting it horribly fine to catch the 6 a.m. flight the next day.

'Don't worry. I'll manage, darling.' But her voice was tight with pain.

I resigned myself to the fact that I wouldn't be going or, if by some miracle I did manage to make my plane, I'd be frazzled to a crisp of stress. I said, 'Which A&E are you going to? I'll meet you there.'

Rebecca said something I didn't catch in the background.

'I'll pass you over,' Mum said.

'Hello there, I'm very happy to go to the hospital with your mum. Really. There's no point in you wasting time waiting around. I'd planned to be at your mum's all day anyway. I'll keep you posted.'

I felt a rush of relief, mixed with worry and guilt. If I was totally honest, I was also selfishly disappointed at the prospect of missing out on this trip. I didn't think I'd ever get over the kick of swanning into the frequent-flyer lounge and helping myself to a glass of champagne. I still felt like an imposter, as though someone was going to clap their hand on my shoulder and say, 'This lounge is only for people who went to private school and university.'

'If her ankle's broken, she can't stay in her house on her own.' I wasn't really addressing Rebecca, more ordering my thoughts out loud, my mind flicking to whether I'd be able to find an emergency carer by this evening.

'I'll ring you as soon as we know something.'

I realised with a flash of remorse that, in the couple of months Rebecca had been helping Mum, I'd relied on her to pick up quite a few of the pieces of Mum's life that were usually down to me.

So, five hours later, vacillating between the conviction that I should cancel and the selfish hope that I could still go, Mum was struggling into my house on crutches with her foot in a big boot. Rebecca followed with her handbag. She wasn't as old as I'd expected from her voice. I'd envisaged a sturdy woman in her forties, the type that had a large leather wallet with a zip-up pocket of change, who'd hold up a queue in the supermarket fishing out the exact sum in five and ten pence pieces. Instead, she was on the skinny side of slim, with an elfin face and short spiky brown hair. She radiated a nervous but capable energy in her movements as though she was poised to rush off to find a solution before anyone else had even defined the problem. As she filled me in on what the consultant had said, Mum kept patting her arm and repeating, 'Thank goodness you were there. I'm glad you were listening. I don't remember him saying that.' I told myself it was my own conscience making me feel that Mum was having a pop at me for not dropping everything.

Rebecca smiled. 'I'm not surprised you weren't taking it in. You were in a lot of pain.' She turned to me. 'Your mum is an absolute trooper. Amazing. Didn't make a murmur when they were pulling her ankle about.'

A wave of irritation wrinkled through me that Rebecca assumed that it was news to me that my mother was made of stern stuff.

Mum was putting on a brave face, but I could see she was shaken. 'I didn't think I'd broken it. It wasn't much more than a stumble.'

'Shall I cancel Amsterdam?' I asked.

Mum hesitated. 'But won't you get into trouble? They're all expecting you to speak, aren't they?'

I could hear her reluctance to be left. That wasn't like Mum at all. She was a tough old bird, who never made a fuss.

There was no way I could go. 'Yes, I am supposed to be making a speech tomorrow, but you can't even get to the loo without help. Sod's law that Sandy's working in Manchester for the next few days.'

I was conscious of not looking like a self-centred daughter in front of Rebecca. She was probably one of those women who lived round the corner from her mum and dropped in every day without ever being tempted to pretend she was stuck at work and would finish too late to pop in on her way home. It wasn't a tactic I was proud of, but there were some days when a well-meaning 'You look pale, are you working too hard?' comment had me biting back with something unkind and uncalled for.

Then Rebecca said, 'I'm not sure what you'd think of this as an idea...'

Frankly I was prepared to consider anything right now, with a decision about whether to go or not needing to be made in the next forty-five minutes.

'If you and your mum would feel comfortable, I'm happy to stay here for a few days until you get home. I can go and fetch the dog from Dolly's and bring him back here later on. I'd need to spend a few hours a day with my children over at my sister's, but otherwise I could be around.' She paused. 'Obviously you don't know me, so you'd be letting a stranger stay in your house...'

In normal circumstances, I'd have had my assistant ringing round for references from multiple sources, but it was embarrassing how quickly I threw myself on the mercy of this woman that Mum had met in the street two months ago. All I really knew about her was that Mum thought the sun shone out of her backside and she knew the difference between a dandelion and a daffodil. Who was to say she wouldn't start poking about and pocketing the odd bit of jewellery? Or telling all her friends exactly what sort of alarm we had and making a copy of the keys? On the other hand, it was more than likely that she was a really nice woman who was fond of my mum and was trying to help.

I went with the good Samaritan version. Mum was a pretty decent judge of character and seemed to have taken to her. I felt the tightly coiled spring of stress loosen as a solution began to form, especially when Rebecca said, 'Would you like to have a quick chat together? I'll pop to the loo, if that's okay?'

I pointed her in the direction of the downstairs cloakroom. 'What do you think, Mum? Sandy will be on the end of a phone, as will I. But it's whether you feel comfortable?'

Three-quarters of an hour later, I was rushing out of the door, with Mum telling me not to worry. I was garbling out last-minute instructions to Rebecca to phone me, to not hesitate to get cabs, food deliveries, anything that money could solve without my presence being required.

Anxiety that Rebecca was doubtlessly judging me for abandoning Mum had resulted in me offering her a sum of money that made her gasp. 'Are you sure?'

I found it encouraging that she wasn't grabby and greedy. 'Yes, of course. I'm very grateful to you.'

I rang Robin as the cab headed to Heathrow and told him what had happened. He immediately reassured me. 'It's much better that she's with someone she knows. Perhaps Rebecca could go and stay with her in her house and look after her until she's back on her feet.'

'Mum's only got a bathroom upstairs. She'll have to live with me for the foreseeable future, so she can sleep downstairs in the snug with the shower room next door.' I dropped my voice so the cab driver wouldn't be party to my conversation.

'Full house of family wasn't exactly what we bargained on, was it? First Sandy, now Mum.'

There was silence on the end of the phone. For a second, I thought we'd been cut off. Then Robin said, 'Would you like me to move back to the hotel? You've got so much on. Maybe it's just not the right time for us.' His voice was kind, regretful.

A surge of panic rushed through me. 'I'm sorry. The timing is really bad. I don't want you to move out. I promise that it won't be like this forever. It is chaotic at the moment, though. Please don't think I don't want you there.' I could feel the threat of tears and a burst of childish fury that as soon as I had a chance at a relationship, my family decided to disintegrate.

I heard a commotion in the background. 'I've got to go. I'll ring you later,' he said.

I spent the rest of the journey alternating between despair and anger, though I reminded myself of Rebecca's gasp of gratitude when I offered her money to look after Mum. I told myself off for being so self-pitying. At least I wasn't squashed into a house with my pregnant sister and kids, wondering where I was going to live. Or at least that's what Mum had relayed to me, but I had to admit that I'd often been flicking through my emails when she was telling me the ins and outs of Rebecca's life, so I wasn't entirely sure I'd got that right.

While the cab weaved in and out of rush hour traffic on the M4, I allowed myself to think about how quickly I'd got used to the idea of Robin living with me. The thought of him packing up all his belongings and no longer seeing his shaving foam and razor on the shelf made my heart hurt like a teenager pining for a pop star. This wasn't me. I didn't moon about after men like this. But when I was sure the driver wasn't looking in his rear-view mirror, I had a quiet cry.

I didn't feel any better when I got to Amsterdam, where even the winding canals of the city glinting in the May sunshine and the buzzy atmosphere of the vestibule failed to lift my spirits. All I could think about was checking on Mum. I rang her on the landline, then her mobile, which, of course, she only switched on when she wanted to speak to someone. I was becoming increasingly het up at no response. Finally, I resorted to calling Rebecca.

'I've literally just walked in from my sister's. Your mum is fine. We're settling down to watch *Antiques Roadshow*.'

'Oh good, right, thank you.'

There was a funny silence as though I was interrupting their time together. I suddenly felt the need to assert my authority.

'Have you given her something to eat?'

Rebecca said, 'We're seeing how she feels for a bit. I won't let her starve, don't worry.'

We. We! I didn't know why Rebecca's relaxed but somehow proprietorial manner annoyed me. Probably because I didn't want to acknowledge that she appeared to deal with Mum in a much smoother and less fraught way than I did.

I had a quick word with Mum, ending up weirdly offended that she seemed so happy in Rebecca's company, without so much as a sniff of the 'When are you coming home? When will you ring me again?' that I was used to.

I needed to get up and throw myself into the melee downstairs. It was ridiculous for me to move heaven and earth, then lie here poleaxed by guilt. Not to mention worry that Robin would decide it was all too complicated. I loved my family, but there was no denying that being unencumbered as he was by parents, siblings or children made for a much more straightforward life.

I had a shower, dodging out to check Robin hadn't called or messaged before I brushed my teeth. There were so many disadvantages to mobile phones in terms of dating. No convincing yourself that the object of your affections had rung while you were in the bath and you'd missed the call. It made me long for the days when my mother had guarded the landline like a lioness and spoilt every conversation with my friends with a 'What have you got to say to each other when you've been at school together all day?'

I gave in and rang him. It was becoming a pattern that the people who were endlessly glued to phones never answered them when I called. I tried not to be that woman who put her life on hold for a man, telling myself I was better than that, stronger than that, as I reluctantly pulled a clean pair of trousers out of my suitcase.

I reminded myself why I hated hotels when someone banged on the door. All that stupid coming in to 'turn down the bed'. What sort of person was so spoilt that they couldn't pull back the covers themselves? I grumbled out, 'Coming', poised to tell whoever it was that I didn't want a silly chocolate left on my pillow. But it was Robin.

He drew me into his arms.

'Oh my God! What are you doing here? How did you even get here so quickly?'

'As it happened, I'd just finished at the development and was intending to fly back this evening anyway. I already had the hotel address from your assistant for a little something I'd ordered for tomorrow morning to wish you luck with your speech. You sounded so downhearted though, I went straight to the airport and hopped on a plane here instead. There was a KLM flight about to board. I only had hand luggage, so I made a dash for it.'

I stuck my face in his shoulder. Men didn't do big gestures like that for me. Sandy's dad, Andrew, thought he was rolling out the red carpet if he fetched me from the station when it was raining. 'Thank you. Thank you. I was having all sorts of horrible thoughts, especially when you weren't answering your phone.'

'Like what?'

I leaned back and kissed him. 'Can't remember now.'

He pulled my bathrobe to one side, his hands moving over my damp skin. 'Fibber.' He nuzzled my neck. 'Tell me or I'll go home.'

We tumbled onto the bed. 'I am worried that I've got too much baggage – Sandy, Mum, my work commitments and that you'll get fed up with all the demands on my time.'

He stroked my cheek. 'One, I don't think you realise quite how utterly bewitched I am by you. Two, I'm in it for the long haul, so a few tricky relatives aren't going to put me off.'

I felt something unfurl in me, a willingness to gamble, to make myself vulnerable. And with the thought that I'd never 'bewitched' anyone in my entire life, I made no attempt to resist as Robin peeled off the rest of my bathrobe and most of his own clothes. I was starting to believe it was my turn for the fairy tale.

6

REBECCA

Cath wasn't like her mum at all. I'd expected her to be like Dolly – chatty, friendly and a bit chaotic. She reminded me of the sort of people I'd met so many times when I was working as a carer. Instead of being grateful that they only had to swan into a decrepit parent's home once every three weeks and even then, they weren't at the sharp end of bodily functions, they immediately strode about questioning every decision and trying to catch me out. Cath had the same twitchy look about her, glancing around the room while she weighed up whether there was anything she should 'put away for safekeeping' despite being quite happy to leave me in charge of her mother.

However, the three days in Amsterdam seemed to have done her good. She gave Dolly a big hug and didn't hurry her along when she launched into a story about how a man on *Antiques Roadshow* had a vase worth £25,000 that he'd found in a charity shop. 'Ugly, ugly as anything it was!'

When I came back downstairs with my stuff, I said, 'I'll be off then. Let me know when you're back home, Dolly, and I'll come over and give you a hand with the garden again.' I patted Alfie. 'No more using the dog as a skateboard, though.' Dolly had been such great company, I felt quite sad to leave her, though I was glad to be able to concentrate on my own family again. I didn't dare ask Debs to pick up the slack with my kids any more than absolutely necessary.

Dolly laughed. 'Go on with you, I'll be doing the three-legged race with you soon.'

Cath showed me to the front door and suddenly did a big sigh, as though a great plume of stress was puffing out of her. 'I hope this isn't out of order, but I'm not sure what you've got planned job-wise. I wondered if you'd be interested in doing some cleaning here and taking care of Mum for the next five or six weeks until she's out of plaster. She said you've looked after her brilliantly – and Mum hates accepting any help from anyone.'

The unexpectedness of both the compliment and opportunity made me slow to answer. Since I'd moved in with Debs, I'd picked up some temporary shifts at the newsagents round the corner from her house and a few hours' gardening a week with Dolly, but despite my best efforts, I was a long way from securing a reliable income.

Cath rushed on. 'I don't want to put you in a difficult position if you've got something better to go to. I'll pay you well.'

My heart was leaping about with excitement. This was exactly what I needed. Better than I could have hoped. 'That would be great, thank you.'

Before I could ask anything else, the gates slid back and a black Audi came up the drive. Cath's face lit up and I lost my audience. She practically waved me away. 'Just come as soon as you can tomorrow and we'll take it from there. Thank you so much for everything.'

I set off down the drive. The man getting out of the car was evidently the mysterious Robin that Dolly had told me with a sniff was 'very charming but remains to be seen if he's decent husband material'.

He was tall and good-looking, with messy hair curling over his collar. I could imagine him playing an electric guitar in smoky pubs. But Dolly had probably hit the nail on the head when she said, 'Bit film-starish, but you need more than looks to make a marriage survive.'

I expected him to be one of those men who didn't even nod in the direction of anyone who was paid to make life easier, but he walked straight over to me and stuck his hand out. 'You must be Rebecca. Thank you so much for looking after Dolly. You really saved Cath's bacon there.'

I blushed. 'It was no problem. I hope you had a nice time in Amsterdam.'

'We did indeed, thank you. Can I pay for you to get a cab home?'

I had to hand it to him, very few employers ever thought about how their staff got home, let alone offered to pay. I supposed to a man like him, a ten-quid cab fare was peanuts. 'No, thank you. I've got my car outside.'

He smiled. 'Drive safely then – traffic's heavy out there' – as though he had all the time in the world to chat to me, despite the crunch of Cath's feet as she clattered down the gravel drive.

'You're back already! You're early! I thought you were going into London on your way back from Heathrow?' She was practically clapping her hands. Clearly, she hadn't read the bit in the dating handbook about not appearing overeager.

Robin said, 'I decided to go tomorrow. Couldn't stay away.'

I hurried off, anxious not to witness any employer/boyfriend intimacy.

But Robin shouted over to me, 'Thanks again, Rebecca.'

I could see why Cath thought her ship had come in.

The next morning, Eddie was finding every which way to be irritating, from putting his school shirt on back to front and pretending to be a zombie to flicking Cheerios at Megan over the breakfast table. With Megan crying because Eddie had splashed milk down her blouse, Eddie laughing with his mouth full and spraying cereal everywhere and me shouting, Jason lost it.

'For God's sake, grow up, Eddie. Stop acting like a pig at the table.'

Eddie went quiet. His face clouded over.

Debs followed Jason out into the hallway. I pretended not to hear him telling her in an angry whisper that he couldn't carry on living squashed in with us any more. The front door slammed and Debs came back in, looking stressed and flustered.

'Sorry about Jason. He's not really used to children.'

'No, I'm sorry. You're both very kind to have us. I'm hoping that with the money Cath pays me, I'll be able to get the deposit together to rent somewhere. We'll definitely be gone by the time the baby arrives. Don't worry.'

Debs frowned. 'You're going to have to pull your finger out to be out in three months.'

I hugged her. 'I'll think of something.'

'Like what?'

'Have faith.' I wasn't ready to share the plan that kept me awake at two o'clock in the morning. She'd kill me for even considering it.

I dropped the kids at school and arrived at Cath's in good time. The jury was out on whether she'd be like so many women I'd worked for in my life, who, because I wasn't swirling about like them in tailored trousers and blouses that could only be dry-cleaned, assumed I was thick.

This morning, Cath was friendly but efficient, like a doctor who didn't want me taking up more than my allotted ten minutes.

'Rebecca, hello. Mum's still in bed, so you might want to go through to her in an hour or so. Let me give you a quick tour – you'll speed up when you get used to the house, so don't worry if you don't get it all done.'

This was not going to be a cosy chat job where I pulled out my phone and showed her pictures of my kids. Fine by me. I needed to earn some cash, not make new friends.

'You've probably seen some of the rooms already,' she said, as she led me through the house, pausing outside the door to the main bedroom.

As I took in the enormous sleigh bed and the half-open door to a dressing room bigger than the nursery at Debs', she seemed awkward. I suppose there was something a bit weird about a stranger coming in and passing judgement on how clean your house was. Let alone the thought that they might be digging about in your drawers and trying on your clothes. I wanted to say, 'Look, love, I'm not interested in looking through your thongs or raising my eyebrows because the men in your life can't aim straight, I'm just here to keep a roof over my kids' heads.'

I blurted out the first thing that came into my mind. 'It must be a bit odd having a new cleaner when your mum's looked after the house for so long. Let me know if I'm not doing it how you like it.'

At that, she seemed to relax. 'Robin is here some of the time – though he's got meetings in Oxford today – so it's probably a good idea to knock before you come in, in case he's having a shower or something. He's already left this morning. So much energy that man, he's amazing,' she said, as though she couldn't stop herself talking about him. Thankfully, she remembered that I wasn't here to chat about the wonders of her boyfriend and marched back down the landing. 'You haven't met my son, Sandy, have you?'

'No, Dolly said he was at a garden festival near Manchester when you were away?'

'Yes, he runs a business putting up stands at events, as well as landscape gardening.' She paused. 'He's living here at the moment too. I'll introduce you.' She glanced at her phone. 'I've got a meeting in half an hour.' I followed her downstairs. 'Sandy? Are you about?'

Another surprise for me. A man with scruffy blonde hair, a frayed T-shirt and slouchy jeans walked into the hallway. 'Hi! You must be Rebecca; my grandma has been singing your praises. Mum says you're going to be running around after her for a few weeks. And keep us all on the straight and narrow too. I'll try not to be too messy... seem to turn into a teenager whenever I come home, don't I, Mum?'

Cath gave him a smile that had as much warmth as a November dawn. I felt caught in some kind of odd crossfire, unable to fathom whether Cath's increased chilliness was directed at me or Sandy.

She turned back to me. 'How would you like me to pay you? Monthly or weekly?'

How on earth I still had any pride left when I'd watched the bailiffs carry out my television with all the neighbours pretending not to rubberneck was something I'd never be able to explain, but I still had to force the words 'Weekly, please' from the back of my throat.

She nodded. 'Let me have your bank details.'

She darted out of the door, another tick on her to-do list completed.

Sandy ushered me into the kitchen. 'Would you like a cup of coffee? How about some toast?'

That small kindness made my eyes fill unexpectedly. I lowered my face into the basket of cleaning products, swiping angrily at my tears. I cleared my throat. 'That would be brilliant, thank you.' I didn't want his first impression of me to be a sobbing wreck. 'I'm going to make a start in the downstairs toilet.'

I remembered too late that Cath had called it a 'cloakroom'.

But Sandy didn't seem like he'd care about that sort of thing. As I ate the toast he'd left on the side for me, I wondered why he was back at home. I didn't have to wait long to find out. When I helped Dolly up, I said, 'I met Sandy this morning.'

It was like winding up the little dog Megan used to love as a child – one twist of the key and it scampered frantically across the kitchen floor in random patterns. Dolly was a great one for indiscretions. 'Did he tell you about his wife? Went off with the man who came to do the loft conversion? I never liked her anyway.' She paused to rub some hand cream in. 'Little trollop.' With the bluntness of someone who's lived a long time and no longer bothers to filter their thoughts, she said, 'What about you? How did you end up on your own?'

Her directness jolted me into blurting out the truth. 'My husband put our house up as security for a loan without telling me and we lost everything. I couldn't trust him after that.'

Dolly tutted. 'Stupid man. Fancy doing that. Mind you, men get up to all sorts, don't they? Better not to know half the time and stick your head in the sand.'

I wasn't thinking that Dolly was going to be at the forefront of the #MeToo movement. I shouldn't have brought up losing the house. Thinking about where we were going to live in three months' time made my brain thump with anxiety. 'Anyway, I'm off to clean upstairs.'

I started in Cath's bedroom. I dusted her dressing table, looking at the various necklaces and rings all tangled up in a bowl. I wished I had some expensive jewellery to flog, but even my wedding ring wouldn't cover a month's rent.

I jerked round as Sandy appeared at the door. 'I'm off now. Grandma's watching *Lorraine* and shouting questionable opinions at the screen. I'm only local today, so call me if there are any problems.'

'I'm sure we'll be fine, thank you. Robin should be back before I leave, I think your mum said.'

'He's not going to be much help with Grandma.' His voice took on a hard edge, his smiley face tightening.

Ah. Not a fan of Robin. I wondered why that was.

7

CATH

With Mum nattering on about what she'd seen on telly the second I walked in the door, Sandy either turning up for dinner when I hadn't expected him or texting five minutes before it was ready to say he wasn't coming back, I wasn't exactly the 'anything goes, what a blast you'll have if you stick with me' girlfriend I'd hoped to be. Especially on this particular Monday when I'd reluctantly decided I couldn't join Robin in Spain at the end of May as we'd planned because I couldn't leave Mum. Spending three days in Amsterdam on a work trip I'd committed to felt very different from jaunting off for a week's jolly with my new man.

To cap it all, Robin came sulking in, monosyllabic. Instead of giving me a kiss as he usually did, he muttered a hello and went straight upstairs. I finished slicing the potatoes and stuck them in the oven. All the time, I was caught between being annoyed at Robin acting like a child and wanting to run upstairs to see if I'd done something wrong.

Eventually, I took up a cup of coffee to my bedroom where he was lying on the bed and asked if he was okay.

'It's not been a great day.'

If someone behaved like this at work, making me drag bad news out of them, I would lose it. But, instead, I passed him the coffee, sat on the bed and stroked his foot. 'Can I help?'

He grunted. 'Probably not, unless you can talk some sense into my ex-wife. Moira told me today that she won't move out until after Christmas, which means I'm stuck in limbo land as far as buying a new house goes.' He screwed up his fists in frustration. 'I want my own home, somewhere we can be together, get some privacy, without worrying about leaving the bedroom door open.'

I should have bristled at his ingratitude, but he said it wistfully, as though he could never get enough of me.

He took my hand. 'I'm sorry. I want to make things so perfect for you. I keep bouncing from disaster to disaster. Every time I think I'm getting close to being able to offer you something, to being a proper partner rather than a leech, something else crops up. I had some other bad news today.'

I braced myself, strangely frightened that it would impact on us, take Robin away from me, just when I'd allowed myself to dream.

He carried on. 'The Spanish have decided to slap a tax on new developments from September, which means until we sell a few more off-plan, we can't afford to finish the last batch.'

I was so glad it wasn't anything to do with me. 'Can they turn round and do that in such a short time frame?'

Robin shrugged irritably. 'One rule for the Spanish, one rule for foreigners. If we don't pay, they'll impound our machinery until we do.'

I didn't recognise this Robin. He was so beaten, so negative. So different from his normal charismatic self.

'Why don't you come down for dinner and we can discuss what the options might be?'

'I'm going to have a little sleep. I'll get myself something later.'

He was shutting me out, closing off, as though what I had to say couldn't possibly be of any value. I was starting to doubt myself. Maybe everything I'd learnt in my own business didn't translate to property development.

I plodded downstairs, reflecting on the major differences between men and women. I couldn't think of a single time when I'd assumed the solution to anything lay in crawling under the duvet. I'd subscribed to my mum's philosophy on life, which was to pull yourself together and get on with it. But despite my irritation at this lame-duck version of Robin, I still felt the draw towards making it right, fixing things.

Undeniably, I was quietly competitive with Moira. On the rare occasions that Robin had spoken about the problems in their marriage, the recurring theme had been that he couldn't ever talk to her about work because her solution was to take to the internet and order a whole load of clothes she didn't need in case the money ran out. I'd said, 'I can't imagine you getting together with a woman like that. You can't stand flaky people.'

His explanation was that they'd met young – 'Before I knew that women like you, who are street-smart, resourceful and independent, existed. I could never burden her with work issues the way I discuss things with you. Back then, I found that fragility quite attractive, but it gets wearing over time. She's not robust like you. She was always fussing about her food, what to wear, if she was going to be too cold.' There was something satisfying about being the poster girl for women he wished he'd known, but I wasn't sure 'robust' was the compliment I was looking for. I wasn't actually hoping to be the apple-cheeked farmer's wife to her ethereal nymph.

When I said as much, he'd laughed. 'You're far more beautiful than she is.' I prided myself on not being that woman who judged other women on their looks, but when he'd pulled out his phone and said, 'I've deleted all my pictures of her, but look, this is her,' I couldn't resist peering at her Facebook profile.

Which was of a woman with long chestnut hair, wide-set blue eyes, a good ten years my junior. Reassurance factor: zero. It immediately made me want to call for an appointment to get my roots done. I'd restrained myself to 'She's a bit younger than I thought?'

'Even though it pains me to say it, she does look good for her age – but then she's spent all my money in spas and facials and God knows what. She's actually forty-seven, only six years younger than me.'

I'd tried to make a joke. 'And now you've hooked up with someone four years older than you!'

He'd pulled me to him. 'One, you don't look it, and two, I'm not having to babysit you, which after all these years is so appealing.'

He hadn't managed to reassure me completely as, now and again, I still had a sneaky search for her on Facebook, flicking through the frustratingly limited photos I could access. The experience reminded me of my mother's mantra: 'Eavesdroppers never hear any good of themselves.' My modern equivalent was going to be 'Snooping at pictures of ex-wives rarely makes one feel better about one's bingo wings.'

And now I was dithering between being a partner who indulged his work worries and following my natural inclination to tell him to buck up and eat dinner.

In the end, I dished up without him, trying not to feel defensive when Sandy asked why Robin wasn't joining us.

As soon as I could, I escaped back upstairs.

Robin jumped up when I walked in. 'Cath. I'm so sorry for being such a misery. I don't know why you put up with me.' He came over and put his arms around my waist. 'It's really depressing that I'm having to throw myself on your mercy to avoid living in a hotel, especially when there are several million pounds owing to me that I can't touch. If I could find some way of getting the Spanish planners off our back, I could be shot of this development by the end of next year, or the following one at the latest, and we could be living the life of Riley.'

'Could you get a bridging loan?' I perched on the edge of the bed.

Robin sighed. 'That's a great idea, but since Brexit, the banks are running shy of lending on overseas property, especially new developments.' He stroked my hand. 'It means I'm going to have to spend much more time over there, and that, my darling, is not what I want when I've just met you.'

I'd made it my mission to be a grown-up and not criticise Moira, but this power play over money was testing my resolve. 'Any chance you could get a loan against your house?'

He shook his head. 'Moira won't agree to that. The house is in joint names and she'd never sign the paperwork. Unless—' He tutted. 'No, stupid idea.'

'What? Might as well explore every avenue.'

Robin sat down next to me. 'It's a long shot anyway and you won't like it.'

'Go on.'

'Well, one of the reasons Moira is being so difficult is because she doesn't really want the divorce. Although she originally agreed to it, she's dragging her heels over signing the last few papers before the divorce application can be processed. And no matter what I say about our marriage being over, she won't accept it unless I go back home for a bit and drum it into her.'

I had an immediate picture of Moira bringing out the wedding albums and the best champagne and them tumbling into bed on a wave of nostalgia. 'Surely you can email her a very strong and definite letter? Phone her up and be totally categoric? If you go back and stay there, she's obviously going to think she's in with a chance.'

'I said you wouldn't like it. Part of the problem is that things are starting to go wrong in the house and she's getting overwhelmed. She's so stressed by the shower not working and a leak in the attic. I could sort all that stuff out so the house is ready for sale and also reiterate that there's no going back.'

'For goodness' sake. Please don't tell me that a grown woman can't ring a plumber or a handyman. Are you really going to trot up there with your toolbox?'

'You've no idea how much she relied on me for everything. And now her only way of controlling me is to place hurdles in the way of our divorce and financial settlement.'

'She's certainly discovered a bit of backbone for that.'

Robin jerked away from me. 'I'm just trying to think of solutions to hurry things along so I can concentrate on what matters. You.'

Despite my fury, I still softened at the idea of his rush to get on with our lives together. 'I don't think that's the answer. She's bound to try to get you into bed at some point. How would you handle that? I think you're going to open up a hornet's nest with that strategy.'

'That wouldn't happen. That's not what makes her tick.' His lips twitched into a ghost of a smile. 'Unlike a certain someone not too far away from here.'

This wasn't what I signed up for. A still-married man going back to live with his wife to convince her their relationship was finished. But there was some ridiculous proud part of me that didn't want to look insecure and needy.

I fiddled with my bracelets. 'Why don't you tell her that you've met someone else? Leave her in no doubt it's over?'

'Of course I will in due course, but not yet. I don't think that will help get her out of the house. If anything, she'll probably ramp up the obstacles – just to spite me.'

I sat in silence, aware of jealousy, an emotion that I hadn't felt in years, burning through me.

Robin reached for me. I snatched my hands away and tucked them into my lap.

He groaned. 'I'm sorry to drag you into my mess. I'm wondering whether it would be kinder to you if we took a rain check for a bit? Wait until I've resolved the development in Spain and sorted my divorce settlement?'

'What, split up?'

'Well, not forever, but until I get back on a more stable footing. I hate sponging off you like this.'

The cosy yet exciting feeling of being with Robin was fast descending into one of despair.

I turned to face him. 'Let's get one thing straight, I don't see you as sponging off me, and even if you were, I know it's only temporary. If money is the stumbling block to you being with me, why don't I give you a loan and then you can pay me back when you've sold the rest of the apartments? Then it won't matter how long Moira takes to get out of the house.'

'I don't think you understand. I need fifty thousand pounds, not a couple of grand to tide me over.'

Again, I felt as though Robin thought I was a two-bit player running a little recruitment consultancy that placed a few office staff in temporary jobs rather than a successful head-hunting company with a turnover of several million. 'I've got that in the business. I could lend it to you as an investment.'

Robin gave me a big hug. 'You are very sweet, but I couldn't possibly take your money. I'd feel so responsible if the development went bust. That hasn't happened in the last twenty-five years, but I'm always terrified it might. I never mix friends and business. And certainly not business and women I love.'

I went very still. I lay back on the bed and looked at him out of the corner of my eye.

That smile of his when he was being cheeky or teasing me was playing on his lips. 'What?'

I didn't want to make a fool of myself, so I said, 'Nothing' in case he was joking or I'd somehow heard wrongly.

'You don't believe me, do you?'

'I don't know what to think.'

'I can promise this, Ms Cath Randell, I have never ever felt about anyone the way I feel about you in such a short space of time.'

My brain was whirling with the about-turn from thinking he was going to dump me to accepting that he was so unselfish that he wanted to do what was right, despite being in love with me.

'But a moment ago you wanted to split up.'

'No, no, no, no. Let's get that absolutely straight. I will be heartbroken if you leave me, but I wanted to give you the option of getting out now because everything about me is so complicated. You, you're sorted. You've got a high-earning business and a lovely house. Why would you want to get involved with someone like me?'

'Because I love you?' The words came out before I'd even acknowledged them to myself.

I suppressed the stab of conscience that I'd promised to watch *Endeavour* with Mum at nine o'clock, as we became quite unseemly in our haste to prove to each other how much we meant what we said. And by bedtime, Robin had abandoned any idea of spending a few weeks back at his old house and agreed to let me transfer fifty thousand pounds to him in the morning in return for shares. I could barely sleep for the new sense of exciting certainty that we were in this for keeps.

8

REBECCA

Three weeks after I'd started working for Cath, I walked in to find Robin in the kitchen in his dressing gown. I wished I could sit at a breakfast bar at nine o'clock, reading the paper and sprinkling blueberries on my granola.

'Morning, Rebecca. How are you doing? Cup of tea?' Robin asked.

'That would be great, thanks.'

He handed me a mug. 'So what's on the agenda for today?'

I summoned up the cheery, salt-of-the-earth voice that people expected from me. 'I thought I'd clean the windows on the top floor today after I've got Dolly sorted.'

'Great idea. Only I'll be working in the office next to the snug and I've got an important call, so I'd appreciate it if you didn't hoover outside the door or anything.'

I longed to live a life where my worst problem was a two-minute buzz of the vacuum cleaner rather than bedding down on a settee, falling asleep too late every night because Debs and Jason went to bed at midnight, never having five minutes of privacy and having zero clue about where I'd be living in two and a half months' time. 'Sure, of course, no problem.'

I settled Dolly on the patio outside with the *Express* that she'd persuaded me to buy for her every morning on the way to work. 'Cath gets *The Times*, but it's so serious. I can't get into it. There's not much to read, is there? Cath doesn't approve, but I'm far more interested in Prince William and Kate than anything that the Prime Minister has to say.'

I gathered up all my cleaning gear and bumped into Sandy in the hallway, standing with an envelope in one hand and something that looked like a bill in the other. He wasn't his usual friendly self, barely lifting his hand in a half-wave, before ignoring me. Minutes later, as I dragged myself upstairs, I heard him shouting. 'Why is she transferring fifty thousand pounds to you? You've only known her four months. How did you manage that?'

I'd always been nosey, so I tiptoed over to the banister, straining my ears.

Robin's voice was measured. 'Woah, woah, calm down. Sandy, I don't think your mother would appreciate you opening her mail.'

'I told you, it was an accident. I thought it was my new bank card. The name was hidden by the envelope.'

I knelt down and wiped the landing skirting boards. Robin was mumbling something that I couldn't hear. Sandy's voice rang out loud and angry, though.

'It's an investment, but you're going to pay her back "when the house sale happens". Of course. That's getting a bit same old, same old.'

I ran my cloth along the dado rail, barely daring to move. This was better than *Coronation Street*.

There was some kind of slamming, as though someone had slapped a book down on a table. Then a door banged. I heard it open again. 'Sandy, can we speak about this in an adult way? I understand how protective you feel about your mother. That's a great quality. But I only want the best for her too, really I do.'

'Yes, of course. As long as the best for her includes subbing your lifestyle.'

'That's not it at all. Cath and I are in it for the long term. As soon as my divorce comes through and my ex agrees to move out of the marital home, I will pay every last penny back and more. I should walk away with at least seven or eight hundred thousand.'

'Bullshit.' Sandy stomped across the hall.

I tried to scuttle up the stairs to the top floor, but a can of polish fell out of my carrier. Sandy glared at me and flounced off into his bedroom. I didn't even bother to pretend I hadn't overheard. Not my fault if the family I worked for decided to wash all their dirty laundry within my earshot. Made a change from Debs and Jason having their hissed exchanges in the kitchen about how Jason couldn't stand the way Eddie slurped his drinks and when exactly Debs was going to chuck us out 'otherwise the baby will be here and we'll have to put the Moses basket in the bathtub!' To be fair, Debs did try to defend us, hushing Jason and telling him to think about what an upheaval we'd all had to face.

I was interested to know that Sandy had a bit of character. I'd slightly dismissed him as someone who mooned around singing to his plants and fretting about how bad weedkiller was for bees, a bit too love and peace to ever stand his ground. Maybe he was planning to retire aged thirty-two and was hoping Cath was going to bankroll him rather than Robin. As far as I could see, he'd taken against Robin from the start and had even started arguing with Dolly about him. Dolly was very live and let live. 'If she's happy, what does it matter to you? You went out with that awful girl whose father owned the cash and carry. The one who smelt of incense and looked like she'd never been near a bath. Had about fifty earrings in one ear. And that scruffy little dog she used to carry about in a rucksack.'

To his credit, he bent down to stroke Alfie without pointing

out that her dog was one of the scruffiest dogs that pattered
about this planet. 'Grandma, I was sixteen. Not fifty-seven.
Anyway, don't exaggerate. She had two studs and a nose
piercing.'

'But what I'm saying is no one can tell you. Your mother
said she'd seen her kissing that lad from football, what was his
name? You wouldn't believe her until she showed up with one
of those love bites. Little hussy.'

At that point, Sandy had shaken his head and walked out.
I'd whispered, 'Good job she didn't know me when I was
sixteen.'

He'd smiled. 'And she thinks the love bites were the big
deal...' I'd laughed. Thank God for someone a bit normal.

9

CATH

After the showdown about the money transfer, I couldn't let go of the fear that with Sandy now so hostile and Mum unable to go home for another couple of weeks, Robin might decide that our unholy trinity was more than he could stand.

When I tried to clear the air with Sandy – 'Darling, I can see you're worried about me, but I do know what I'm doing' – he put his palms up in surrender.

'Okay. I won't say any more about it. It's your money.'

Short of stamping my foot and stating the obvious – that yes, it was my money – I was left down a cul-de-sac of a conversation with all the resentments still bubbling about, nothing resolved, but the discussion truncated. He reminded me so much of his father, who made cutting off the air to any argument an art form.

Sandy's resistance to Robin made my heart ache. Even though I kept telling myself that he'd come round, his opposition dragged me down. Robin more or less ignored him, which I understood, but it still made me sad. Instead, he directed his attempts to lighten the atmosphere towards Mum, taking refuge in hearty jokes about how he was going to fix her up with a sexy

Spanish grandfather. 'That's what you need to get you back on your feet, Dolly. I'll get the lads on my development to introduce you to their grandads.'

Mum would laugh along out of politeness, but despite seventeen years passing since Dad died, she took any suggestion that she might one day meet someone else as an insult. 'I don't want another husband. I've only had one love of my life and that was Arthur.'

I decided the time had come to prove to Robin that I did know people who would adore him. I couldn't deny that I was looking forward to showing him off to the friends who'd been nagging me for years about my single status. Not only was he more than presentable, his tall slim frame showcasing his beautiful suits, but he was genuinely interested in everyone he met, asking lots of questions and bothering to remember the answers. The following day, I told him about my plan to invite my best friend, Jax, and her husband, Dan, over that Friday evening.

'Thought I'd keep it small to start with so you can have a proper conversation with them, rather than a whole gang of people chatting about old times. And it's bank holiday on Monday, so we'll have an extra day to recover.'

'Who's to say I wouldn't love to hear a bit more about your "old times"? Knowledge is power and all that.'

'Ha. I'm an entirely open book. What do you want to know? Ask me anything.'

'Why did you and Andrew split up?'

I felt the air change in the room. Apart from discussions around Robin's house and how to get Moira to leave, we'd been very grown up about not needing to involve ourselves in the nitty-gritty of each other's past relationships.

I busied myself wiping the crumbs from the work surfaces. It still hurt. 'He was a bit of a womaniser and I didn't want to keep looking over my shoulder.' I swung round. 'My turn to ask a question.'

He threw his arms open. 'Whatever you want. I've got nothing to hide.'

I was on the verge of enquiring why Robin had never had children, but at the last minute, I lost my nerve. In the rush to change tack, I forgot to get my filter in place and burst out with another question I longed to ask but had resolved never to articulate. 'Do you definitely want to divorce Moira?'

A flash of anger passed over his face. 'I find that question rather insulting.' Within minutes, he'd scraped his chair back and shut himself in the study until bedtime.

I went up first, resolute in my determination not to apologise but hating being at odds with him.

When he slipped into bed, I lay there waiting to see what would happen. He leaned over me, all minty and fresh smelling. 'Sorry. You hit a nerve. With Sandy, let's say, doubting me all the time, it hurts me when I feel like you don't believe me either. I love you. I want to be with you. I'm doing the best I can to move things along.' He wriggled on top of me. 'Just be patient for a bit longer.'

Robin's words stopped short of the one hundred per cent 'I am pulling out all the stops to make my divorce happen' that I needed to be reassured. I was becoming a woman who was very difficult to please.

The rest of the week passed in a blur, with meetings coming at me thick and fast and Robin taking the train up to London several days in a row. By Thursday evening, we were both exhausted. I congratulated myself on Jax and I agreeing to a casual supper at home on Friday night, so we could all chill out with a few glasses of wine and not have to get dressed up.

Despite saying I'd keep it simple, I left work early so I could marinade the pork and make the table pretty.

I texted Jax. *I'm nervous!*

A whole string of emojis came back, with hearts and balloons and flowers – *You don't need to be, I'm sure we'll love him. Dan and he can talk about cars while we drink ALL the wine. See you at seven.*

Quickly followed by a gun emoji. *Hopefully won't need this but might bring it anyway so he knows your friends mean business.*

I hoped Jax wasn't going to be too overwhelming. Twenty-five years of friendship since we met at our sons' primary school meant she rather took it for granted that she could say anything she liked. 'Let's face it, Cath, I'm more of a sister than a friend by now. That gives me special privileges.'

Thankfully, Robin wasn't a shrinking violet. I really wanted him to warm to her. Dan was so laid-back; he was always my first choice for sitting next to any tricky dinner guest. He never took offence, not even on the occasion when Jax got very drunk and started asking everyone at the table for suggestions to pep up their sex life. He'd just laughed and offered to take her to Ann Summers.

By quarter past six, I'd done my hair and make-up and was putting out the olives and salmon blinis, wondering where Robin had got to. I'd been expecting him half an hour ago. The trains were always a nightmare back from London Bridge on a Friday night. I texted him. *Are you nearly home?*

No reply. I prepared the Hasselback potatoes but kept slicing them wrongly as I was glancing at my mobile every few seconds.

At twenty to seven, I rang him. His phone was switched off. I tried to relax, telling myself he was probably in a tunnel with no signal. I checked on my train app but couldn't see any delays.

At five to seven, the doorbell rang. I was sure it was Robin forgetting his keys, but it was Rebecca. I'd asked her to come and watch TV with Mum for the evening so I wouldn't feel guilty about not asking her to join us for dinner.

'Hi there, thanks for coming. Can you see yourself through to Mum's snug? My guests are about to arrive.'

'Yes of course, I'll just pop to the toilet.'

And with that, I heard Jax's voice booming out as she did the code on the gate. She came up the drive, her dark hair flying about in unruly corkscrews, with Dan, her huge bear of a husband, beside her. 'Woooo! We're here.'

She and Dan came whirling into the entrance hall bearing wine and a bunch of lilies as Rebecca came out of the cloakroom.

Jax giggled. 'You're not Robin, are you?'

I did the introductions. Rebecca called to Alfie, who'd belatedly come out to bark, and went off to find Mum. We decamped to the kitchen.

Jax looked around in an exaggerated and comical way. 'Where are you hiding him then?'

'I'm sorry, I think there must be an issue with the trains. He'll be here any minute. Anyway, gives us a chance to catch up.' I felt the anticipation and pleasure of the evening ebbing away, feeling strangely robbed of that moment I'd been looking forward to: my two friends who'd been married forever walking into my kitchen and seeing me standing next to a man, that intimate aura of a couple, for the first time in decades.

I poured some wine and we lapsed into the easy chat of people who've known each other for years and can weave in and out of numerous topics without the need for explanation.

One bottle of wine and several bowls of crisps later, with the pork ready to serve, I was starting to get agitated. 'I'm so sorry. I'm going to try ringing him again.'

'Has he texted? Do you know for sure he's actually on a train?'

I didn't want to admit that he hadn't even bothered to let me know he was going to be late, but it was now quarter past eight. I ignored the question and went out into the hallway, feeling like I might cry. He'd promised that he'd be back at 5.45 p.m. to give himself time to have a shower and 'make myself beautiful for your friends'.

I was just ringing his number for the third time, when the front door opened and Robin walked in. Only the fact that I didn't want Dan and Jax's first impression of our shiny new relationship to be us snapping and snarling at each other stopped me completely losing the plot.

'Hello, love. Were the trains up the spout?'

'No. Why?'

'You were supposed to be home at quarter to six?' I kept my tone playful, as though I was lightly puzzled rather than smothering a bunch of emotions, none of which were pretty, with the flimsiest of control.

'I always said I wouldn't be back until quarter past eight and I'd have to do a really quick turn-around.'

He pulled me into a hug. I couldn't make my body comply.

'Shall I come through and meet your friends and then I'll nip up for a shower?'

'We've been waiting to eat for ages.' I kept my voice down, praying that Dan and Jax weren't listening.

'But I never said I'd be ready for seven. My last meeting finished at seven-thirty. I came as soon as I could. Fine, I'll skip the shower.'

Robin beckoned me through to the kitchen as though the matter was closed.

Without waiting for me to introduce him, he shook hands with Dan and kissed Jax on each cheek. 'So nice to meet you both. I'm sorry if you were expecting me earlier. Cath got a bit confused about what time I'd be able to get home.'

I brushed it away with 'I lose track of everything these days, so much going on with Sandy and Mum,' but I was trawling through my memories of our conversation about tonight. Robin seemed so certain about the timings. Maybe I really did have too much in my head. Perhaps it was the menopause fogging my brain. I'd work it out later. Right now, I wanted my friends to like Robin and to be happy for me.

I took a bottle of Sauvignon Blanc out of the fridge.

'Oh come on, Cath, we can drink that any time. Tonight's a celebration. Surely it's an evening for champagne? Shall I get the Moët?'

I felt wrong-footed, as though I'd somehow been ungenerous or lacking in imagination. 'Of course, why not?' I tried to make a joke. 'Far cry from when we first met, eh, Jax? We thought we were pushing the boat out with a bottle of Piat d'Or.'

She screwed up her face. 'Or a round of Pernod and black. I can't even bear the smell of it now. Good times, though, good times.'

Robin disappeared into the utility room and came back with two bottles.

'You know how to party,' Dan said.

And with that, Robin launched into a long story about how lavishly he used to be entertained when he first started working in property development. 'Those were the days. Champagne fountains, lobster by the trolley load, pretty girls.'

I nudged him. 'You sound like a throwback to the 1970s.' I was acutely conscious of Jax and how she might be judging Robin. I didn't want her to think he was always ogling other women and take against him. I'd never heard Dan make a single appreciative comment about another woman's looks.

Despite Dan's appearance making me think he missed his calling as a rugby prop and being married for well over thirty years, he only ever spoke about Jax as though he was the luckiest man alive. Always slow to shout about his own successful career as a structural engineer, he was the first to tell everyone what an incredible English teacher Jax was. 'I don't know how she does it. I wish I'd had someone as inspirational as her teaching me. I might not have had to take my English O level three times.'

I changed the subject by telling Dan about Robin's development in Spain and relaxed a bit as they started discussing various building projects. Jax and I did our usual thing of talking about our sons, lamenting their inability to find a decent partner. She asked all about Mum, and in return, filled me in on her worries about her own mother, who seemed to be more and more confused. When Jax went off to the loo, she looked slightly unsteady on her feet. I asked Robin to fetch some sparkling water from the garage. While he was gone, I hoped Dan would give me the discreet thumbs up, but he started asking about Sandy and how I was getting on having him back at home. 'We love it when George stays for a few days, but I'm not going to lie, he brings so much chaos and mess with him. It's like he's still a student,' he said.

Then Jax came back in, so the moment was lost.

Robin eventually reappeared. 'Sorry I couldn't find the sparkling water. That garage is such a cavern.'

I tutted. 'Typical man, can't see it unless it's on the end of his nose. Don't think you're going to be one of those men who does jobs so badly that you never get asked again.' I then felt I'd been a bit mean and launched into a long speech about how good Robin was at DIY. 'Saving me a fortune!'

I tried to pour Jax some water, but she waved it away and topped up her wine. Over banoffee pie, she descended into the outrageous lairy self that I recognised of old, a tipping point where the booze took her from outspoken and witty to deliberately provocative. I glanced at the clock. Eleven-thirty. I started to make murmurs about what a busy day we had tomorrow, going over to Mum's house to see what needed doing before she moved back in.

But Jax was in full flow. 'So, Robin, what's your story? Why should we trust you to take care of Cath? How can we be sure that you have her best interests at heart?'

'Jax! You can't put him on the spot like that!'

She put her hand up for quiet. 'Shhh. Your dad's no longer around, so I'm having to do the whole "what are your intentions, young man?"'

I peered at Robin to see if he was coping with Jax's onslaught. 'You don't have to answer this interrogation.'

He leaned back in his chair. 'It's my pleasure. Great to know that you have good people around who are looking out for you. The answer, Jax, is that Cath is everything I've ever wanted.'

I squeezed his hand. 'Thank you.' I loved that he was prepared to make himself vulnerable in front of my friends.

Jax had the devil in her. 'And what did you always want?'

I glanced at Dan to see if he was picking up on my 'nice evening, let's leave on a high' vibes, but he looked genuinely interested in the answer, as though Jax was posing a perfectly reasonable question rather than giving Robin the third degree.

Robin didn't miss a beat, though he'd started tapping his index finger on the table. 'I wanted someone smart, kind and capable.'

Jax opened her arms and gestured round the kitchen. 'This isn't so bad either though, is it?'

Robin deflected with a wry 'It'll do until we find our own place. I'm waiting for my divorce to come through so I can sell my house and release the capital.' He sounded vaguely amused, as though he'd clocked what she was up to and was having a bit of fun teasing her.

Through the fug of alcohol, I felt cross with Jax that she was being so hard on him, though I was sure it was because she felt protective. I could look after myself. Two bottles of champagne on top of the wine we'd already drunk had been a bad idea. I'd hate it if one of Robin's friends gave me a grilling. Alongside that thought came the realisation that he'd never suggested that I meet any of his friends. In the morning, I'd present it to him as a chance to get his own back.

Thankfully at that point, Rebecca appeared in the kitchen. 'Your mum is ready for bed. Could I just make her a hot-water bottle? She's complaining of a sore muscle in her neck.'

I was delighted with the distraction, so I welcomed her in like she was the party piece we'd all been waiting for. Rebecca's milling about seemed to interrupt Jax's laser beam locked onto Robin and by the time Rebecca had finished, she was talking about making a move.

As I showed them out, I was way too enthusiastic with my 'thank you so much for coming, great to see you!' which was totally at odds with the deflated feeling inside me that Jax hadn't whispered in my ear, 'I can absolutely see why you're so happy with him, he's lovely!'

I went back inside and threw my arms around Robin. 'You were brilliant. They loved you.' I hoped that the thread of unease winding through me was down to overthinking every little thing.

'I thought they were great fun. That Jax is quite the card. Fantastic company. Dan's a really solid bloke too.'

My heart lifted. 'Perhaps we could all come out to Spain to visit your development at some point? Dan would be really interested in seeing what you're doing out there.'

There was a pause.

I rushed in with 'When you know them better, of course.'

'Sure,' Robin said.

He sounded like me when I bumped into someone I hadn't seen for years and said, 'We must catch up for a coffee some-time' because I couldn't think of an elegant way to escape. I hoped I was wrong.

10

CATH

I was dying to ask Jax what she thought of Robin. She hadn't given anything away on her 'thank you' text the next morning, which focused on my generosity with the champagne and food rather than what I wanted to know: did she find Robin as charming as I did? But despite my fishing with *Robin thought you were great company both of you*, she just came back with a thumbs up and a kiss-blowing emoji. I told myself that she'd been out of the dating game for so long, she wouldn't have a clue that all the feelings I had now were no different to when I was twenty, hoping that everyone could see what I saw in my new boyfriend. In truth, my love for Robin was far more terrifying because I knew how fragile relationships could be, how difficult it was to retain your own identity while compromising enough for the partnership to work.

The rest of the bank holiday weekend flew by. Tuesday morning rolled around and I set off to work feeling unsettled in a way I couldn't quite put my finger on. I oscillated between thinking that Robin and my best friends were perfectly fine and my expectations that they would become best buddies after one evening were ridiculous, and upset that all of the people I loved appeared lukewarm towards him at best. In Sandy's case, down-right antagonistic.

I also seemed to be muddling so many things that I was wondering whether I had early-onset dementia. After the debacle of Robin turning up late on Friday, I'd managed to forget that he was staying in London with a client that night. He was slightly exasperated when I rang him at 8.30 p.m. to find out where he was. 'I told you I was taking a new investor for dinner and staying up there because I didn't want to be worrying about trains back. We talked about it on Sunday.'

It had to be the menopause. I was becoming so unreliable. Robin never made any reference to the fact that I was four years older than him – at our age, it was neither here nor there. But that was before I started acting like a woman who'd forget where she'd parked her car if I didn't draw myself a map with 'X' marks the spot.

So when Robin messaged me first thing Wednesday to say he was going to be home by three and was there any chance I could finish work early, I told my assistant to forward anything urgent and took the rest of the afternoon off.

I'd made it home with twenty minutes to spare – just time to shower, change and check Mum had everything she needed – before Robin was due to arrive. She waved me away: 'Rebecca's taken good care of me. You go and get on with your work.'

I muttered something about a few more emails to do before dinner and texted Robin to come in through the garage and round the back so we could sneak upstairs without Mum seeing. There was something supremely teenage about it, but, selfishly, I wanted Robin to myself without him getting caught up again in explaining why he'd chosen to build houses in Spain to Mum. 'I would have thought that with all the demand for houses here, you could have found somewhere a bit closer.'

We crept upstairs, giggling. Robin clicked the bedroom door

shut and produced a bottle of cava from his briefcase. In between kisses, he said, 'Today is a celebration.'

'Of course it is. You're home early.'

'No, beyond that. Guess what has happened?'

I felt oddly nervous of mistakenly going for something huge and exciting and taking the wind out of Robin's sails. 'I don't know, what?'

He poured the cava into our water glasses – 'Sorry not very elegant, but today is a good day. I've had notice that the first stage of my divorce will be through by the middle of June.'

'That's brilliant news! How amazing that you can get it through that quickly. Are you sure?' I hadn't realised how much the idea of Robin's divorce dragging on for months, if not years, had been weighing on me.

Robin tapped the side of his nose. 'Money talks. After our conversation when I suggested moving back home and I saw what a lead balloon that was, I offered Moira a slightly bigger percentage of the house sale. Then I told my solicitor he'd get a bonus if he could pull strings to get the case to the top of the pile in court.'

I was torn between shock at my naivety that solicitors could speed things up for the right money and admiration and relief that Robin was a man of action.

'And Moira changed her tune, simple as that?'

'I also agreed she could stay in our house until January – she didn't want to move before Christmas. That and the extra money seemed to be the magic bullet to shuffle things along. She signed everything and my solicitor got the ball rolling the very next day.' He clinked his glass against mine. 'That means you've got me as a penniless lodger for a bit longer, but at least I am going to be a free man sometime soon.'

He looked so happy that I abandoned my usual checklist of potential problems, took a gulp of cava and drew the curtains, whispering to Robin that Mum was in the room below. 'Hopefully she won't hear anything over the TV.'

We kept laughing as we tried not to make the bed creak, though by the time we'd finished the bottle, we were becoming rather blasé. Afterwards, we lay there, half-dozing and the busyness in my brain had dulled to a warm contentment.

Robin lifted himself up onto one elbow. 'Do you know why I am so happy?'

'Apart from agreeing your divorce?'

'Because I can marry you now.'

'Haha.'

'I'm not joking. I want to marry you. That's why I've been so grumpy and preoccupied. If life has taught me anything, it's to go for what you want, not to wait. I'm not going to waste any more time. If you'll have me, I'd like you to be my wife. Marry me. Please.'

Of all the things on the list of what might happen today when I stood watching the green woodpeckers searching for ants on the lawn this morning, a marriage proposal had never entered my head. Maybe it was the growing sense I'd had over the last few years that I didn't look forward to things with the same amount of excitement any more. That feeling that I'd achieved what I wanted to at work, but the weeks all blurred into one, with very little to distinguish one year from another. That slight envy I tried hard to suppress when my friends were booking holidays with their husbands, talking about the trips to the Amalfi Coast, the cruises around the Balearics, the rail journeys across Canada that they'd do when they retired. Or perhaps it was the cava making me reckless, filling me with a desire to live before it was too late. Possibly the need to prove to everyone that Robin wasn't a stopgap, someone I'd hooked up with briefly but who would quickly become 'That property developer bloke, what was his name?' Or to show them that we were serious about each other and they should take us seriously too.

So instead of giving in to the hundreds of reasons why I should take my time to think about it, I leaned over, looked into his eyes and said, 'Nothing would make me happier.'

11

CATH

I spent the next week hugging our secret to me, a little burst of disbelief and joy rushing through me every time I thought about it. Robin and I had agreed not to say anything to anyone until Mum was back in her own home and I wasn't so thinly stretched. I wanted the headspace to break the news to Sandy without Mum chirping up with her opinions in the background – she'd mean well, but in this particular instance, I felt the stakes were complicated enough without it being a free-for-all.

That alone was enough to motivate me to sort things out for Mum to return home. Disappointingly, the five and a half weeks Mum had been living with us had strained our relationship. The constant hobbling to stand behind me every time I was cooking, saying, 'I think you need a bit of cornflour in that sauce' made me want to introduce her to some swear words she hadn't heard before. And now it was obvious she couldn't clean for me any more, she'd gone the other way. Every surface in the kitchen had some trace of Mum's existence: a coffee ring, a few toast crumbs, a smear of margarine. I could have sworn she was trying to keep Rebecca in work.

Without mentioning it to Mum, Rebecca, Robin and I had

popped over to her house to see what needed doing before she could move back in. As we'd walked up the garden path, the gate latch crumbled, the rust finally finishing it off. The whole house had a musty, stagnant air to it.

Rebecca had immediately offered to come in and give the house a thorough spring clean.

'Are you sure?' I'd said. 'I'm a bit ashamed of how bad it is.' And how much she would judge me for letting it get like that.

'Don't forget I've been a carer. I've been in houses where I've had to scrub shit off the loo walls.'

I couldn't make out this woman. Half the time, I felt as though she was a thoroughly capable person, a godsend who alleviated a lot of stress. The other half, she made me so self-conscious, embarrassed to ask, 'Would you mind just having a little clean of the windows in the gym?' as though I was some lady of leisure who spent her life having spa days. Every time I heard the word 'just' come out of my mouth, as though I was asking her to do a little thing, nothing important, as though she had a choice, I cringed. I rushed around with the bleach every Wednesday morning when I knew she was going to clean my bathroom, making sure there wasn't a single stray hair in sight and emptying the bin.

'My only worry is what to do with all these bits and pieces,' Rebecca had said, gesturing to the shoeboxes stacked in the corner of the living room. My mother was saving them to fill with Christmas gifts for children who didn't have anything. Though they'd been standing there for about the last three years.

Robin had stepped in. 'It all needs chucking out. I'm surprised there aren't rats in here.'

I'd immediately thought about vermin when I'd walked in, but I didn't want him criticising Mum.

I could have hugged Rebecca, who leapt to her defence. 'She is eighty. A lot of the people I've cared for can't see as well as they used to, so they miss things. They're also of that make-do-and-mend generation, so they find it harder to get rid of stuff in case it comes in useful one day.'

Robin had looked surprised that Rebecca was challenging him, but she was probably right. In any event, I couldn't miss this chance to sort the house out. 'It's hard, but we probably need to get on top of it now while she's not here.'

Rebecca had rescued me. 'Why don't I start upstairs, clean as much as I can and put all the extra stuff in a tidy pile so I can go through it with your mum when she comes home?' I'd felt a surge of gratitude to this dispassionate outsider, unclouded by emotion.

So today, when I brought Mum home after her final check-up at the hospital, the huge guilt I felt about never spending enough time organising her affairs had melted away. The whole house was brighter, lighter and smelt of lemon rather than old raincoats left on a peg too long.

Alfie scampered about sniffing at all the new smells. Mum looked underwhelmed and nowhere near as delighted as I'd hoped. 'Where are all my boxes? I've been collecting little pens, notebooks and games for children in need.'

I tried not to jump down her throat. 'We didn't throw them out. They're probably in your new shed. Look, Robin took the other one down and replaced it.'

Mum frowned. 'Your dad made that shed from some offcuts left over at the factory.' Her voice went small. 'I didn't know you were going to get rid of it.'

'Mum, it was falling apart. The roof was rotten and everything inside was sodden. Your lawnmower would have rusted to bits if we'd left it like it was.'

'I could have patched that up myself with a bit of felt and tarpaulin.'

Yes, that's just what was required. Mum, with her newly healed ankle, up a ladder repairing the shed roof.

The temptation to throw myself on the hall floor and bang my feet and fists up and down very nearly got the better of me. I dug deep for a sliver of patience. 'I know change is hard, but we wanted to make it nice for you, a bit easier to manage on your own.'

'I've lived on my own for seventeen years and haven't collapsed in a heap yet.'

I resisted pointing out that she had actually collapsed in a heap – and broken her ankle into the bargain.

Mum started tutting and opening and closing cupboards. 'I hope she hasn't thrown all my tins of corned beef away. I was going to make a salad with it tonight.'

Of course she was. As opposed to eating the smoked salmon, chicken or mackerel that we'd bought fresh for her. 'I'm sure she hasn't. Here, have your tea and we'll sort it out in a minute.'

But Mum was rummaging in her cupboards as though her life depended on a tin of corned beef from circa 1987, when I couldn't recall her eating any in the last five years.

My phone pinged. Sandy had messaged. *We need to talk as soon as possible.*

Why did men always make everything sound like an emergency? I had no idea what this was about. Sandy didn't really differentiate between life-threatening and 'I've been thinking of buying a new running machine for the gym'. I should install a text rating system for urgency and priority.

Was he in trouble with the police? Deciding to move out? My heart did a little leap of hope, immediately followed by regret that I wanted my son to go and live somewhere else. I simply was not in the mood for another moan about Robin. It was like having two toddlers running in and out, snitching on each other.

I turned back to Mum, who said, 'Can you ring Rebecca and ask her what she did with my tins?'

'I'll ask her tomorrow. I don't like to disturb her when she's busy with her children.'

Mum harrumphed. 'You get off. I've taken up enough of your time.' She picked a couple of dead leaves off her spider plant. 'Thank you for having me.' She sounded like a ten-year-old who'd been told by her mother to thank her friend's parents for a party she hadn't enjoyed.

I decided to bowl her over with excess generosity rather than allow myself to be disappointed she wasn't excited to come home to a clean and tidy house. 'It was absolutely lovely having the chance to spend some proper time with you. I'll ring you tomorrow.' I hugged her, suddenly aware of how little she was.

As I drove away, I was immediately filled with self-loathing that I should have been more understanding. I would miss my mum so much when she died, I knew that already. However, there was a part of my brain that remained resolutely childish, utterly unable to accept that she could easily be gone in ten years, five, even one. I was incapable of translating how much I would miss her in the future to patience in the present.

But seeing Sandy's face when I drew up knocked all the space for thinking about my mum right out of my head.

He didn't even wait for me to get inside, just stood, arms folded and said, 'Why didn't you tell me you were getting married?'

A swell of nausea rushed through me. The hurt in his eyes drilled right down into the deepest place of regret in my heart, that tiny space where a special shame resides for when you recognise you've done something so wrong, so hurtful, that it isn't easily rectified.

'I haven't really decided what we're doing yet.'

'You're lying to me. There's a quote from a caterer for a "wedding breakfast" on the dining table.'

I felt the air leave my lungs. Given that we probably wouldn't get married for at least another year, I hadn't under-

stood Robin's hurry to start gathering quotes for catering, decorations, honeymoons and a thousand other things he spent
hours every evening researching on the internet. But nor had I
wanted to be a killjoy, so I insisted that he lock all the paperwork in a drawer in my office, while I picked the right moment
to tell Sandy.

'Not too long though,' Robin had said. He'd been hopping
about from foot to foot. 'I want to share it with everyone. I can't
wait to tell the world how lucky I am. It might come as a shock
to people, but once they realise we're serious about each other,
they'll start to accept it.'

I knew he meant Sandy and I also knew he was right. I'd
left the conversation with a renewed determination to tell
everyone as soon as possible, but when the moment came to say
the words, I seized up. I wasn't ready for Sandy to distance
himself from me, the inevitable consequence of my increasing
closeness to Robin. My new husband would crowd out some of
the space that Sandy claimed, as he withdrew and I shifted
focus. However, now my hand had been forced, I couldn't put it
off any longer.

Robin must have been in a hurry to catch his flight and
forgotten to tidy the papers away. My voice crawled out. 'I was
going to tell you, darling. I know you're a bit uncertain about
him and I was hoping that, with time, you'd come round to
seeing what I appreciate about him.'

'I hope you're signing a pre-nup. When is the big day,
anyway?'

There was such sarcasm in his tone that I snapped. 'We
haven't firmed up a date yet.'

I should have been calm, absorbed his misgivings and
proved to him I was more than capable of making a rational
considered decision about my future. But his response, 'Perhaps
you'll tell me to my face when you've decided, rather than

leaving a wedding invitation lying on the table' tipped me over the edge.

I shouted at his departing back that he was a selfish sod and shouldn't take his unhappiness out on me. The whoosh of regret that came from hurting Sandy when I spent ninety-nine per cent of my time building him up and sheltering him from harm followed immediately.

I was just catching my breath when Mum's name flashed up on my mobile, a sure sign of impending doom. I didn't have the tolerance for more drama about missing corned beef tins.

I barely managed a hello before Mum launched in with 'That gold bracelet that your dad bought me on our honeymoon has disappeared and so has my mother's engagement ring.'

Eloping, with or without a husband in tow, was looking more attractive by the second.

12

CATH

I didn't sleep. My mind was vacillating between Sandy's resistance to my marrying Robin and Mum's upset that her jewellery had gone missing. She'd started crying when I asked if she thought that perhaps in all the hoo-ha of breaking her ankle, she might have mislaid it. 'If you hadn't interfered and had everyone poking about in my house, I wouldn't have lost it.'

Mum's ingratitude winded me. I explained that I'd wanted to give her a hand to get on top of things, as she'd been doing for me all these years.

'But you never asked me what I wanted. You wait until all you've got left of someone you love is a few bits of jewellery and memories and then see how much it bothers you when the things they gave you vanish.'

I didn't know what to say. She kept muttering about 'people not always being what they seem'. I was ninety-nine per cent sure Mum had put them in a safe place that she'd now forgotten or knocked down the back of her bedside table, but when I ran through those options, she got more and more offended. 'I'm not senile, you know.'

In the end, I had no option but to ask Mum outright. 'So, do you think Rebecca took them?'

Mum sniffed. 'I can't really think of any other explanation. She seemed honest enough, but maybe being here on her own was too tempting. I know she's struggling for money. You need to ask her. And check she hasn't taken anything from you.'

Mum made that conversation of 'Are you stealing from us?' sound so easy. My gut didn't have Rebecca down as a thief. She'd had loads of opportunity to dip into my handbag and I'd never noticed any cash missing. I still thought Mum's stuff would turn up when we stopped searching for it. However, I ran upstairs to look in my jewellery box. My platinum bracelet with diamonds was still there. Plus a couple of gold bangles and my emerald earrings. But did that just mean she was smart enough not to steal from me?

I tossed and turned all night, wondering whether to broach the subject, and if I did, how to do it without accusing her straight out. I'd grown used to her help, her quiet and effective sorting of boring chores, and not least the way she handled Mum, lightening the load on the tail end of my to-do list that I never managed to reach.

Robin would have to be away when I needed him. His phone flipped to voicemail. Now I'd lent him the money to deal with the Spanish authorities, he'd promised me that next year, he'd only need to be on site four days a month, instead of the current rate of about fifteen. 'There's no way I'm going to spend half of my life away from you. We're going to go travelling ourselves... I've always wanted to have a nice little road trip round Tuscany.'

And my mind filled with images of hilltop villages and sitting outside on sunny terraces with glasses of Chianti. I thanked my lucky stars that I'd met someone dynamic enough to do all the glorious things that I'd seen other couples do together, while I'd been slogging my guts out, building up the business and trying to be a reasonable mum to Sandy and a good daughter to my own mother. I wasn't sure I'd succeeded on either count.

I dragged myself downstairs, calling my assistant to tell her to postpone my first two meetings. I couldn't have Rebecca in my house if I harboured the slightest suspicion she was stealing. At the very least, I needed to see her reaction. This wasn't something I could discuss on the phone.

She looked surprised to see me when she let herself in. 'Hello, not at work today?'

'I'm going in later.' I swallowed. If this was happening at work, I would have an HR protocol in place and I would be dispassionate and businesslike. But a cleaner in your own home was different. For a start, there was such an imbalance of knowledge. Despite my best efforts at discretion, Rebecca probably knew that I was on HRT, was quite slovenly at cleaning up cheese crumbs in the fridge and threw away an obscene amount of bagged salad that I bought in order to kid myself I was eating healthily. I, on the other hand, knew... what did I know? That she had two kids. Two boys? No. A boy and a girl. Single mum, but I wasn't sure if the dad was in the picture at all or not. Lived with her sister. Used awful sweet perfume that reminded me of the scent I used to wear to the school disco. Did everything I asked her to and never ever objected, yet I still sensed some underlying resistance that I couldn't quite put my finger on. Something that made me feel criticised and apologetic, especially when Robin came in with bags of designer shirts or talked loudly about how he'd test-driven a new Porsche when he was in Spain.

I prevaricated. 'I'm just making some coffee. Would you like one?'

She accepted but didn't follow me through to the kitchen, instead putting her bags down and assembling what she needed to clean the gym.

I carried a mug through to the utility room. 'Rebecca, this is really awkward, and I don't want you to think for a moment I'm accusing you of anything...'

I studied her carefully. She already looked blotchy and upset.

'What?' The word came out sullen and defiant.

I explained and she practically crumpled in front of my eyes. For a second, I thought Mum was right and my brain flitted between demanding the return of the jewellery and whether to call the police. Then Rebecca started crying, something that I'd never associated with her. She always seemed so tightly held, so contained.

'Well, it feels like you are accusing me. I didn't take the jewellery, but I'm sure you won't believe me. Why should you? You know I'm desperate, that I'm living with my sister – who has just asked me to move out by the end of next week because she's got pre-eclampsia and needs bed rest and calm. And, of course, they're worried sick that the baby will have to be delivered much earlier. At any rate, I think she'll be induced in the next month or so. The basic upshot is that I need to find somewhere for me and my two kids, otherwise I'll be homeless and they'll have to go and live with their dad down in Shoreham-by-Sea. To cap it all, we heard yesterday that when the bank auctioned off our old house, the sale only covered the debts, so there's nothing left to put towards me renting somewhere. So yeah, it probably does follow in your mind that if I had the opportunity, I'd have filled my pockets with stuff I could flog from your mum's house.'

I was shocked that I'd had no idea how dire her circumstances were. I'd done what I never thought I would do, which was stick her in the category of 'staff', without ever stopping to consider what might be going on for her. If she'd dropped any hints, they'd been white noise washing over me before I could instruct her about the eco-friendly furniture polish I wanted her to use in future.

'Oh my goodness. I didn't realise that you were having such a difficult time.' I wasn't sure if she'd answered my question about whether she'd stolen from Mum or not.

She walked out, saying, 'I'm just going to blow my nose.'

I stood looking around my utility room with its Fired Earth grey tiles and granite worktop. If she gave the jewellery back, I'd still have to sack her.

She came back in. 'You'll never believe me, but I didn't take anything. I love your mum. There's no way I would do that.'

There was something about her words – unless she was a brilliant actress – that sounded beaten, but also rebellious and sincere. I'd built my whole business on following my instincts and done very nicely out of it. I cursed Mum. We'd probably find the ring hidden in a teapot or hanging on one of her cacti where she'd put it for safekeeping.

'I believe you.'

The effect on Rebecca was so powerful, it brought a lump to my throat. 'Thank you.' She paused and looked down. 'Are you happy for me to carry on cleaning as usual?'

I nodded, feeling an urgent need to make up for even raising the subject. 'Sorry, Rebecca. I had to ask. I honestly didn't think you had taken anything, it's just that Mum was so convinced that the ring and bracelet were in her dressing table. She does get confused though.'

I didn't want to see the expression on Rebecca's face. I felt petty, and ashamed that I'd become like the bosses who'd taken advantage of my situation as a single mother to make me work unpaid overtime or lose my job. I was gathering up my briefcase, feeling knackered before I even got to work when Sandy came in.

'Why is Rebecca crying? Did you accuse her of stealing from Grandma?'

I shook my head. 'No. I just asked her if she had seen any of the things that were missing.'

Sandy's mouth dropped open in disbelief. 'She's upstairs pushing a Hoover round with one hand and sobbing into a tissue in the other. Grandma doesn't know where she's put her handbag half of the time. You don't seriously believe that Rebecca has gone round there and pocketed her jewellery? For one thing, she's bright enough to know she'd be the first suspect.'

I couldn't fault his logic. 'I thought that myself, I must admit.'

Sandy ranted on: 'You do know she's about to be made homeless?'

'I found out this morning.'

'I've been telling you for weeks that she has to get out of her sister's.'

'That's not the only thing I have to think about, darling. I'm sorry if I didn't take it on board, but I have thirty-five employees with all their problems, Mum with her broken ankle, you to worry about... I can't be responsible for everyone's issues.'

'You have found time to agree to marry a man you've known for five months and to transfer enormous sums of money to him though.'

I felt like sitting down and crying myself. 'I hoped it was my turn for a bit of fun, and that everyone might be happy for me. I didn't think that was too much to ask.'

Sandy wrinkled his nose as though the concept of parental happiness hadn't really occurred to him. Not for the first time, I recognised that streak in Sandy that came from his dad, that obstinate insistence on fact, untouched by emotion or human frailty. This was the point where tougher mothers than I would say, 'Too bad. My house, my rules. You don't like what I'm doing, you are free to leave.' But I wasn't that mother. I was a mother, who, despite her son being in his thirties, still wanted to make his face light up with joy, the kind of delighted excitement that an unexpected ice cream could deliver when he was four.

Sandy carried on. 'I am happy for you, if it's the right thing. It's a bit sudden and fast, that's all.'

I appreciated the enormous effort he was making to meet me halfway.

'I understand that. But at my age, when it's right, it's right, you kind of know. And then there doesn't seem any point in messing about.'

Sandy tried and failed to subdue an eyebrow flicker. 'Anyway, you are going to have to become a bit involved in Rebecca's life, because up until now, Grandma has really got on with her and we can't afford to lose her.'

I smiled. We knew Mum taking to anyone who was going to 'meddle about' in her house was a miracle. 'I don't know whether she'll agree to having Rebecca back now.'

'She will if you are very definite that the missing jewellery isn't anything to do with her. Grandma does listen to you. And she trusts your judgement even though she pretends not to.'

I hoped he was right. My heart sank at the thought of everything from tying back Mum's roses to making an appointment at the doctor's – 'I can't get the hang of that stupid press one, choose this. I want to speak to a human being' – plopping back into my lap.

Sandy saw me weakening and attacked with ruthless precision. 'Couldn't Rebecca stay in the guest suite on the top floor until she finds somewhere to go?'

I wasn't quite sure how I'd gone from doubting my cleaner's integrity to being responsible for providing accommodation for her. 'I don't think that would work, love. It's a nice idea, but that's way too much blurring of the professional boundaries.'

'So you'd rather see her on the streets with her kids than clogging up one of four spare rooms in this house?'

'She must have somewhere she can go, surely? Hasn't she got any parents?'

Sandy's face clouded with disgust. 'What was it you used to say when I was small? A hand up at the right time when someone is down costs you nothing but can change a life? Or are you worried about what Robin will say?'

Like a hygienist prodding into dark recesses and hitting a nerve, Sandy had drilled right into my reservations. Of course, I didn't want to have someone who worked for me living in my house. It was bad enough that she knew I was so spoilt I used a clean towel every day and never bothered to finish a bottle of shampoo before moving on to the next miracle cure for my menopausal frizz. But the truth was Robin had been a lot more relaxed last week when he knew Mum was going home and I was pretty sure he'd be sunnier still when Sandy left. The last thing he'd want would be for my cleaner to move in.

I mumbled about the dangers of the pool, how I wasn't sure two primary school children would understand that I sometimes worked from home and couldn't have a lot of shouting in the background, not to mention what we'd do if she refused to leave.

My brain darted about, searching for a solution, one that wouldn't make me a villain in Sandy's eyes but wouldn't mean opening up my home to my cleaner and her kids. But Sandy had that gaze, that determination about him, the stance that had worn me down over the years, the skill he'd had at extending an eleven o'clock curfew to 1 a.m., the refusal to go to university in favour of a qualification in horticulture. Experience had taught me to start off generously rather than be pincered into a far more drastic position later on.

'I'm not happy with her being in the house, but what about the tennis pavilion? There's a shower room in there.'

'The tennis pavilion? That's barely better than a shed!'

'I can't have two children under ten running around in here. That's a step too far. I'm prepared to offer her that for a few weeks over the summer. It should be warm enough now we're in June. Perhaps you can help her sweep it out and have a clean-up. We could put those trundle beds in there for the kids and the sofa bed out of the snug for Rebecca?'

Sandy looked doubtful, then brightened. 'Have you still got that hotplate you used when the kitchen was being redone? And that little fridge?'

He darted off upstairs to tell her before I could say anything else. The muffled sound of her saying, 'Oh my God, thank you. Thank you so much' went some way towards balancing the sinking feeling I had about telling Robin.

13

REBECCA

I'd forgotten who I was and what I was doing in Cath's house when Sandy had offered me the tennis pavilion. I'd even forgotten that moments before, Cath had practically accused me of stealing from Dolly. I hugged him. Properly flung myself at him and squeezed him like I was trying to get the last bit of toothpaste out. It was only later that I'd panicked that I'd left a snot trail on his shirt. But he worked in gardens with worms and slugs so he'd probably forgive me. He was so unlike Cath with her silk pillowcases so her hair didn't frizz up. And Robin was equally bad with his Chanel shaving foam. I could have bought Eddie a new pair of trainers with what that cost.

I'd shoved all those thoughts to one side as Sandy had led me right to the bottom of the garden. I'd never been down that end before, only into the orchard to hang out the sheets on the line.

'It's nothing special, but there are two changing rooms that the kids could use as bedrooms, and we could put a sofa bed in the main bit. There's a little shower room through there. I'll check the immersion heater still works. No one plays tennis since I moved out, so I doubt anyone has really been in here for a few years.' The door was sticking. 'I'll get that planed down.'

Give me a man with a toolbox any day.

Cobwebs hung from the ceiling and piles of leaves had gathered in the corners. Sandy had frowned. 'It's not exactly a palace. It's worse than I remembered. What do you think? It might be okay during these summer months, as a stopgap? I'll help you clear it up.'

'This is brilliant, thank you. I'm really grateful to you – and your mum.' I didn't care if Cath had made the offer out of guilt, an apology for even considering that I'd been making off with Dolly's treasures. In that moment, I was just relieved to have a solution to my current crisis.

Sandy was trying to disguise his shock that I was so thankful to be offered a spidery shed. I didn't want his pity, so I rambled on. 'Do you think your mum will mind me staying here? And Robin? I mean, I'll do my best to keep the kids out of his way, but he's not used to them, is he?'

Sandy's response was robust. 'Don't forget Mum was a single parent herself. She hasn't forgotten how hard it was. And as far as Robin's concerned, it's nothing to do with him. It's not his house. If he dares to say anything to you, you come to me.'

'Oh, I wouldn't put you in that situation,' I'd said, though I'd quietly chalked Sandy into the 'useful ally' category.

Sandy had sighed, a great huff of unhappiness. 'Relationships. Honestly, you've got to wonder why we all bother. No one ever seems to get it quite right. There's my wife running off with the guy who came to do our loft conversion – which she said we needed if we were going to start a family. So that went well. There's Mum marrying a bloke she hardly knows, Grandma pining after someone who's been dead for seventeen years...'

I'd chimed in. 'Me not noticing my husband was signing away the house under my nose and leaving us all penniless...'

Sandy had suddenly realised he'd been lulled into indiscretions and clicked into business mode. 'Right. I'll crack on checking the plumbing, you go and fetch the cleaning paraphernalia from the house, and we'll see if we can transform it into a liveable state by next Saturday. That's your deadline, isn't it?'

I'd nodded, my relief fading into a realisation that the first sight of a single spider and Megan's screams would be livening up the neighbourhood. I'd have to get Eddie on board and make the whole experience into a Bear Grylls survival adventure. I'd felt like wilting down the cobwebby wall at the energy I'd require to keep up the 'that scratching is a hedgehog running across the lawn to curl up with its babies' commentary, but I'd have to suck it up. It was the best option I had. The only one.

But before I could move into Cath's, I had to square things with Dolly. I couldn't bear it if she suddenly seemed twitchy when I went upstairs when I was cleaning for her, or started following me into the kitchen every time she'd left her handbag in there. Before she'd moved back home, Cath had agreed that, for now, I should go over to Dolly's every other day to keep on top of the house, and take Alfie for a walk. Cath said, 'Keep a general eye on her. She's a great one for telling me everything's fine and then I discover that she's been taking some random antibiotics she's been hanging on to since the last century "because her chest didn't feel quite right". She'll get grumpy with me if I ask her if she's been doing the exercises the physio recommended, but she seems to respond better to you.'

I'd smiled then. I'd had plenty of practice when I'd worked as a carer at persuading even the most cantankerous patients to do what was in their best interests. Nonetheless, the first time I visited Dolly after Cath had asked me about her bracelet and the engagement ring, I felt ridiculously nervous. Cath had brushed my concerns off as 'She never believed you'd stolen anything but couldn't work out what had happened to them'. On the other hand, it suited Cath to convince herself that was the case because without my help, she'd be seriously stretched between her own work and Dolly's needs.

When Dolly opened the door to me, I hid myself in making a fuss of Alfie. I hadn't done anything wrong but my face was flaming as surely as if I'd been filching fivers out of her purse at every opportunity. She stood back to let me in, her 'Hello, Rebecca', lacking its usual exuberance.

I stood in the hallway. 'Dolly. I know you're upset about your jewellery and I promise you, I'll help you look for it. But I need you to believe me when I say I didn't take it. I've never stolen anything in my life and I'm not going to start now. I can't work for you if you don't trust me. I really can't.'

Dolly shuffled through to the kitchen, harrumphing and shrugging. 'I know what Cath thinks. That I'm losing my marbles. Is that what she told you?'

'No! She didn't say anything of the sort. And I don't think that either. You're one of the sharpest eighty-year-olds I know.' I didn't think it would be a good time to mention that Cath had said Dolly got 'confused', not when I could sense a weakening, a willingness in Dolly to take me at my word.

Alfie pawed at my legs, wanting me to play with him. 'So are we okay? Are you happy for me to keep coming?' My tone was teasing. 'If you want, I can empty out my pockets and handbag every time I leave.'

Dolly's face broke into a smile. 'Go on with you. I never really thought you'd taken anything. You don't seem the sort. And anyway, Alfie likes you and he can sniff out a scoundrel at fifty paces.'

I'd bring some special treats for my doggy ally next time I came. He'd probably write me the best reference I'd ever had.

14

CATH

I picked Robin up from Gatwick late on Monday evening three days later. He was already waiting for me even though I was early, obscured by a huge bunch of roses. I wondered if his ex-wife was one of those women who automatically expected a present every time he went on a trip. I squashed the churlish thought that arranging flowers was another job to do when really I just wanted to sit down and have a glass of wine.

'How's my bride-to-be? I've missed you so much. I'm so sick of being away from you, especially at weekends,' he said, pulling me into such a close embrace that we squished a few petals. My ingratitude soon vanished when he said, 'Want to hear my excellent news? The judge has granted the first stage of my divorce. Forty-three days to go and I am officially free!'

He filled in the details on the way home. 'It's all coming together. You really helped with that loan and my solicitor rang to say Moira's changed her mind about staying in the house until next year. And, even better, she's agreed to put it on the market at one of the lower valuations so we can sell the house quickly and I can pay you back.'

The knot of worry that Sandy stoked up in me, that I was

being taken for a ride, eased every time I was actually with Robin, when I saw how decent he was and how much he cared for me. I really had to stop letting other people's views act like fertiliser on my natural inclination to distrust.

'What was the difference in valuations?' I asked.

'About one hundred and fifty thousand. I've agreed to take a hit of one hundred thousand, so I can get your money back to you as soon as possible.'

'You don't need to do that. I'm not in a hurry.'

'No. I hate owing you money. With all my cash being tied up in Spain, it will be ages before I get a proper cash flow to pay for our wedding otherwise.' He squeezed my knee. 'I want you to become Mrs Franklin sooner rather than later so we can cement our life together. I've been so lucky to find you.'

'Mrs Franklin? You'll be lucky. I've always been Cath Randell, even when I was married to Andrew. Never quite subscribed to the idea of "belonging" to a man.' I laughed as though it was something so obvious, so part of me. On one of our earliest dates, he'd chuckled in admiration as I'd told him I'd kept my maiden name when I got married. 'Independent,' he'd said. 'I like that.'

Now a silence permeated the car, the sort that engulfed us.

I glanced sideways. 'Were you expecting me to become Cath Franklin?'

I couldn't. I couldn't do it. The name felt uncomfortable and cumbersome on my tongue.

'Not if you don't want to,' he said, in the tone of someone who was properly offended.

I tried to explain. 'I've been Cath Randell for fifty-seven years. I don't think I can take on a different surname now. I'm too old.'

He stared straight ahead, jaw clenched.

I didn't know why I couldn't come straight out with, 'Stop being so childish. You change your name to mine if it matters that much.' But I couldn't. Robin had this aura about him. A sense of purpose, a man who was quite clear about his place in the world. Given that I'd trained myself to see off ninety-five per cent of blokes who mansplained their way through the basics of recruitment, there was a strength about him that I didn't encounter often and that I respected. And, if I was honest, that I needed, to stop me walking all over him.

I pulled into the drive. 'Sorry. I didn't mean to get the evening off to a bad start. I was so excited about you coming home.'

Robin's face softened. 'I'm just disappointed. I was looking forward to gliding about with you on my arm and introducing you to all my colleagues in Spain, "Señora Franklin".'

'I'll think about it.' My first rule at work: deliver bad news quickly and never let the client think you might change your mind. But Robin's face lit up so much that I decided to park it until another day. 'There's one more thing before we go in.'

I filled him in on Rebecca moving into the pavilion with her children. I was braced for him reacting grumpily, but he pulled me into his arms. 'How lovely are you? You're such a kind person.'

'It was Sandy really. I wasn't very keen, but he persuaded me.'

'I knew he'd have to have inherited some of your generous ways. Couldn't be all his father.'

I pushed away the stab of defensiveness that I felt a veiled criticism within the compliment. But I didn't have time to brood. As soon as we walked into the kitchen, Sandy, right on cue, picked up his beer, mumbled a hello and disappeared upstairs.

'Sorry about that. He's still getting used to the idea that I'm marrying again.'

'Don't worry, darling. It's a lot for him to take in, when he's had you to himself for all these years. I'm sure we'll all adapt over time.'

I was so grateful to Robin for meeting Sandy's hostility with understanding that I felt my whole body relax.

'I've been meaning to talk to you about our wedding though. Now my divorce should be finalised by the end of July, why don't we get married in September?'

'That soon? I thought you wanted to get married next summer.' My heart leapt at the thought of being that woman, the one who 'just knew', who'd be telling her grandchildren about her whirlwind romance, about how we married eight months after we met. I'd always thought such women were so different from me, reckless, irresponsible. But now I understood that they'd instantly recognised when they'd met the right person.

'The more I'm away from you, the more I realise that I want to be with you. If we keep it fairly small, your family and a few of our closest friends, we should be able to make it happen,' he said.

He leaned over and kissed me. I let go of thoughts about my mum, about Sandy, about the tricky work call I had at 9 a.m. the next day and relaxed into the unfamiliar luxury of being the focus of someone else's world. I wondered if it was possible to get everything organised in less than three months. I nurtured the forlorn hope that Sandy would give up his ridiculous opposition. No doubt his reaction was bound up in some misplaced loyalty to his dad, who, it was tempting to point out, had thought emptying the dishwasher would somehow emasculate him, yet also didn't consider bringing home the bacon his arena either.

With renewed purpose, I started emailing caterers to ascertain their availability in September.

15

REBECCA

Sandy was as good as his word and had carried on refurbishing the pavilion every evening after he finished work. And now here I was a week later, shoehorning the kids into the car and our duvets, laptop and suitcases around them. I'd billed a second move in less than four months as a great adventure, but the truth was I was so relieved to escape Jason and Debs, I'd have slept on the bare floorboards among rat droppings if necessary. We'd just about managed to cling on to a semblance of civility, but it had been a close-run thing all round. Jason moaning to Debs about how he was never going to let his kids be so fussy about their vegetables, me pretending not to hear, Debs not knowing whether to glare at Jason or Eddie and Megan. Secretly, I hoped that their baby would clamp its mouth shut at the mere sight of broccoli and refuse to open it again until it was allowed to mainline chocolate mousse.

Debs hugged me as I got into the car. 'Come and see the baby as soon as it's born. Whenever that is. Hopefully not too soon.'

I squeezed her as tightly as I could without squashing her bump. 'Try not to worry. They're monitoring you really well.

And by the time you get to thirty-seven weeks you might be dying to get it out, especially if we have a really hot July.' I felt a sudden pang of protectiveness that made my impatience with her seem so uncalled for. Tears sprang to my eyes. I blinked them away. 'Thank you so much. I know we've put you out, but I don't know what we'd have done otherwise.'

'Don't be daft.' She gave the children a cuddle. 'Come and see your cousin as soon as she or he arrives, won't you?'

They leapt into the car, pulling faces and waving.

I followed, thanking Jason as I went. He didn't quite manage to look me in the eye as he said, 'It's been lovely spending time with you.'

We drove over to Cath's singing, 'Jason's feet smell, Jason's feet smell, keep them far away from meeeee'. Clearly as well as making peas an optional extra, I had yet to exhaust the many other ways I could be a terrible mother.

But the hilarity of breaking loose from the 'Who used the last piece of toilet roll?/Don't go in the lounge with your shoes on!/Do you have to shout all the time?' monitoring soon faded when I presented Megan with her new home. Thankfully, Cath had said, 'You know the way. I'll let you settle in' when she greeted us, so she didn't witness Megan's wide-eyed horror when a moth flew across the room. I hoped she didn't get a job as a cleaner when she grew up, otherwise there were plenty of houses she'd run screaming from when she saw the state of their plugholes. It probably wasn't the right time to tell her how I'd once found an escaped gerbil riddled with maggots when I moved a chest of drawers.

Eddie was at the other end of the scale, shouting about the tennis court and the pool, despite me reminding him that he needed to use his inside voice. Just as Megan's crying reached a crescendo, along with my yelling at Eddie to calm down because the last tiny staple holding my patience together had well and truly gone AWOL, Sandy appeared.

'Sorry about the noise.' In that moment, I hated Graham with an energy that could have lit up half of London. No doubt he was strolling along the beach, paddling in the sea, while I was on moth, tears and boisterousness duty. I was my own worst enemy because Graham would have had them more than every other weekend, but while it was term-time, I didn't want them endlessly shunting between two houses. It was already a miracle if Eddie arrived at school on time with what he needed for that day and Megan, in particular, became very unsettled by moving from one house to another.

Sandy beckoned to the kids. 'Shall I show you my favourite secret spot in the garden?'

Amazingly, they both followed him out, moderate decibels from Eddie and minimal snivelling from Megan.

I slumped onto my settee, wishing I could close my eyes and sleep for a fortnight.

When Sandy brought Megan and Eddie back, he said, 'We were thinking, if you haven't got any plans, they could have a swim and then we could order some pizzas?' He corrected himself. 'I could treat you to pizza?' Sandy gave me that stare, the one that said, 'For once, don't argue and go with it.'

I hesitated, despite the children clamouring for me to say yes. My whole existence at Cath's house was becoming a right old tangle of emotions. I'd never expected for one minute that this job would be the one that got me a roof over my head. And I certainly hadn't bargained on liking the people. Or rather, one person in particular. Despite trying my hardest, there was no doubt that in the trudge of surviving, Sandy's cheery face popping up now and again brought a flicker of hope to my heart. Of all the hazards I'd expected, I hadn't foreseen that complication.

I couldn't allow an ill-fated romance to derail me.

CATH

I couldn't risk Sandy finding out by accident that we were getting married in September, so I bided my time until Robin was back in Spain the following week and told him over dinner.

Something between contempt and incredulity settled over his features. 'What's the rush? You were with Dad for two years before you got married. Why is Robin any different?'

I explained how things moved more quickly when you were older, that you knew yourself better and what you needed in a partner, which helped you make decisions more swiftly. I hoped that was the case anyway. Robin seemed to understand me so well. When we were on our own, I was in a bubble of contentment. It was just the outside world that complicated things for us. Not least Sandy, who, despite my entreaties to talk through his concerns, pushed his plate back, picked up his jacket and mumbled something about going to the pub.

After Sandy's caustic reaction to my happy news, the thought of telling my mother and friends became more and more daunting as the week ticked past. I begged Sandy not to breathe a word to anyone yet. 'You know what Grandma's like.

She blows hot and cold about everyone. I need to catch her on a good day.'

He shrugged. 'None of my business when you tell anyone.'

In the end, when it got to Friday with Robin coming home that evening, I couldn't put it off any longer. Who cared if no one understood why we were getting married so quickly? I'd been on my own for twenty-one years and I was going to seize the moment. But I still felt nervous when I hurried out of work for the grand reveal at Mum's, wishing I could crash in front of a box set instead.

As I fought my way through rush-hour traffic, I felt ratty and irritable at the thought of Mum giving me the third degree about why I was rushing into it – she probably wouldn't understand the philosophy of carpe diem. I was definitely not in the mood for our inevitable stand-off about crumble and custard – or, even worse, tinned fruit cocktail and evaporated milk, which, if I tried to refuse, Mum would say, 'During the war, we were lucky to get an orange once a year!' Too many late nights at the office sustaining myself on biscuits and peanuts, and my old foe, the menopause, meant that I was going to have to be super-strict if I wasn't going to look at our wedding photos and think 'Who ate all the pies?'

Robin had never been anything other than complimentary about my body, but he often commented on women on TV in a way that made me lift my thighs off the sofa slightly. If I said anything, he'd immediately protest, 'I wouldn't change a thing about you!' but even so, with his naturally slim build and golden skin, not rocking up to my wedding day with a crumble-filled stomach hanging over my pants seemed like a reasonable insurance strategy.

By the time I pulled up outside Mum's, I had talked myself into a more positive frame of mind with the help of my favourite playlist. Which rapidly disappeared when Mum came scuttling down the path and hovered outside the window while I gathered up my phone and handbag.

'Was the traffic bad?' she asked.

I tried not to snap that I'd left work as soon as I could, both resentful that Mum had no understanding of how demanding my job was and sorry that I was later than I'd hoped to be.

I followed her into the house, itching to gather up the stack of newspapers and throw them in the recycling bin. I made a mental note to suggest to Rebecca that she had a discreet cull of reading material every time she came over to clean.

Despite it being the hottest day of June so far, Mum had cooked steak and kidney pie. After fifty-seven years of reminding her that offal wasn't really my thing, I accepted defeat without a word. I tried not to think about Robin just boarding a flight back to Heathrow. No doubt he'd be sipping a nice glass of wine in business class, while I steeled myself for a mouthful of kidney, washed down with lemon barley water. Meanwhile, Mum chattered on about the next-door neighbour's dog barking at all hours and setting Alfie off, before launching into a moan about the branches overhanging her garden from the other side.

As she cleared away the plates, I took the plunge. 'I've got some good news.' She peered over her shoulder as she washed up. I rushed on. 'Robin's asked me to marry him.'

Mum put down the pot she was scrubbing and peeled off her rubber gloves. She sat back at the table. 'Did you say yes?' I couldn't tell from her tone what answer she was hoping for.

'I did. We've decided not to hang around now his divorce is nearly finalised. We're intending to get married in September, if everything goes to plan.' I hated that my voice sounded apologetic, as though even I knew how ridiculous it was to marry someone so quickly.

Mum looked properly shocked. 'This September?'

I couldn't expect someone who last fell in love sixty years

ago to remember that feeling of completeness that comes with being part of a couple. That sense of complex alchemy that is unique and, as I was starting to understand, often incomprehensible to everyone else. For me, Robin encompassed cosiness, sexiness, excitement and hope, all wrapped in a package that made me feel as though he cared about my happiness more than his own. Someone who flew all the way to Amsterdam because I sounded upset on the phone, who was moving heaven and earth to sort out his finances so we could choose a new house together.

'Yes, Mum. We're only having a small wedding,' I said, as though that made the decision so much more reasonable. 'You're invited, of course.'

'I should hope so.'

I waited for her to say congratulations, but she went back to her washing up.

'What's the big hurry? Your dad and I were engaged for two and a half years before we got married.'

'You were twenty, Mum. I'm fifty-seven. It's different. Can you just be happy for me, please?' I was becoming so weary of battling with other people's expectations.

'I am. But after last time, with Andrew, and all his shenanigans, I don't want you to make another mistake.'

'Don't you like Robin?'

'I do, of course I do. I'd hate to see you get hurt again though.' But she was pursing her lips, as though she couldn't quite believe my lunacy.

I sat through another half an hour of Mum's relationship wisdom – 'You make sure he pays his way. I don't care what anyone says, you need to keep control of your money. That's Sandy's inheritance when all's said and done.' I had the sneaking feeling that Sandy had been undermining Robin on the sly. In Mum's eyes, Sandy could do no wrong. Even when he got into a fight at school, Mum would always say, 'The other boy must have started it,' despite compelling evidence to the contrary.

Disappointment that she hadn't been absolutely thrilled coursed through me. I got to my feet. 'Thanks for dinner, Mum. I'll catch up with you again soon. Perhaps you'd like to help me choose my wedding dress?' As soon as the words left my mouth, I wanted to go and boil my brain as the strong possibility of my mother raising her eyebrows and saying, 'Isn't that a bit low-cut for someone your age?' sank in.

I was both relieved and offended when she said, 'Oh, you go with one of your friends to do that. I bet Jax would love to come with you. I did it last time.'

Although Andrew turned out to be a total womaniser, my mother was obviously going to cling on to that event as my 'proper' marriage.

Mum hadn't quite finished her observations though. 'You're not going to truss yourself up in a big meringue again at your age, are you?'

I took my leave before all the words I wanted to say burst free in an unfettered and irreversible torrent. I just about managed to hug her, registering her slightness, the hollows where soft curves used to be. I walked away, annoyance swirling alongside regret that our interactions never quite lived up to the jolly mother and daughter occasions that other women seemed to manage with ease.

I got into the car while she stood waving at the door. I phoned Jax on my way home and said, 'Can you pop out and meet me in the wine bar? I need a friend and a drink.'

At least, I hoped she was the friend I needed.

17

CATH

Jax burst into the wine bar, a whirl of big hair and platform shoes that made her tower above the average man in there. She slid into the booth. 'What's going on? You sounded upset.'

Before I'd even explained, I felt the age-old comfort of being in the company of someone who would really understand me. 'I am upset, mainly because I should be so happy – Robin and I have decided to get married – and Mum and Sandy are acting like I've booked my plot in the cemetery.'

Jax didn't even crack a smile, despite my playing by our unspoken rules of finding a glimmer of humour in tough times.

'Married? Already? You're not pregnant, are you?'

I was starting to think that the world supply of the word 'congratulations' as a response to 'I'm getting married' had dried up. 'That would be a turn-up for the books at fifty-seven. No, we love each other and don't want to waste any time.'

'But you've only known him for five months. And he's worked away half of that time. You've probably only spent about a hundred days together. We've only met him once.'

I was still sore about the fact that she hadn't shown her most charming side to Robin, going over the top with her questions. I couldn't really blame him for not rushing to repeat the experience when I'd suggested that we might catch up with them last weekend – 'It's been a long week. Can we just snuggle up and watch a film?'

She put her glasses on. 'That's better, you were all blurry. So what's the issue? That Sandy and your mum think it's too soon?'

I told her about Sandy's behaviour, but could feel myself leaning heavily towards emphasising that it was my son who was unreasonable, not Robin. I did make her laugh about Mum's tactlessness.

'But do they have a point?' She flicked up her hands, her long red nails darting about.

'I kind of think it's nothing to do with them.'

'It is a bit to do with them, because they want you to be happy. And even though you think they are worrying unnecessarily, it's not that unreasonable for them to be concerned because it's all happened so quickly.'

I ordered another glass of wine, recognising the unpalatable truth that I didn't want an objective opinion from Jax. I wanted her to tell me that Robin was beyond lovely, that my mum and Sandy would have to like it or lump it and that her and Dan were really looking forward to spending loads of time with us.

But Jax steepled her fingers. 'Okay, let's look at this as though it was a business proposition, because marriage is a transaction at the end of the day.'

I should have ordered a whole bottle of wine to ease me through Jax's 'advice'. 'How romantic. Is that what Dan thinks?'

'Nah, but we were stupidly young when we met. I was all about the dinners out and the roses on Valentine's Day then. It's pure luck that we've grown together. But you, you're old enough to be clinical about it.'

'Really? Are you suggesting I get out a spreadsheet and

weigh up the pros and cons? Where does love feature in all of this?'

Jax leaned back in her seat. 'Love? Come on, girl. You've been together such a short time that lust will be fogging up your brain.' She cackled. 'Humour me.'

What I really wanted was for someone to consider humouring me but I knew Jax wouldn't desist until she'd made her point. I resigned myself to a lecture.

'We all agree he's charming and fun and trots out to Amsterdam because you've had a meltdown and is a big fan of the grand gesture.' She said it in a way that sounded dismissive.

'That's not nothing. Andrew barely got off the sofa to find out what he could do to help when my dad had his first heart attack.'

'I get that, but you're a successful woman, one sexy momma and good all-round catch for any bloke. So if I were in your shoes, I'd be wanting to make very, very sure that I was marrying an equal, not someone I was going to have to carry. You know, similar affluence, ability to take responsibility for their own stuff, emotionally stable. I mean, do you know roughly how wealthy he is?'

I explained about the house and the property developments.

Jax pulled a face. 'It all sounds good.'

'But?'

'I couldn't help feeling he was showing off when we came for dinner. It made him seem a bit flash. On the one hand, he was full of how much money he was making out of his property development, but he's been pestering Danny to invest since we came to yours. He comes across as rather desperate.'

I was so angry with Robin for putting me in this position. His philosophy on life was all 'If you don't ask, you don't get,' but I was furious that he'd contacted my friends without discussing it with me.

'Sorry. I didn't know he was going to do that.' I didn't really blame Jax and Dan for finding it a bit odd. It was.

Now I'd conceded that I didn't know about it, Jax revved up the big guns.

'Danny looked on Companies House and he's got at least six dissolved companies in the last ten years. I mean, there might be a good reason for that, of course.'

'I don't think that's anything to worry about. He had a partner for a while and they went their separate ways, then I think the law changed around property developments and he had to find a more tax-efficient way of working.' I sieved through my memory for other snippets of information, but the truth was my main interest in his business was how soon he could cut down the amount of time he spent in Spain.

'I also felt that he kept putting you down.'

'No, not at all. No, you've got him wrong there. He's been great for my confidence.'

Jax didn't meet my eye. 'Maybe.'

I knew, though, that she would say what she needed to say, either now or at a later date. I decided to get it over with, in a bonanza of being irritated with everyone around me. 'What made you think that?'

'Does anyone our age go on about all the pretty girls they'd known at parties thirty years ago? I thought it was really disrespectful. And when I went out to the loo, the door was sticking. He started going on about the house, and how it was too big for you, what a state it was when he moved in and thank goodness he was a great handyman. Your house is beautiful!'

Hurt and anger made me burst out with, 'Well, he's happy enough to live there for free!'

I regretted it immediately when Jax said, 'You are sure his house is actually on the market?'

'Yes. I mean, it's been on and off a few times because his

wife has been using it as leverage, but even she seems keen to
sell now.'

'Do you know the address?'

'It's in London. Sartre Street, Fulham.'

She whipped out her phone. Uncertainty, disappointment
and resentment that Jax was looking for reasons not to like
Robin and treating me as though I was so gormless, I'd go along
with anything churned in my chest. Despite all that, I was
finding it hard to ignore the fear that she had spotted something
I hadn't. She brought up Rightmove on her screen, tapped in
the street and turned the phone to me. 'Is that the one? The
four-bedroom maisonette? One point nine million. Hopefully
that's nearly a million quid winging its way towards him some-
time soon.'

I felt a huge surge of relief that I didn't have to come up
with a hundred excuses why the house might not be on there.

She then started on the video tour – 'Ooh, nice stained
glass. That bathroom could do with an update. That's a lovely
painting. I've always wanted a roof terrace. That fridge is like
something my grandma used to have.' She carried on watching.
'Imagine owning a house worth nearly two million quid and still
having neighbours underneath to complain about your noise.'

'Stop it,' I said half-heartedly but couldn't resist leaning over
the table to see what she was gawking at. Too chintzy for my
taste, all brocade curtains and oriental rugs. Privately, I thought
my house was much nicer, but I didn't articulate that in case Jax
twisted my words into evidence that Robin lacked taste.

Jax was studying every picture with great gusto. 'She's into
her ornaments, isn't she? No wonder he likes your house. Must
be so relaxing after living with all that clutter. Will you really
sell up and buy somewhere else with him?'

I drained my wineglass. 'Nothing is set in stone yet.'

Jax stopped scrolling. 'But you're definitely getting married.'

I nodded, feeling sad that she wasn't excited for me and

protective towards Robin. 'Give him a chance. He might have been trying too hard to win you over, but you're also quite a force of nature.' I tried to make a joke. 'A wonderful force of nature, but still quite intimidating before people get to know you. He perhaps wanted to impress you and went about it the wrong way.' I got up. 'Come on, Robin's texted to say he'll swing by to pick us up on his way back from the airport. We'll give you a lift home.'

Jax stabbed at her mobile. 'No, it's out of your way. I'll get an Uber.' Before I could protest, she'd clicked on her app. 'Five minutes.'

I hugged her and she said, 'We just want the best for you.'

Tears prickled in my eyes. I felt as though I was going to spend the rest of my life defending Robin. I couldn't remember a single person expressing the slightest concern about Andrew and look how that turned out. Here I was, marrying again thirty-three years after the first time, much wiser, yet everyone was acting as though I knew nothing about life.

18

REBECCA

Since we took up residence in the Wimbledon Hotel, as Eddie called it, Cath couldn't seem to find the right balance in her attitude towards me. Half the time, she seemed terrified that now I'd got my feet under the table, I'd turn into a slacker. 'Did you manage to get through to the pharmacy and get Mum's medication ordered?'

'Yes, the prescription hadn't been issued, but I managed to sort it all out. I'll drop it off at the weekend when the kids go to their dad's.'

She smiled absentmindedly. 'Thank you, that would be brilliant. I hope you didn't waste too much time on it.'

I was daring her to say, 'I wondered why you hadn't managed to clean the gym.' She didn't quite get the words out into the air, but I could tell she was thinking them. I put her right. There was no way she was going to get the impression that I'd been sitting in my hut watching the clouds go by. 'Robin was on the rowing machine and told me not to bother cleaning in there. I did tell him that you'd specifically asked me to.'

Then, at other times, like this morning, she acted as though she was my mate. 'I thought we'd have the wedding reception here... get some fairy lights and bunting up. Do you think solar lights would still work in September? I've seen some quite funky ones with little white geese on them... I don't want to be that old bride doing hearts and bells at my age.'

Solar-powered geese. Roll on the day that instead of worrying about paying my electricity bill, I could focus on whether my geese were going to get enough sunlight to quack into life.

'So have you set a date yet?'

Cath looked away. 'We're hoping for the fourth of September. I'm trying to confirm it all at the moment – it's a bit complicated because you can't get a marriage licence until you can show proof that you're officially divorced. That won't be until the end of July.'

I had all this ahead of me, but at least Graham and I wouldn't have to wrangle over how to divide up our assets as he'd ensured that there weren't any left. I was still smarting from the knowledge that after paying a mortgage every month for nearly eleven years, I'd come out with nothing. I couldn't help wondering why people even bothered to get married any more. Cath looked as though she had the weight of the world on her shoulders, rather than preparing to skip off into the sunset with her handsome new husband.

'I was hoping you might be able to help with some of the organisation if I pay you extra, because it's all going to be a bit last minute and there's always far more running around to do than you bargain on, isn't there?'

'I'd certainly be up for that, thank you.' I didn't think this was the moment to point out that I'd stayed up until 2 a.m. the night before I got married sorting out the flowers for everyone's buttonholes. As far as I could see so far, Cath had delegated the 'running around'. I shouldn't be churlish though. This wedding was delivering windfalls in all manner of ways that I hadn't foreseen. The more indispensable I could make myself, the better.

'Shall I do the office now?' I said.

As she picked up her bag, I was twitching for her to leave so I could get in there before Robin needed to start work. He was very particular, hated me moving anything on his desk. I'd even resorted to taking pictures, so I could put it all back just so. He always made me a cappuccino though, very concerned about whether it was strong and hot enough. That was part of his charm. He never made me feel as though I was a cleaner, more like someone who was a valued member of Team Robin, working towards the common goal of keeping everything organised and running smoothly. Such a chivalrous man, carrying the Hoover upstairs for me or giving me a hand moving the settee in the lounge.

As soon as Cath's car disappeared down the drive, I shot into the office, took a photo of the desk and began dusting. I'd never understood some of my cleaning colleagues who said they never looked at any of their customers' private paperwork. I couldn't help it. Born nosey, I supposed. And, in an odd sort of way, quite entertaining, an insight into how people thought. A reality TV programme where a psychologist analyses what cleaners discover about their clients would knock the spots off *I'm a Celebrity* and *Love Island*.

I flicked through the quotes – flowers, wedding favours, caterers, marquee, chair hire. Thousands of pounds. A proper princess affair. Yet Cath still bought the thinnest, cheapest bleach and smoothed out and saved the tissue paper from the endless bouquets Robin gave her. I studied the quote for wedding flowers (nine hundred quid!) and tutted at the picture Cath had ticked of pale vintage pink roses. How boring. I turned over the page. I much preferred the vibrant deep pink dahlias, the bright orange Californian poppies and lavender. I was so deep in thought about how snapdragons looked gorgeous next to echinacea that I didn't hear Robin come into the kitchen until he shouted through, 'Coffee?'

I jumped and hastily patted the quotes into a pile, making a big palaver out of squirting polish and rubbing the arms of the chair. He put down a mug on the coaster. I tried to read his face to work out if he realised I'd had a good beak at their private stuff.

His eyes flicked to the neat stack of letters. 'Have you finished in here?'

'Nearly. I just need to run the Hoover around.' I did an elaborate wipe of the computer screen, to show that I had a reason for hovering around the desk and took a sip of my drink. 'Thank you. You make such good coffee.'

He smiled. 'Had plenty of practice. Drink about ten cups a day. Probably shouldn't at my age, but then again, I'd be falling asleep if I didn't.'

'Well, you're much fitter than I am. I could never do all that rowing and running you do.' Flattery felt like a good distraction technique.

He puffed up his chest. 'You move around a lot for work. I'm stuck at a desk. You're probably fitter than me.'

I laughed. 'Go on with you. You're not going to need to diet for the big day.'

'Thank goodness for that. If all the paperwork comes through on time, I've only got about two months to get into shape.'

'Crikey. That's coming around quickly.'

His face took on a self-satisfied air, all cat got the cream that he'd bagged someone like Cath. Though, to be fair, he did look after her. He always had his head under the bonnet of her car filling up the washer bottle or checking the oil. If that whole knight in shining armour thing was your bag, Robin definitely ticked that box with his 'After you, let me carry that for you, you put your feet up' twaddle. Though even I'd been impressed when I saw him rigging up a fancy new sound system in the gym. If Graham had been in charge of wiring like that, I'd have been running a sweepstake at the bookies on the chances of him lighting up his ears.

I wondered whether I could ever get used to a bloke fluttering helpfully around me after living with Graham lumping about on the settee, shouting, 'I'll do it in a minute' for so many years. Before I could have a proper poke at that thought, Robin jolted me back into the present by saying, 'Once we've got the wedding out of the way, we'll be putting this house on the market.'

I sensed a warning in there. A smiling, cheery torpedo across the bows not to get too comfortable. I pulled a few books out of the bookcase and dusted underneath. 'Always good to make a fresh start when you meet someone new,' I said, keeping my voice light. If he hoped to rattle me, I was going to disappoint him.

But Robin had lost interest in me, hadn't given a moment's thought to the fact that if they moved, the cleaner who washed his whiskers out of the sink would be made homeless. To most people, I was an invisible presence, a non-entity in bleach-stained leggings and an old T-shirt. One day I hoped to surprise everyone.

19

CATH

In the days following my chat with Jax, I found unwanted suspicions creeping into my mind. Over dinner one night with Robin, I said casually, 'When I had a drink with Jax the other evening, she said you were hoping Dan would invest in your business?'

He made a face as though I'd spoilt a lovely surprise. 'He's not really the calibre of investor I normally encourage, but he was telling me how they couldn't afford to build an annexe for Jax's mother and they were worried about finding fees for a nursing home.' He forked a piece of chicken into his mouth. 'I wanted to help him out. He's your friend, after all, so I was prepared to offer him a short-term investment of a year. I reckon he'd make the fifty grand he needs by next Christmas at the latest.'

'You didn't mention it.'

He tilted his head on one side and frowned. 'We talked about it when they were here. You were definitely in the conversation because you and Jax both argued that it would be much cheaper to build an extension to their house than to pay nursing fees.'

I felt wrong-footed.

Robin waved his glass of wine at me. 'I think you've got champagne-induced amnesia.'

It was shameful that I had zero recollection of that debate. It was about time I learnt not to drink on an empty stomach.

'He's very keen and keeps ringing and badgering me for more details. I've been so busy, I haven't managed to set up a meeting with him yet, but I will.'

I didn't ask any more. I didn't know what was going on. Perhaps Robin was overenthusiastic and had misunderstood Dan's polite interest. Perhaps Dan had played it down to Jax because they had different views, or he hadn't actually admitted to her that they couldn't bankroll accommodation for her mother. My mind hummed trying to make sense of it all. I changed the subject to the far safer topic of which wines we were going to choose for our wedding day, but the dizzy thrill of getting married when Robin proposed a month ago might as well have been centuries away. We were like a couple of shire horses hauling a dray of naysayers and nitpickers towards the finish line.

Suddenly he clattered his cutlery onto his plate. 'Cath, is everything all right? You do want to get married, don't you?'

'Yes, of course I do. I'm just trying to please so many people and I know they've got my best interests at heart, but everywhere I turn, someone is asking me if I'm doing the right thing.'

'Is that because they don't like me?'

'No! No. It's nothing to do with that. I suppose they've seen how long it took me to get my life back together after Andrew left and they don't want to see me hurt like that again.' I yawned. 'I could fall out with all of them at the moment.'

Robin leant over to kiss me. 'It's only because they love you and they don't know me yet. And, let's face it, it hasn't been plain sailing extricating myself from Moira. It's not ideal having an ex-wife still pulling the financial strings.'

I loved him for being so understanding. 'Yes, I think that's what Jax was worried about. She really likes you,' I said, with absolutely no evidence that was the case, 'but she's a bit concerned about how difficult Moira might make life for us. She even looked up the house on Rightmove.'

A shadow crossed Robin's face. 'She really is something else, isn't she?'

I cursed myself for not keeping that little bit of information under wraps. 'She was messing about, being nosey and seeing how much you were selling it for. She's interested in property – fancies herself as someone who can predict the market.' I couldn't hold his gaze and started stuttering.

'You mean, she was checking up on me.'

'No, not at all. She was just curious. She's lovely, honestly. When you're more at ease with each other, you'll have a great laugh. She's really generous and funny.'

Robin didn't look convinced, but said, 'I look forward to getting to know her better.' He scraped his chair back. 'I'm going up to the house this Saturday to get Moira to agree to my settlement terms for our finances. She'll hold us up by faffing about otherwise. I was wondering if you'd like to come with me? I could use the company on the journey and we could go out for dinner afterwards?'

The taut band of tension squeezing my stomach loosened slightly. 'I'm happy to come to London, but I'm not sure it's going to smooth anything over with Moira if I turn up.'

'Too right. We'll have to make sure she doesn't see you. I'll park down the road and you can stay in the car. Hopefully it'll be a quick in and out, then we can get a bite to eat – where do you fancy? Moro? Ottolenghi?'

Eating was the last thing on my mind. I couldn't think past Robin finally being free of Moira if all went to plan. But I didn't want to rain on his parade, so I smiled and said he should choose.

. . .

On the morning we were leaving for London, Robin was pacing about at the bottom of the garden on the phone. He'd covered the mouthpiece and waved me away when I went down to check if everything was okay. 'Just a couple of details to authorise and then I can relax.' I went back inside to get ready and I bumped into Rebecca in the hallway.

'Where are you off to? Anywhere nice?' she asked as I put on my lipstick.

My ridiculously high spirits that Robin was being proactive over his finances made me far chattier than I would be normally. 'Don't think you could call it nice – we're driving up to London so that Robin can conclude some matters with his ex-wife – but after that, we'll probably grab something to eat and go for a walk.'

I was aware that I was trying to make it sound like we'd get a sandwich and sit in Hyde Park rather than the Michelin-starred restaurant Robin had booked. I would have quite liked to picnic in a London park, but Robin was addicted to trying out the latest restaurants he'd seen reviewed in the Sunday papers.

'What about you?' My voice tapered away, slightly embarrassed because I was pretty sure her Saturday wasn't going to be anywhere near as enjoyable as mine.

She took a deep breath as though she had a whole list of wonderful things planned. 'I'm dropping the kids down to their dad, so I'll probably go and spend the day at the beach.' She stretched out her arms. 'Could do with a bit of sunshine on my skin.'

I recognised the effort she was making to sound as though it was no big deal taking the kids back. But I remembered the ache that dogged me all the way home, seeping into the stillness of the house and stretching into the silence of the evening whenever I left Sandy at his dad's. I touched her hand. 'You do get used to it. I promise. It's always hard, but eventually, you do stop saying to yourself, "they'll be having their dinner now" and wondering if they are getting to sleep okay.'

Rebecca blinked hard. 'Thank you. That's very nice to know.' She turned away, wishing me a good day and I couldn't help thinking about how much women carry, absorb and withstand in the name of motherhood. I admired her. She never complained, but quietly and efficiently accepted her lot and did what she had to do.

As we joined the motorway towards London, the playlist that Robin had made for our wedding blaring out, I was in the sunniest of moods. We belted out everything from Neil Diamond to Boney M., finishing with Lou Reed's 'Perfect Day' as we drove through Fulham and turned into Sartre Street. He parked, took his briefcase off the back seat and said, 'I won't be too long.' He slammed the door. 'If you see her chasing after me with a carving knife, send for help!'

'I might have a little walk and stretch my legs.'

He gave me a hug and set off up the road. I waited by the car until he was walking up a black and white tiled path to a handsome Victorian house with a 'For Sale' sign in the front garden. He rang the bell. I tucked myself behind a tree, waiting for a glimpse of my predecessor. He glanced at his watch and knocked, then stepped back and stared up at the upstairs windows.

He pulled some keys out of his pocket and opened the front door. I looked forward to telling Jax that I'd seen his home with my own eyes and could vouch for the fact that he had lived there. I'd have to make an effort not to appear too smug. On the other hand, I was disappointed not to catch sight of Moira – I was hoping that the real-life version would be more fluffy slippers and baggy-kneed leggings than her Facebook pictures suggested. Though I couldn't deny I was also relieved that she wouldn't somehow sense my presence and come tearing out on the warpath.

I wandered further up the road, pressing myself into the shadows, careful not to make it obvious that I was glancing up at the top windows every now and again. There was no sign of her. I didn't know what I'd expected, that I'd spot her gliding past in a negligee beckoning to Robin with a bottle of champagne in her hand? It was far more likely that she'd deliberately gone out when she knew he was coming or perhaps she was just playing mind games and not answering the door.

As every minute ticked past, I imagined Moira begging Robin to reconsider, pleading with him to call a halt to the divorce before it was too late. Or playing hardball and asking for an even bigger percentage of the assets. Or her not being there at all and Robin wandering from room to room, looking at everything they'd bought together, reminiscing about the good times. That idea I didn't want to dwell on and reverted back to focusing on the possibility of an antagonistic meeting.

Part of me regretted Robin's rush to get married, which made us vulnerable to Moira's whims as he tried to tie up the loose ends. But I couldn't deny there was something incredibly flattering about being with a man who was in a hurry to make me his wife. Especially at our age, when I'd all but given up on ever feeling romantic again. I'd begun to think that fluttery sensation died off beyond the age of thirty-five and everything else after that was just about the quality of the cocoa. Discovering that being fifty-seven was no barrier to listening out for Robin's car and experiencing a burst of excitement when he walked through the door was a revelation.

I was starting to pace now. I was sure that Moira wouldn't be able to talk him round, but my relationship with Robin felt so hard fought for, he and I against the world, that I couldn't shake off the fear that, one day, our love wouldn't be able to withstand the avalanche of people who were campaigning for us to fail.

About three quarters of an hour later, as my mind was regressing to all sorts of possibilities I didn't want to consider, Robin reappeared in the street. I waited for him to reach his Audi, double-checking that Moira wasn't following him before I hurried along to where we were parked. I dived into the car, braced for a drama of some sort.

He was resting his forehead on his hand, looking every inch a man exhausted by life.

'Well, what happened? Was she even there?'

He lifted his head. 'She was. Asleep on the sofa. Been out with her toy boy to the Sanderson Hotel for cocktails, didn't get in till three and didn't hear the bell apparently.'

'Did she accept your proposal, though?'

He thrust a large brown envelope at me and started the car. 'Yes, with a bit of persuasion. The financial settlement is agreed. Finally! Hallelujah. And even better, there's been a decent offer on the house.' He leaned over and kissed me and all the dread, all my worry that Moira would ruin our happiness melted away.

We drove to lunch with an air of festivity and hilarity that made me feel as though we really were on the cusp of the rest of our lives.

CATH

Despite the good news about Robin and Moira finally agreeing their finances, money issues dogged the following week. I was increasingly uncomfortable about how much Robin wanted to push the boat out for our wedding. Every time I said, 'I'm not bothered about the palate-cleansing sorbet and the petits-fours' which added another few hundred onto the already shocking catering bill, he mocked my misgivings, making me feel as though I'd suggested eating off paper plates.

He kept saying, 'I am going to foot the whole bill eventually, so let me treat us to the best possible time we can have.'

When I protested that in this day and age, women should pay their share of everything, he got quite offended.

'Maybe the men you know want their wives to divide everything down to the last toothbrush, but our big day is on me. It marks a break with my past life and our new start.'

And, as always, he won me round, persuading me that any restraint was a curb on living freely and fully. He'd lift my chin, kiss me and say, 'Why wouldn't we kickstart our future together with a huge celebration? I'm never going to have another wedding, so this is my line in the sand, my megaphone announcement that, finally, I have met the woman of my dreams, my absolute soulmate.'

I tried to relax into it, to not dwell on how hard I'd had to work for the money I had to keep transferring. Initially I'd been so happy to hand over all the organisation to him – I found getting samples of menus, talking to different florists, tying down the detail of what would happen when unutterably boring. I also loved how arty Robin was, his eye for which colours and shapes complemented each other.

But when I stopped to look at how much we would end up spending, I struggled not to be a killjoy. I didn't want to be the person who tied their shoes up with string, but, essentially, I was still the person whose first commission for placing someone twenty-one years ago had meant that I could afford to take Mum and Dad and Sandy to a holiday park in Weymouth. Despite a leaking chalet and torrential rain, we'd had the best time, sitting in the clubhouse, joining in with all the quizzes, Dad forgetting to whisper the answer to me in his excitement and Mum being furious that the table next to us had overheard and pipped us to the bottle of Malibu. The whole week cost a mere fraction of what we were spending on Antigua. When I tried to explain that to Robin, he would say, 'But that was then, and this is now. You don't want to honeymoon in a caravan, do you?'

Which I didn't, but I couldn't shake off the feeling that it was so profligate to blow such a lot of money when I saw how grateful Rebecca was when I gave her food for dinner. I'd got into a habit of saying, 'Tesco sent the wrong cheese/fruit/bread', because I didn't want to offend her. Even so, I didn't know why it mattered to me what she thought, but I was mortified when Robin discussed whether we needed a private jacuzzi and butler service on honeymoon in front of her. I felt the need to say afterwards, 'I'd be happy with something low-key, but Robin really wants to celebrate.'

She never took advantage, though. I couldn't believe I'd suspected for a second that she'd taken Mum's jewellery. Thankfully, for all our sakes, Mum seemed to have accepted that Rebecca wasn't responsible for its disappearance even though it hadn't yet turned up. As we settled into a routine of Rebecca going over to Mum's on a regular basis, I realised I'd rarely had someone as trustworthy as her working for me. The company was good for Mum, as well. On the odd occasion that the kids weren't at school and Rebecca had to take them over with her, Mum was always buzzing about how much fun they'd had playing with Alfie. Despite the obvious gulf between what Rebecca had and what I had, she never expected more than I offered, always doing the hours she was supposed to and giving me the right change and receipts when I asked her to buy something on my behalf. Frankly, I was becoming far more annoyed with Robin's attitude when he said things like, 'I see, now I'm a done deal, we're on the supermarket shower gel. It was all ginger and lemongrass fancy stuff when I first moved in.'

I knew he was joking. However, given that his contribution to date had mainly been wine deliveries and some random fancy items he'd picked up in Harrods food hall when he was in London – everything from capers to honey-covered cashews but nothing you could make a whole meal from – the comment immediately made me want to draw up a balance sheet of who'd paid for what so far. As fast as I handed over money, another bill popped up – a deposit on a marquee, a delivery of champagne and the one that really had me gritting my teeth – a handmade suit from Savile Row. When I'd said, only half-jokingly, 'What's wrong with Moss Bros?' he'd replied, 'The best bride deserves the best-dressed groom.'

I tried to push away the creeping unease that he was very generous with himself on my cash. But before I could stop myself, I'd asked, 'Have your buyers organised their survey yet?'

He'd sounded snappy when he said, 'Their surveyor is away

for the next couple of weeks until the end of July. I'll pay you
back with interest, if that's what's worrying you.'

I'd screwed up my face. 'I'm not expecting you to pay interest. Don't be silly.' Though I would be happy when we could
stop living under this uneasy cloud where money was such a
touchy subject. I didn't feel quite so stressed about it now I'd
seen his actual house with the 'For Sale' sign. I'd taken a surreptitious photo and texted it to Jax with a jokey comment,
*Waiting outside while Robin's in the marital home – I'm
shaking in my shoes in case the ex-wife comes out on her broom-
stick*! She'd sent laughing emojis back, but I felt the quiet satisfaction of proving to her that the house and wife were just as
he'd said.

However, the awkwardness around finances was nothing
compared to the arguments we had about Sandy. The real row
had come when he'd told me that he thought Sandy needed to
move out. 'I'm not being funny, but a thirty-two-year-old
shouldn't be living rent-free and sponging off his mother when
he's earning perfectly adequate money.'

'He's still having to pay his own mortgage until they sell the
house.'

'But he doesn't give you money for anything.'

And that was it. My knee-jerk reaction. I'd never been able
to accept anyone criticising my son. 'Neither do you yet.'

I saw a side to Robin that I'd never seen before. He marched
over to the wardrobe, pulled out his holdall and said, 'No one
has ever accused me of not paying my way and they're not going
to start now.'

I'd stood, my brain trying to catch up with the grown man
chucking his underpants into a bag. It was almost laughable.
'What are you doing?' I was waiting for him to turn round and
say, 'Ha! Had you going there!'

He didn't. He'd carried on pulling shirts off hangers and
shoving them in. I couldn't seem to get my head around his reac-

tion, resisting the temptation to say, 'Fold them up properly. Rebecca spent ages ironing those.'

Finally, he'd said, 'I can't be married to someone who doesn't trust me and accuses me of freeloading.'

'So, what, that's it? You're going to walk out without a discussion?' For the moment, anger had the upper hand, but I could feel tears gathering, distantly, amassing like clouds over a far-off valley. 'If you throw all your toys out of your pram like this when I say one thing you don't like, it doesn't bode well for married life.'

Robin had sat down on the bed, with his face in his hands. 'You've no idea how much it hurts me not to be able to provide for you at the moment. I've got so much going on, there simply aren't enough hours in a day to sort everything out and I'm getting it in the neck everywhere – from the site managers in Spain, from Moira and from you as well, when I'm doing my absolute best to give you the wedding you deserve.'

I'd stopped being angry and felt guilty that I'd carried on working as hard as ever, occasionally nodding at a picture of a wedding cake, popping out one lunchtime to buy our rings in forty minutes flat and answering most questions about cutlery, chairs and crockery with 'I'll be delighted with whatever you decide.' In retrospect, given that of the thirty guests, ninety-five per cent were mine, as Robin didn't have any family apart from a few distant cousins, I probably should have shouldered more of the organisation. But he'd seemed so happy doing it, spending hours searching for 'the perfect thing' on the internet.

I'd knelt down at his feet and put my hands on his knees. 'I'm sorry. I know you're carrying a heavy load at the moment. I didn't mean to upset you.'

He'd grabbed my wrist. 'You know that you're the most important thing in the world to me. What you think really matters. I couldn't bear it if you thought I was letting you down.'

I shook my head. 'You're not letting me down. You're the

best thing that's happened to me in years.' I wished we could sort the money issues out once and for all, so the insistent nagging worry that was starting to accompany every request for a transfer could keel over and die.

His shoulders had relaxed. 'Do you mean that?'

I did. I thought my lot was to work until I dropped, increasingly embroiled in the administration of Mum's life, hoping that one day Sandy might have children of his own. I'd given up thinking that I might find a man who didn't mind my full-on career, who wasn't threatened by my success. Now, I was allowing myself to fantasise about touring round Galicia in an open-topped car, taking ourselves off for winter sun in the Caribbean, spontaneous weekends in the Cotswolds. All the things that never appealed to me on my own, but now hovered in front of me like fireflies lighting up an August sky. I'd pushed away my frustration that Robin's house sale was taking so long and said, 'Maybe we should postpone the wedding for a while, so you're not under so much pressure.'

'No! No. I'm not going to let all the other things become more important than marrying you. How about we take off this weekend, just us, and reconnect? We need some time away to focus on each other.'

I was so relieved that I wasn't having to phone everyone with the news that the wedding was off and prove all the doubters right – 'Crikey, that was a bit quick, are you sure?' – that I ignored the irritation that I was so busy at work that planning a weekend away felt like another chore on my to-do list. 'That would be lovely. Where would you like to go? Do you want me to sort it out?' I'd smiled in apology.

Robin had tapped his nose. 'I know a brilliant hotel in Herne Bay on the Kent coast. Leave it to me.'

· · ·

So mid-morning on a baking-hot July Saturday, we set off to the seaside. Robin had casually announced that morning that we were going to Deal, not Herne Bay. 'They were very apologetic, but they'd overbooked. They've upgraded us though, so it should be lovely.' I tried not to be annoyed that I'd wasted ages researching places to eat and walks in Herne Bay and quietly cancelled the reservations, then phoned almost every restaurant in Deal before I could find a table.

An hour and a half later when we arrived in the town under the bluest of skies, Robin's enthusiasm for this part of the world was rubbing off on me. 'You'll love it here. I used to come here as a kid. My dad couldn't bear sandy beaches, but he liked this one because of the pebbles. The pace is much slower than Surrey; people seem friendlier.'

I wanted to mooch around the shops and look in the art galleries, but Robin had other plans.

'Let's go for a coffee at the Italianate Glasshouse in Ramsgate, while the weather is so gorgeous. It's beautiful there, and knowing the Great British summer, it will be pouring down tomorrow. We can do the shops then.'

I knew he was anxious to show off the area, so I went along with it, and we spent a happy couple of hours sitting in the sunshine over tea and scones. We were so content in each other's company that I had the strongest sense yet that our future was becoming a concrete reality, something to look forward to, rather than a nebulous pipe dream mired in Moira's whims and Sandy's objections. We spent ages discussing our fantasy home with his and hers offices, and a master bedroom with two en suites, bantering about who needed what and which items fell into the 'luxury, nice-to-have' category.

As we drove back into Deal, I wanted to prolong the moment and suggested having a drink on the seafront.

'This early?'

'It's six o'clock. The sun's over the yardarm somewhere. And we are on a sort of holiday. I'm not suggesting we drink ourselves into oblivion, just sit and have a glass of wine and people-watch.'

Robin frowned. 'I was hoping to go back to the hotel and have a little siesta before we go out.'

Robin was very fond of 'siestas', which often didn't involve sleep. After so many years of intermittent sex, being with a man who couldn't get enough of me was a bit of a shock.

'Let's enjoy the sea air for an hour or so. It's so long since I've been to the coast.'

My tone was teasing, but Robin pursed his lips. 'You don't fancy me as much as you used to, do you?'

I leaned in and kissed him. 'I most definitely do.'

He pulled back. 'Then why would you prioritise a glass of wine over me?'

I reached for his hand. 'I didn't realise it was such a big deal. Let's go back then.'

'No, because you're doing it to please me now, not because you really want to.'

I lost my temper. 'You can be such a child. Right, you please yourself, but I'm going to have a walk along the beach and have a drink in the sunshine.'

'That's another thing. I think you're becoming alcohol-dependent.'

I walked off, overwhelmed by the peculiar sort of anger that comes from the frustration of everything being in place to have a wonderful time but ruining it all with a stupid and avoidable argument.

I couldn't be bothered to explore and opted for the nearest outdoor terrace. I ordered a glass of Sauvignon while grumping about the accusation of being alcohol-dependent. My breathing settled as I looked towards the horizon. I took a sip of the wine, expecting Robin to slide into a chair opposite me at any moment and make amends with a bottle of champagne – 'Nothing sorts out a quarrel as easily as remembering all the reasons you have to celebrate each other.'

I kept glancing at my phone, waiting for *Sorry for being grumpy, please forgive me* to ping up, but nothing. I tried to concentrate on the sun shining on the water, the seagulls wheeling around in the sky, the noise of the waves, but the bruise of being at odds with Robin consumed me, weighing on my heart and making it impossible to relax. In the end, I paid and left, eager to get back to the hotel, make up and salvage the rest of the weekend.

I let myself into the room. No Robin. I had a moment of panic that he'd returned home without me, until I saw his overnight case still there. My favourite green shirt of his was gone. He must have come back and changed. He knew I always loved him in it. We'd obviously just missed each other. I texted him. *I'm at the hotel waiting for you x.* I stared at the message watching for him to read it.

Minutes, then half an hour, an hour passed. If he didn't materialise soon, we'd be late for our dinner reservation. Plus, there was the inconvenient fact that the longer this went on, the harder I was going to find it not to explode when he did finally walk through the door. I never managed a whole weekend off work. There were always emails to catch up on, issues that I didn't have time to think about during the week. Days like these were precious.

I rang him, but the call went to voicemail. My frustration mounted at the total waste of time and energy. I stretched out on the bed; the doubts that I'd been shooing away like curious chickens pecking at my certainty crowded in.

Seven o'clock came and went. I vacillated between angry and worried. The downside of Robin was that he was such an impetuous man, so passionate. He probably needed longer to calm down. Sandy's dad had always maintained I had a clinical, logical brain. Maybe I was the odd one. I said my piece, then got over it.

I cancelled the reservation at the restaurant where I'd already scrutinised the menu and salivated over the fresh fish of the day. Even if he did show up now, we needed to have a serious talk and there was no way I wanted a waiter butting in with 'Any pepper? How is everything? More water?' when we were stuck into the nitty-gritty of sorting out the fundamentals of our relationship.

As the hours dragged past, the gradual realisation dawned that Robin wasn't coming back. At midnight, I slipped out of the hotel and walked to where we'd left the car. There was a group of teenagers on the beach, their laughter carrying on the still air. I felt a burst of envy. Carefree nights under the stars seemed the preserve of another lifetime. I trudged along the street towards the car park, not knowing whether I hoped the car would be there or not. It would have been odd for him to have brought the spare key anyway. I tried not to imagine how miserable it would be having to catch the train home on my own. What would I do with Robin's stuff? Leave it there? But the Range Rover was sitting in the same spot. I opened the doors to check that Robin wasn't sleeping on the rear seat. I then had a vision of someone leaping out from behind one of the other cars and kidnapping me at knifepoint. My heart hammered as I scooted out onto the road. I couldn't believe that calm, logical me had become this person, wandering about a strange town in the early hours of the morning, conjuring up ever more extreme pictures of doom. I plunged back into the hotel hoping that I'd find Robin curled up on our bed, but there was still no sign of him.

After ringing several times and leaving angry, then desperate and tearful messages – 'Please just let me know you're okay' – I finally took refuge in sleep, waking up as dawn was breaking to look at my phone, staring out at the slivers of orange rising over the sea. What if he'd had an accident? Where could he even be at four-thirty in the morning? I couldn't imagine him in a sweaty nightclub drinking whisky chasers.

Feeling ridiculously dramatic, I googled when to report a missing person, both hoping and dreading that it would instruct me to wait twenty-four hours, but the advice was to call the local police as soon as you believe a person is missing. I lay there wishing I had a different life. Surely I wouldn't end up having to trouble the police with 'It was like this, my boyfriend' – could I even say boyfriend with a straight face at my age? – 'wanted sex and I wanted to go and have a drink. I'm not an alcoholic or anything, I hadn't been to the coast for ages and fancied sitting by the sea...' Maybe I'd rattle on nervously and they'd end up assuming I had something to hide.

Though I could far more easily imagine a scenario with a fresh-faced PC going through to his colleagues and saying, 'Another bloke who's "gone missing" and saved himself from marrying while he still could. Bless her. She thinks something's happened to him. I'll tell you what's happened, he's woken up and headed for the hills.' Followed by shouts of laughter that would drift over to me as I exited past the reception, feeling like the frumpiest, most deluded woman in the world.

I still didn't really believe we were in a situation that required the involvement of the authorities. It was far more probable that he'd huffed back to Surrey to wait for me there. I turned over in my mind how I could find out from Sandy if Robin was at home, without alerting him to the fact that I didn't know where he was. I couldn't. Instead, at nine o'clock, I phoned Rebecca.

'I was wondering if you'd seen Robin this morning.'

'No, I haven't.' I could hear the puzzlement in her voice. 'I thought he was with you?'

'Unfortunately, he'd left behind some papers he needed and was going to pop home for them. He'd gone before I woke up this morning and his phone has obviously gone flat, so I was trying to get an idea of when he might reappear. No worries. I'll just have to be patient.'

I knew I was gabbling in the way that people do when they're trying to cover something up. But Rebecca and I didn't have a super-chatty relationship – I was terrified of being over-friendly in case I had to ask her to leave – so she wasn't in the habit of asking for detail.

'Shall I get him to call you if he comes in?'

'Yes, that would be great. Thank you.'

I rang off. I felt as though I might cry, but I wasn't the sort of person to sit snivelling in my room. I got ready to go out and traipsed downstairs, pride making me wave cheerily to the bloke on reception, given that Robin had regaled him with details of our upcoming wedding the day before. I'd do a quick sweep of town, then what? For the first time, I accepted that I might have to seek out the police station.

Police station. The closest I'd ever got to a police station was checking to see whether anyone had handed in the bag my mum had left at the bus stop. There was no doubt I'd been plodding along before I met Robin. His arrival in my life had awakened long-dormant emotions, the like of which I didn't think I'd experienced since my twenties, accompanied by the uncertainty that went hand-in-hand with such intensity.

Serve me right for daring to believe that this was my moment, a chance for me to explore what it was like to be with someone who had my back, someone to plan, laugh, be quiet with. How did other people do it? How did they make relationships that lasted? I hadn't even managed a year, let alone forever.

My mind fumbled around for explanations, but aside from a terrible accident or being dumped without Robin actually communicating that to me, I was coming up blank. The optimism that had carried me through life was refusing to wither on the vine, however, and my heart was still insisting that there was some rational explanation that my dullard brain had so far failed to grasp.

As I swung out of the hotel, I scanned the seafront. All these normal people with normal lives, posing for photos, buying ice creams, debating about the best spot on the beach. Then a familiar figure in a green shirt. Robin was walking towards me, dishevelled, as though he hadn't slept all night. When I imagined seeing him again, what that might feel like, I thought I'd run to him, fall on him with relief, weak with joy that I didn't have to immerse myself in an alien world of police, of Jax being sympathetic but right, of my mother saying over and over again, 'The more I see of men, the less I understand them.'

But I did none of that. I looked at him, then sat down on the nearest bench and stared at the sea, great surges of anger rolling through me and crashing against a swell of despair.

He took a seat beside me. 'I can explain.'

'Is it worth it? Is it going to make a difference to what I think? Because, right now, what I'm thinking is that I don't know you at all and I'd be an absolute fool to marry someone who can vanish for a whole night without so much as a message to say you're okay. It's so selfish. I've been so worried.'

He put his hand out to cover mine, but I snatched it away. 'Hear me out.'

I wanted to listen. I wanted to hear the explanation that would leave my future intact, that wouldn't lead to pity on people's faces, to unsolicited observations of 'It was a narrow escape if you ask me.'

Robin leaned forwards, his elbows on his knees. 'I've been walking the coastline all night, asking myself if I can really drag you into my complicated life.'

I interrupted, lack of sleep making me impatient. 'We've been through all this.'

He put his hand up. 'I'm sorry I was so childish and stupid yesterday. I'd intended to walk round the block and come and join you, but before I got back, Moira texted, saying she'd pulled out of the house sale because her solicitor said she was entitled to a bigger share of the proceeds and she shouldn't move out until we'd agreed it.'

'So why didn't you tell me that instead of flitting into the night like some latter-day Lord Lucan?'

Robin sighed. 'I knew I couldn't think clearly if I was with you. I love you, that's not the issue... Well, it is really, because I want to be that person who makes you happy, not the man who keeps promising things but can never give you what you deserve. Everyone already thinks I'm taking advantage of you, and this could go on for years. You've already invested in my company and it isn't fair that you have to bankroll the rest of my life.'

'Who is everyone? You've only met Jax and Dan very briefly. I haven't discussed how the finances work with them.'

'Jax doesn't like me. She thinks I'm freeloading.'

'You've only spent one evening with her – how would you even know what she thinks about you? But, for the record, she's never given me any indication that she thinks you're not paying your way.' I tried to block out her words, 'All that talk about five-star hotels and travelling first-class. He was also very generous with your champagne. Be careful you don't become his sugar mummy.'

Robin grunted. 'You're a hopeless liar.'

'If she gave you that impression, it's because she feels very protective towards me. She knows how tough I found it after Andrew left me. She did a lot of picking up the pieces.'

Robin scratched at his unshaven chin – I'd never seen him anything less than perfectly groomed. It felt oddly comforting to note that I wasn't the only one who'd been through the wringer. 'But it's not just her though.'

'Who else? Sandy?'

'He's your son so I don't want to criticise him.'

My body ached with the effort of working out where this conversation was leading. I seemed to be making excuses for everyone I loved. 'It's hard for him because he's never had to adjust to another man. I've never had a serious relationship – or at least, not one that he was aware of – since his dad left over twenty years ago. Kids always think their parents have no idea what they're doing.'

'I'm pretty sure that I would act like him if the boot was on the other foot. But the point I'm making is I don't want to be dead wood, dragging you down. You deserve better than that.'

He looked so downcast and miserable that I felt myself weakening. I forced myself to ask the difficult questions, exactly as I would in a business situation. 'So your solution is to disappear, call the wedding off without asking me what I think? Only you get a say and I'm the little woman who has to go along with it? And instead of having a grown-up discussion, I have to toss and turn all night imagining that you've been stabbed to death? How is that fair?'

Robin examined his hands. 'It's not. I'm sorry. It's just that I love you so much, I knew I wouldn't be able to do what's right. I've come back now to say we should postpone the wedding, I'll finish up in Spain, return your investment with interest, and then we can see where we're at after that. I can't rely on the money from the house any time soon.'

'But you said it was at least another year or two before you'll be finished in Spain.' I felt tears start to run down my face. So much for tough-talking me. I turned in towards Robin, weirdly conscious of everyone walking past, witnesses to our misery.

Robin looked as though he might cry himself. 'I should never have got involved with you. I knew it was too soon, but I couldn't resist asking you out when I saw you at that workshop.

You had so much drive and energy. I don't think I'd ever met a woman like you.'

'But you're still assuming that I'm too pathetic to cope with whatever life throws at us.' As I spoke, I became convinced of the need to show him how strong I was. He was probably used to women like Sandy's wife, Chloe, who cowered in a corner if there was a wasp in the kitchen. I was a fixer, a stayer, someone who could not only weather a storm, but also direct people to shelter.

Robin shook his head. 'You're not pathetic at all. You're one of the strongest people I know.'

'So this is it? Nice knowing you, I'll give you a ring in a couple of years and see if you've still got a slot for a husband?'

He pulled me to him and I sobbed on his shoulder for a brief moment before my need for privacy cut through my grief.

'We can't talk here. Let's go back to the hotel.'

Robin helped me up. 'I need to get my things anyway.'

I still couldn't believe he was serious. My mind rebelled at the monumental task of cancelling the wedding, the explaining, the sorting out of refunds. Sandy's satisfaction. Mum's bewilderment.

I trailed behind Robin through the hotel reception, where the cheery chap at the desk looked over to catch my eye and then discreetly busied himself on the computer when he saw the state of us.

I slumped onto the bed when we got to the room, searching for the words that would give us other options, other choices. 'Is this just about money? Or is that a convenient excuse because you've got cold feet?'

Robin knelt on the floor and put his hands in my lap. 'I would love nothing more than to marry you. You know that. But I don't know what my future holds – it's easier for me because my parents are dead and I've never had kids – so I'm not having to manage a whole raft of expectations from other people close to me. I simply can't let you live defending me all the time. It will wear you down in the end and I'd rather let you go now.' He paused. 'If I don't leave now, I'll never be able to.'

'Can you give me a hug? I don't want you to leave.' I didn't recognise myself. I'd never begged anyone for anything in my life.

Robin sat on the bed and put his arms around me. 'Don't make this harder than it is.' He laid me down gently and I raised my face to kiss him. And with that peculiar passion that comes from heightened emotion, we forgot about how difficult life might be, what obstacles we might have to overcome and lost ourselves in each other.

Afterwards, Robin smoothed my hair back from my face. 'I did try to leave.'

'I don't want you to. For better, for worse.'

'On your head be it, Mrs Franklin.'

21

REBECCA

After Cath phoned to see whether Robin had appeared, I'd glimpsed Sandy drive off with his kayak on the top of his van and felt that sinking sense of knowing that I had several hours to fill until I could travel down to Shoreham-by-Sea and pick up the kids from Graham. I'd got used to Sandy poddling down with a little table one of his gardening clients was throwing out, or a rugby ball he'd found in the attic that he thought Eddie might like.

Instead of lying on the settee, I forced myself out into the sunshine, trying to take the advice I always gave to the kids. 'You'll feel better if you've had some fresh air.' I pottered about deadheading the calendula and geraniums, wondering whether the hydrangeas in my old garden would be surviving without me watering them in this dry spell. I still couldn't believe how easily we'd lost everything. Slipping down into homelessness on the Snakes and Ladders board of life had been far swifter with fewer safety nets than I'd ever imagined.

The distant chime of the doorbell reverberating through the kitchen window broke into my navel-gazing. I hurried through the side gate, expecting Robin without his keys.

But it was a blonde woman, about forty, smartly dressed, birdlike, as though she'd never opened a packet of chocolate digestives and not known when to stop. All skinny decaf cappuccino and gluten-free banana bread.

She looked surprised when she saw me. 'Hello there, I'm looking for Cath, Cath Randell?' She said the surname as though she wasn't quite sure she'd got it right.

'She's not here at the moment. Can I take a message?'

Her face cleared. The penny dropped. She didn't know what Cath looked like, but she certainly hadn't expected someone in an old pair of Nike tracksuit bottoms and flip-flops. 'Do you know when she'll be back?'

I didn't like the way she was having a little crafty gaze at the house and garden, as though she was drinking it all in and working out the weak spot to break in. Or maybe too many nights on my own watching Netflix made me think that any passing stranger was about to demand access to the house and beat the code to the safe out of me.

I ignored the question. I didn't want to sound like Michael Caine – 'Who wants 'er?' – in some gangster movie, but it didn't seem wise to start spilling too many details. 'I'm not sure. Is it something to do with the wedding? I can take your name and get her to call you?'

The woman gasped. 'The wedding? Is Cath getting married? Oh my God.'

I folded my arms. 'Sorry, I don't want to be nosey, but would you mind telling me who you are?'

'Who are you?' she countered.

I couldn't help wondering how long we were going to keep ping-ponging backwards and forwards answering each other's questions with one that we found far more interesting.

'I work for Cath.' I wasn't about to say that I was her house-keeper, though she probably wouldn't mistake me for her yoga teacher.

'It's really important that I talk to her.'

I started to get a creeping sense of dread. 'Are you a friend of Robin's?'

She almost shouted 'No!' in my face.

'But you know him?' I asked.

She didn't speak, just stood there as though she was trying not to breathe, a bit like I did when Cath leaned right in to explain something and I'd gone heavy on the garlic the night before. Eventually though, she let out a big gust of air and with it came a sob. 'I know him, yes, you could say that.'

I wasn't going to need a specially tuned wronged woman antenna to work this one out, but there was no harm in double-checking.

'Are you Moira?'

She looked at me as though I was so far off the mark. 'No. I'm Amy, Robin's girlfriend. Or, more accurately, ex-girlfriend.'

No good was going to come from this exchange. Cath wouldn't want me talking to her, let alone telling her anything about their plans. I knew instinctively that whatever she told me meant I'd be between a rock and a hard place. It wouldn't be the first time a messenger had been shot. And once I knew whatever this woman had come to say, I couldn't unknow it. It would become another secret weighing on me, someone else's fat baggage to consider. As if I didn't have enough to carry around already.

Inevitably, however, curiosity got the better of me. 'How long were you with him?'

'Five years. We split up yesterday.'

'What? They're getting married in less than two months.' Surprise had sent all my intentions of keeping my mouth firmly shut packing.

'That's why I'm trying to warn you. That's what Cath needs to know.' She pressed a business card into my hand. 'Make sure she calls me. I promise I only have her best interests at heart. If she doesn't believe me, get her to ask Robin where he was last night. With me, in Deal. And for goodness' sake, tell her not to lend him any money.'

A cog whirred and clicked into place in my mind. The weird phone call from Cath, all hesitant, asking if I'd seen Robin. She hadn't known where he was. And now I did.

Was he really capable of what this woman claimed? Five years? I felt tired just thinking about it. How did he fit in Amy alongside zipping off to Spain and planning a wedding with Cath? Let alone all the flaming time he spent ordering designer gear – 'What do you think, Rebecca, this pink shirt to go with my dark suit, or the lilac one?' He said it as though he valued my opinion. And although I'd restricted myself to paying lip service to keep on the right side of him, he was so charming that before I knew it, I'd be suggesting a tie that I thought would look good.

I felt oddly protective of Cath as though I didn't want this woman to go away thinking she was a soft-hearted idiot who'd been sucked in like Amy herself. Followed by a strong desire to chase her away and tell her to keep her black crow bad news far away from my life. 'Cath's very private. I don't think she'd want to talk to you. Actually, I'm sure she wouldn't want to talk to you.'

'She has to. She has no idea what she's dealing with.' She turned to get into her car. 'I'm not mad. I am telling the truth.'

I was highly tempted to say, 'Please keep your truth to your-self and don't throw a spanner into my works.'

I looked down at the business card. Amy Barron had put me in a very difficult position, but what she'd told me could and did change everything.

I ran through the various possibilities in my head. 'Cath, I wondered if I could have a word...' 'Cath, I'm not sure whether you already knew this...' However much Cath rolled her eyes and pretended to be all 'if it wasn't for Robin, there's no way I'd be making such a song and dance about my wedding day', there was something soft, something vulnerable about her, as though she couldn't believe that someone loved her enough to make such a public declaration. That wasn't looking quite as promising right now.

My mouth was hanging open in disbelief. Was he really stringing one woman along while planning to marry another? I had every reason to be cynical, but with all the bunches of flowers, and the little notes stuck on her dressing table – 'I never knew how good life could be until I met you' – Robin gave every impression of being in love with Cath. Now Amy was blowing everything I thought out of the water. I could and should tell Cath what I knew. But the more I mulled it over, the more I became certain that the biggest casualty of the fallout would be me. Out on my ear, long before I was ready, without even a shed to offer my kids. If everything was about to go up in a big puff of smoke, I needed to get some plans in place. I shoved the business card into my sweatshirt pocket.

Amy seemed genuine but what if she was nothing more than a disgruntled ex-girlfriend with an elaborate plan to get her own back? Even as I examined the likelihood, I knew I was clutching at straws. Could I really let Cath go ahead with her wedding without at least giving her a hint that Robin might be taking her for a ride? I was pretty sure she wouldn't want to hear it, wouldn't welcome me stamping on her dreams with my size six cleaning clogs. But had I become so hard-hearted that I was happy to let someone else blunder into their own nightmare?

The guilt at saving myself started as a trickle, and swelled to a tide by the time I got back to the pavilion. I couldn't quite believe how my own lack of options had made me so self-centred. But the fact remained: I couldn't let myself be distracted by what was best for Cath. I had to focus on what was best for me. For us.

22

REBECCA

Panic was coursing through me. I leaned against the pavilion door, before pulling out the card she'd given me. Amy Barron, personal stylist. What if Cath found out I'd spoken to her and said nothing? Was I really going to have my life derailed by a woman who organised clothes by colour in people's wardrobes?

I glanced at my watch. After worrying about how I was going to fill my day, if I didn't leave right now, I was going to be late fetching Megan and Eddie from Graham. My mobile rang, making me jump. For one minute, I thought it was Cath with a secret camera trained on me, asking me what I was playing at. But it was Graham.

'You haven't left yet, have you?'

'No, I'm just about to. Is there a problem?'

'Megan doesn't want to come back to yours. She's begging to stay here.'

I wasn't having that nonsense. 'Don't be silly. They've got school in the morning. In case you've forgotten, they don't break up for the summer holidays for another two weeks.'

'I don't mind getting up early and driving them. It's only

forty-five minutes. I washed their uniforms when I picked them up on Friday.'

'No, you're not starting that. They come to you one weekend in two and during the week in term-time they're with me. We can look at it again in the holidays.'

'Rebecca, listen to me. They're having such a nice time at the beach. The weather is supposed to be boiling at least for the rest of this week. It's so good for Eddie to run around after he's been cooped up in lessons all day. It does help him concentrate better. And his swimming is coming on really well.'

'No, Graham, you listen to me. You're the one that made us lose our home. You're not making me lose my kids as well. They need me.'

'Rebecca, this isn't about that. It's what's best for the children. Megan was up all night crying her eyes out about how she hates the place you're living because of the insects.'

'So you get to keep the kids because you've been lucky enough to be able to move in with your mum? Nice try, mate. No, they come back here.' I hoped I sounded tougher than I felt. The thought that Meg was sobbing into her pillow during the night and I wasn't there to comfort her ripped at my heart. Every little bit of me ached to give her a hug, to tell her everything would be okay.

Graham and I delivered punches to and fro, my fury growing by the second that he was able to continue playing happy families and go to the beach while every day brought me a new problem to solve. Then Megan came on the line, sobbing. 'Mum, don't make me come back. Please. I can't sleep there. I want to stay at Grandma's.'

I felt the fight in me collapse like an underdone Yorkshire pudding. Megan handed the phone to Graham. 'I'd better not find out that you encouraged her. What about Eddie?'

'Eddie doesn't want you to be on your own, so he said he'd go with you.' He lowered his voice. 'I know you don't want to hear this, but he's made some little friends at the beach and they're having a ball playing French cricket. It's up to you, but I think he'd really love to stay another week.'

I couldn't let my seven-year-old son take responsibility for me. I imagined him pulling at his fringe the way he did when he was full of feelings. My soul hurt for him. But it was still nice to know that I hadn't become totally irrelevant. 'Fine. Pass me to the kids.'

I kept my voice steady as I told them I'd see them soon and to have a good time, not to worry about me, I had loads of work to do and they'd have much more fun at the seaside. Then I put my head in my hands and cried.

I sniffled about on the decking outside the pavilion and tried to cheer myself up by playing my radio full blast and singing to every song I knew. It didn't help.

In the end, I resigned myself to being miserable and crumpled in a self-indulgent heap on the settee, watching a spider with a body like a hairy barnacle weaving a web on the ceiling, briefly thankful that Megan wasn't here. I was tempted to go over to Dolly's, spend the day mooching about in her garden, but I'd never be able to hide my upset from her beady eyes. It wasn't right to unload all my woes onto an eighty-year-old and I didn't have the stomach for being told that life wasn't fair but you had to get on with it. I already knew that, but I was finding it hard to put it into practice. Instead, I dozed on and off until nightfall, even considered texting my friends, Ali and Liz, to see if they fancied a few drinks, then remembered that I was no longer in a position to burn money down the pub. I'd been fobbing them off, saying I was flat out organising somewhere to live but I'd be in touch when I was settled. The idea of explaining my life to them, and even worse, them finding it funny exhausted me. 'You're doing what? Living in a garden shed? We'll have to start calling you Swampy.' My old life of nights down the Red Lion, a few bangers on the barbecue in one of our gardens, with Liz making us all have a go on the karaoke seemed like another world. I couldn't invite any of my friends to Cath's house, couldn't have them shrieking about the size of it all and wanting to skinny-dip in her pool.

Just when I thought it wasn't possible to feel any lonelier than I already did, I saw the lights switch on in the house and Cath and Robin come out onto her terrace with a bottle of wine. I flicked the lights off in the pavilion, squatted down on the floor and peered over the windowsill, trying to see whether they looked like they were having an argument. But they kept leaning over to each other and kissing. Her laugh carried across the garden. She laughed at a lot of things Robin said. Fair enough, he was quite witty, but not so hilarious that she needed to be giggling away all the time. Maybe desperation to bag a man made you like that. Or maybe I was becoming a sour-faced grump because I was forty in four years' time and hadn't expected to be heating up tins of rice pudding on a plug-in hotplate because I no longer had a kitchen of my own.

They clinked glasses. It was sod's law that when I was married, I'd loved it when Graham went down the snooker hall with his mates and I could watch what I wanted on telly without a commentary. But now, I missed the rustling of someone else around, the 'Do you want a cup of tea?', even the sound of the fridge opening and closing. Maybe I'd end up like Cath, twittering around any bloke that showed an interest in me, letting them think they'd missed a career in comedy. She'd evidently forgiven him for 'coming back to fetch some papers'. I'd kept a very close eye out after Amy had left and I was pretty sure he hadn't been near the place.

I was about to stand up and stretch my thighs, which were burning with the effort of crouching when Sandy came through the side gate with his kayak. Cath sprang up to greet him. He didn't acknowledge Robin as far as I could see and soon escaped to store his equipment in the shed next to my pavilion.

I quietly tiptoed back to the settee, switched a lamp on and picked up my book. He clattered about for quite some time, then eventually there was a knock at my door. 'All right? Wondered if you wanted to join us for a drink?'

'Thanks, but I was just about to go to bed and read.' There was no way I was going to sit there making polite chit-chat with them. I'd never mastered the 'skivvy fraternising with the masters' small talk. And who knew what I might blurt out if I got a bit squiffy?

Sandy squinted down at me in the dull light. 'Are you all right? Are the kids here?'

Despite working so hard to keep myself to myself, I started crying. 'No, they decided to stay in Shoreham.'

'Hang on a minute. I'll be right back.'

He scooted up the garden and into the house. He returned with a tray and said something to his mother, which made Robin throw up his hands. Marching over to me, Sandy set a couple of bottles of wine down on the table outside.

'It's a night for drinking and sharing sob stories.'

And despite stupid Amy turning up and plunging me into a dilemma, the huge hollow ache that Megan would rather stay with her dad and the general thrust of my life in a disastrous direction, I couldn't help hooting at Sandy's description of his high-maintenance wife. When he got on to how he'd hired a vintage campervan as a surprise for her thirtieth birthday and she'd insisted on booking into a hotel every night they were away – 'I can't sleep in that!' – I laughed so hard that it was a miracle I didn't squirt wine out of my nose.

As the sky darkened, I saw Cath and Robin go inside. 'Does your mum mind you socialising with the cleaner instead of sitting with them?'

Sandy waved his hand dismissively. 'I don't think she thinks of you as a cleaner.'

The wine made me bold. 'Oh, I'm pretty confident she does.'

'If she gives that impression, it's because she's embarrassed. You've seen my grandma's house. That's where Mum grew up and they never had cleaners or anything. Mum was okay when it was Grandma looking after the house because it gave her something to do, but Mum's so terrified of looking like Lady of the Manor ordering the servants about, she's just awkward.'

I wasn't sure that Sandy was bang on the money with his explanation, but it was better than my conviction that Cath saw me as a loser, who by carelessness, laziness or stupidity had ended up in a situation where she and her kids were relying on her charity to stay off the streets.

Even in my three-glasses-of-wine-and-counting state, I realised that discussing Sandy's mother – given that I depended on her for the flimsy stability that I had – would have my paranoia levels bubbling like a cauldron the next morning.

'Anyway, not fair to ask you about your mum. What are you planning to do with your life?'

'Woah! That's a big old question.'

I blushed, as though Sandy would be outraged that I dared to ask him when I was obviously the most clueless out of everyone.

He leaned back in his chair. 'Get divorced. Build the business up. I'm interested in helping people rewild their gardens, encourage them to move away from the manicured look.'

'I'd love you to help me do that.' I screwed up my eyes. 'If I ever have a garden again, that is. I'm going to need an unexpected mystery inheritance for that, sadly.'

'Is there any chance of that?'

'Nah. Mum lost everything about thirteen years ago. Just about survives as it is. And now, history is repeating itself, really.'

Sandy poured us another glass of wine. 'You're still young. You're smart. You'll get there.'

Sandy's faith in me when I barely trusted myself to open a can of beans without making a hash of it made me want to explode out with a million thank yous that someone in the world didn't write me off as a complete moron.

I knew it was a bad idea when he went off to the kitchen to get another bottle of wine. And an even worse one when I told him his wife sounded like an absolute idiot and he should thank his lucky stars that she decided to get it on with the builder. There was that moment when loneliness, alcohol and sheer recklessness made me think about inviting Sandy onto the settee. In my drunken stupor, adding in sex with my employer's son seemed like a top idea for moving my chaotic life in the right direction. But before I could slur out that piece of brilliance, he stood up. 'I'd better go.'

We locked eyes for a moment. He leant over and kissed me gently. I pulled him to me, but he held his ground.

'Not sure you need that complication right now. It's been a lovely evening, sleep well.'

I wanted to throw my arms around his neck, fling off all my clothes and shout that I didn't care about complications, I simply wanted to have someone cuddle me, love me, make me feel *hopeful*. After so many months fitting around other people because I owed them – Jason, Debs, Cath – I'd forgotten what it was like to have a conversation with someone who liked me, someone who maybe more than liked me.

But he opened the door to the pavilion and guided me in. He kissed my cheek. 'Bed. If you need paracetamol tomorrow, text me.'

I lay on the settee trying to focus on the corner of the beam but kept jerking into a sitting position to stop the room spinning. I propped myself up on cushions, smiling with a little burst of warmth as I remembered Sandy's kiss, the first from anyone other than Graham in twelve years. Then out loud, I said, 'Don't even think about Sandy.' Anything to do with Sandy would end in a fiasco. He didn't deserve to be dragged into whatever came next.

I did, however, make one decision I could no longer avoid that I hoped would still seem right in the cold light of day.

23

REBECCA

Now I'd decided, I spent the next nine days in anguished anticipation. My heart thumped every time I thought about it. Part of me hoped that the opportunity would never present itself, but with the wedding taking place in seven weeks, the clock was ticking and if the stars didn't align on their own, I would have to move heaven and earth to make them. A couple of times, Sandy had caught my eye and given me a little intimate smile as he left in the mornings, which made my heart lift with joy, until I reminded myself that Sandy and I were one story that could never have a happy ending.

After a weekend when Sandy and I kept 'bumping' into each other in the garden, our conversations getting longer and longer, my resolve was faltering. I had to do it before I lost my nerve. On Monday evening, Sandy let slip that the next day he was working in North London to install an in-ground trampoline, which seemed like a brilliant idea for anyone with kids, given Eddie's ability to fling himself off anything that was more than five centimetres from the ground. The thought of Eddie and Megan spurred me on. My sister always called me the ballsy one and I had to prove her right. I wouldn't tell her till afterwards though. Debs would go off the deep end if she got a whiff of what I was intending to do.

Just as I was trying to figure out whether Cath and Robin would be working from home the next day, Cath knocked on my door late on Monday night and said, 'Sorry to disturb you, Rebecca. I've spoken to Mum and she's due at the hospital tomorrow afternoon at 3.30 p.m. She forgot to tell me and I'm in London all day. Robin is here, but he's got some important Zoom calls that he can't reschedule. Could you possibly take her?'

My heart beat faster with both dread and anticipation. 'Yes, of course, no worries at all.' I wanted to see Dolly anyway. I hoped she wouldn't think badly of me, wouldn't hate me when she discovered the truth.

Cath sagged with relief. 'Brilliant, thank you.' She paused. 'No Megan and Eddie?'

I didn't mean for my voice to come out all tight and high as I blurted out that they'd chosen to stay with their dad for the time being. It was one of those moments when someone chucks out a casual question and it stabs straight into the heart. Cath probably didn't even care anyway, just felt obliged to pretend for a minute that her interest in me wasn't only about how I could make her life easier.

Surprisingly, she said, 'That must be so hard for you. I used to hate it when Sandy went to his dad's, especially when he came home all full of stories about how great the new girlfriend was.'

I nodded at the unexpected confidence.

She carried on, 'But in the end, I realised that kids are fickle when they are little, they go with the latest shiniest thing, but eventually, they understand. Not as quickly as we'd like them to, probably, but they do know who did what for them, who made them a priority.'

She'd had all these weeks to talk to me, to understand my

life, to be someone other than the person who left notes on the kitchen island about not using an abrasive sponge on the guest-room bath. And she'd chosen right now. The very moment when I needed not to care what effect I was going to have on anyone else's life.

With that, she said, 'If you wouldn't mind popping Mum home afterwards? I've got an appointment at the bridal shop after work, so I'll be late back tomorrow. I'm very grateful for everything you do, you know.' She turned to leave. 'You handle my mum so well. Thank you for being so patient with her. I wish I could be a bit more like you.'

There was something so human, so generous in her words. I rushed to make her feel better. 'It's always so much easier when you're not related to them. You should see how snappy I get with my own mum.'

She laughed. 'You're a good person, Rebecca.'

Right then, I could see so much of Sandy in her. Those bursts of honesty, of stepping back and sizing people up, then delivering a compliment in a sincere way that couldn't help but make you feel good about yourself. I'd miss Sandy. I should never have allowed myself to have any affection for any of them.

Cath rubbed her hands together. 'Right, well, I'll let you get to bed.'

'Thank you. And thank you so much for letting me stay here. It's very kind of you.'

'It's me who should thank you, Rebecca. Goodness knows how I could have organised a wedding if you hadn't been here.'

Her face did a little twitch of happiness, as though she couldn't believe after all these years that she was going to cross back over the line into coupledom, like a pilgrim reaching the Promised Land.

I shut the door, leaning against the wood. I went over the facts for a final time, trying to make sure that I was dealing in cold realities, not family folklore. And then I lay, listening to the rustles and scratching in the garden until the pink light of dawn rose above the sycamore trees.

The next morning, I showered. Put on my best shirt and trousers. Tied my hair back. Ate a leftover piece of pork pie to fortify me. I had to do it early otherwise I'd lose my nerve. And whatever the fallout was going to be, I still had to get Dolly to the hospital on time. I couldn't let her down.

I walked around the front of the house to check Sandy's van and Cath's Range Rover had gone. Then I let myself in through the French windows, counted to three and knocked on the door of Robin's office with nowhere near as much force as I should have done. I opened the door without waiting for an acknowledgement.

He clicked off the computer screen and frowned. 'I'm about to go on a Zoom call. Did you want something?'

'Yes. I need to talk to you.'

'Can it wait?'

'Not really. You see, I had a visit from Amy Barron last weekend.'

He was good, very good, just the slightest intake of breath. 'I'm not sure I know who she is.'

'That's strange. She said she was in a relationship with you.'

Robin leaned back, spluttering. 'Jesus, what do you take me for? Some kind of playboy? Where would I find time to be in a relationship when I spend half my life in Spain and the other half with Cath? Probably some wannabe get-rich-quick woman, hoping to pick my brains about becoming a property developer. You'd be amazed at how many people think building houses is a licence to print money.'

He'd actually come up with the same logic that I had to start with. But he didn't know what I knew. His fingers were drumming on the table.

'Amy seemed worried that Cath had lent you money. Do you have any idea why that might be?'

For a second, his face darkened. I hadn't entirely thought through what I was going to do if he turned nasty. I curled my fingers around the phone in my pocket. However, like the light of a photocopier passing over the screen, his features cleared. 'I know who you mean, now,' he said. 'Tall woman, blonde? A bit scrawny?' He did one of those laughs to indicate he couldn't believe I'd been taken in by her. 'I hold my hands up. I had a fling with her, ages ago, four, maybe five years ago. Long before I met Cath anyway. She bought one of my Spanish flats off-plan and changed her mind before we'd finished building it. I cut her a deal, but she lost a bit of money because the bottom had fallen out of the property market.'

I forced myself to stick to what I understood to be true. I had the proof on my phone, the photos of all the bank statements, with Cath transferring thousands of pounds to Robin. If I'd ever been caught taking pictures of their private papers, the divorce order, the particulars to his house, I'd been ready with my story: that I was making sure I could put everything back in the right place, but really I'd been collecting anything and everything that I could use against Robin. Even so, there was no denying that his easy delivery, his slow and deliberate explanations were scraping away at my conviction, feeding my fear that my desperation had led me to grab at truths that didn't exist. There was only one way to find out.

'The thing is, Robin, I don't think it's fair for you to marry Cath if she doesn't know everything about you.'

Robin got to his feet. 'Rebecca, I'm not sure what you're getting at, but I suggest you stop there in case I get the sense that you are threatening me. If I had my way, Cath would never have let you take up residence in the garden, and I'm pretty sure I can swing things in my direction.'

I curled my toes tightly to stop my legs shaking. 'I'm not threatening you, Robin, I'm just asking for what is mine and when I get it, I'll disappear and you'll never hear from me again.' Now it came to it, the statement sounded fanciful, ridiculous even. 'You owe me two hundred thousand pounds.'

He threw back his head and burst out laughing. 'You sure you don't want half a million quid while you're at it?' He was practically slapping his knee as though it was the funniest thing he'd heard in some time. But underneath I could smell a weakness, a fear, like Graham when I asked him how the business was going and he'd respond with an over-cheery 'Never been better.'

I forced myself to stare him straight in the eye. 'No. Not half a million. Just two hundred thousand. The money you stole from my mother.'

24

REBECCA

I anchored my feet, pushing deep into my trainers. The low-level jazz that Robin always had playing in the background when he worked seemed unnaturally loud and jaunty. I'd dreamt about confronting him for so long, of watching him squirm, of showing him that he might have been able to cheat my mother, but it wasn't a family trait.

Robin went cross-eyed as he sifted through my words, the demands from this nothing person whose purpose was to facilitate his life, not complicate it. 'I don't know what you're on about. Are you feeling quite right, Rebecca?'

'That's the second time your memory has played up today. Let me help you. Lynette Ruddick? Remember her? The woman who sold her home, put the money in your joint bank account so you could buy a farmhouse in France? I flew all the way back from Australia for the wedding that never was. And by the time my mother realised that her charming fiancé had made off with her money, you were long gone. You'd fooled her, you see.'

I couldn't help feeling sorry for my mum now. She didn't stand a chance against a slippery fish like Robin. The memory of her all giddy, so proud she'd caught the eye of this handsome man six years her junior – 'I've still got it at forty-six, Rebecca' – gave me the courage to lift my chin and stare Robin down.

'Until Amy came round, I thought your swindling was a one-off. It didn't really register when she told me because I was so blown away by the revelation that you'd been two-timing Cath all this time. Apparently screwing women out of money is a habit of yours. Did Amy lose her home too? Not that you'll care, but my mum now works at a garage, living in a bedsit, sharing a bathroom and kitchen with strangers, still wondering what she did wrong.'

Robin was shaking his finger at me. 'That's not what happened, Rebecca. Your mother always did have trouble telling the difference between fantasy and fact.'

I put my hands on my hips to stop my certainty of being in the right seeping away. He wasn't smooth-talking his way out of this.

Robin had his hand on his chest like a preacher addressing his flock. 'We were duped by the property owner. I didn't take the money. We both lost out. Your mother blamed me, which was no basis for a marriage. You're mad, accusing people of things like this.'

He was so calm, so convincing, that I wondered whether my mum had told herself that he'd tricked her because it was easier than believing her hysterics over losing the money had driven him away. To put it mildly, Mum wasn't the sort of person you'd hope would be first to stumble across the scene of bloodshed.

I scratched back through my memories of Paris, of the time immediately afterwards when my mother had rocked and cried and gone on about being cursed in life. Which Debs and I had found unexpectedly hurtful. Even at nineteen and twenty-three, we still wanted our mother to say, 'But at least I've got my kids.'

In the end, we'd had to take over. I'd exchanged the last of my Australian dollars to scrape together the money for us all to get the coach back to London.

As Robin opened his hands as though my understanding of what had happened was so far from reality, I reminded myself of Mum's pinched face, pressed against the window as we chugged up the autoroute towards Calais, her navy hat with the little veil on her knee. Just in case my resolve started to crumble, I homed in on what two hundred thousand pounds could mean to Mum, to me, to my kids. I allowed myself to think about all the things I usually pushed from my mind – how she locked her door against the alcoholic who lived down the corridor, how she preferred to wash in the sink in her room than use a bathroom littered with other people's hair and toiletries, how she'd become so isolated, ashamed of where she lived, that she no longer invited her friends. I thought of Amy and her sobbing. And who knew how many other women as well.

The way he was so unruffled, so plausible, confirmed that Robin wasn't a man with a couple of dodgy financial dealings behind him. A man who'd had too many women to choose from and been a bit blurry about the exact timeline of starting one relationship before finishing another. The spark of injustice flamed hot and strong. No. This was a man who knew exactly what he was doing.

'Here's my offer, Robin. You get two hundred thousand pounds to me. What would be fair? We've waited thirteen years, so I'm prepared to be generous. A man of your calibre should manage to get his hands on that money in, say, a month? Do it and I'll be out of your hair forever. You can marry Cath and live happily ever after. If that money isn't in my bank account by the seventeenth of August, I'll tell Cath everything and bring my mum and Amy along too.'

A shadow of doubt passed over Robin's face, as though he couldn't believe that this person he barely noticed, who only caught his attention when she was cleaning the gym and he wanted to get on his rowing machine, could have the bare-faced cheek to challenge him.

He stepped towards me. 'I'm not ripping Cath off. I love her.'

I brandished my phone. 'I'll call the police if you come near me.'

He held his hands in surrender. 'You've got me all wrong. You've been told a pack of lies.'

'Bullshit. You're the serial liar. And I'm not falling for it. I want my mum's money or I'll tell Cath. Simple either/or.'

I backed out of the office. I'd never felt my knees go weak before, thought that was something that happened to people in cartoons about ghosts, but I had to will my leg muscles to carry me down the garden. My fingers were poised over 999 on my mobile, my ears straining for the sound of Robin's footsteps behind me. I wrenched open the pavilion door and turned the key in the lock, securing the bolts. I drew the curtains. My spin of the roulette wheel was over. It was going to be a long month to discover whether my gamble had paid off. In the meantime, I needed to pull myself together and get ready to take Dolly to the hospital. The thought of how hurt she'd be when she realised I'd used her to wheedle my way into Cath's house, and therefore Robin's life, made my stomach churn. She'd never believe how sorry I was.

25

REBECCA

The day after I confronted Robin, Debs was induced because the doctors were becoming concerned about her blood pressure. I hadn't been round there since we'd left a month ago and although we'd FaceTimed a few times, our conversations had that heaviness of people who are pissed off with each other, but also know it's not really anyone's fault, just circumstances. In the end, she'd stepped up when no one else could offer me and the kids a home, but I still felt let down by her siding with Jason. She probably thought I'd been nowhere near as grateful as I needed to be for how they'd crammed us into their little house.

Cath was already home from work when I got the call. She made me jump when I came down from hoovering the attic. I was half-expecting Robin to have marched straight to her to dob me in – 'Do you know what that mad bitch who cleans your loos threatened me with today?'

I braced myself for the 'Ah, Rebecca, I wondered if I could have a word.' But she seemed pretty chipper, mooning about some bud vases that would be 'perfect for the little posies on the tables'. I hoped if it came to it, I'd be tough enough to carry out my threat and come clean with Cath, so that even if I didn't get any money out of Robin, I'd have the satisfaction of saving her from the ordeal my mum had faced. I forced myself not to consider that any decent person would warn her anyway. I couldn't afford to lose my bargaining power. Two hundred grand was a lot of money for Robin to cough up, but as far as I could see, marrying Cath was the golden ticket with bells on it – especially if he divorced her and trotted off with half of everything. Made my stunt of being married to one person, staying faithful, doing lots of poorly paid jobs so I could work around the kids and exiting after eleven years of hard labour with no house, a collection of credit card debts and kids who jumped ship at the first spider look a bit underwhelming.

Cath's face creased into genuine pleasure when I asked if I could leave early so I could be there at visiting time for Debs. She ran over to the fridge. 'Here, take her a bottle of champagne.'

'Are you sure? I don't want to deprive you and Robin tonight.'

She laughed as though I'd said something funny and quaint. 'He's not here anyway. Had to rush out to Spain for an urgent meeting.'

I nearly blurted out, 'Are you sure he's in Spain?' However much I focused on my goal of getting my hands on Mum's money, I was finding it increasingly hard to watch someone as street-smart as Cath sleepwalking towards marrying a man whose track record with women and finance left a lot to be desired.

As far as Mum was concerned, I'd always assumed that Robin had taken advantage of Mum's weak spot – that she wasn't a woman who could exist on this earth without a man. After my dad had died fifteen years ago, she only perked up when she had a bloke on the scene. I'd lost count of how many times I'd listened to wails of 'What's wrong with me?' when it all went belly up. So when she'd emailed me in Australia, where, at twenty-three, I was having a wild time drinking and partying away my own grief, and told me she was selling up, getting married and moving to France, I'd taken it with a pinch of salt. Stuck it in the bucket of 'Yep, looking forward to the next email saying that her "fiancé" turned out to be a wrong 'un, can you believe it?'

Eventually I'd had to take her seriously and Debs, who was only nineteen, had begged me to fly home for the wedding. 'I can't do it on my own, Rebecca. It's only a year and a half since Dad died. She barely knows this bloke.'

I flew, hung-over after an all-night party in Sydney, to Charles De Gaulle airport in Paris. At the arrivals gate, I mistook my mother's tears for joy at being united again. In the end though, Debs had to translate the sobs. 'Robin's left Mum. Turns out the venue he'd "booked" had no record of the wedding. Not replying to her calls. Evaporated into thin air.'

My first reaction was fury that I'd ditched my job in a back-packer hostel and shelled out my hard-earned dollars to get home earlier than planned. The whisky I'd consumed on the plane to help me get off to sleep had merely topped up my hangover without acting as a sleeping pill. I was crotchety, homesick for Sydney and the luxury of living in the moment with no responsibilities. And no need to think. 'You're telling me I've flown seventeen thousand kilometres for no reason?'

Debs did that look I recognised when she was trying to alert me to one of my mother's impending meltdowns. But this time there was no 'impending' to it. Robin ditching Mum wasn't really the big enchilada. Her being stupid enough to put the money from her house sale into a joint account to buy a little farmhouse in France was the real catastrophe. Because, as I understood it, the farmhouse with its blue shutters, oak beams and balcony overlooking the boulangerie had gone the way of the buffalo, along with all Mum's cash.

I couldn't take it in. I stood open-mouthed as people whose

lives weren't imploding filed past, hugging relatives, swinging grandchildren into the air, heading towards good times. 'You mean you've hosed all the money from our house up a wall without ever thinking, "Perhaps I'll just keep this in my name until I've got my hands on the deeds so that I won't end up living under a bridge"?'

Debs tried to shush me and comfort Mum.

Of course, back then, I'd believed in justice, that the law was on the side of people who were essentially decent if a bit short on brain cells. I didn't immediately run around shouting, 'Ooh la la' and thinking we were doomed. But when we got back to England, it became clear that money in a joint account could indeed be hijacked by some man promising sunflowers, honey from their own bees and fresh cheese from a rare-breed goat.

Too broke to fly back to Australia, too angry with Mum for being so stupid, with Debs for not being as furious as me, even with Dad for dying, I took refuge in a relationship with Graham. With hindsight, it was a fling that I never got round to finishing, as though I'd been stuck on a train, missed my first stop, then taken the easy option of staying on to the end of the line. Over the years, Mum showed no signs of getting back on her feet; the days when she'd dance around the kitchen, go over the top with Christmas lights, bring out all her lotions and potions and insist on giving Debs and me a pedicure were a thing of the past.

As I'd become more dissatisfied with Graham and his chaotic attitude to money, my frustration at our lives renewed my focus on Robin and how he'd wronged us. It started with a casual trawl of the internet, with nothing in mind except destructively feeding my own rage. However, as Graham's fortunes took a turn for the worse, and mine along with them, I'd experienced a growing desire for revenge. In the last five years or so, still devoid of a plan or a purpose, I'd tracked the various property-related businesses that Robin had set up, googling for evidence of yet another website full of flashy apartments under his umbrella company. As far as I could see, Mum's money had kick-started his empire. However, it had taken my own desperation to translate my knowledge, my resentment, into concrete action to find him. I wasn't entirely sure what I was going to do, what I really hoped to achieve. Talk to him maybe. Reason with him. At least understand whether Mum's blurry version of events remotely resembled the truth. And even if I couldn't recover Mum's cash, at least I might be able to stop these waves of rage crashing through my body at every opportunity if I could hear his side of the story. But then fate offered up Dolly and a way of getting right up close to him, to get the upper hand without him realising. And once the door to revenge had opened, no amount of shoving would close it again.

As I drove to the hospital cursing the broken fan in my car as I boiled in the hot July sun, I raked back through what I'd seen over the last few months. I still couldn't decide whether Robin was genuinely in love with Cath. He was always walking past and giving her shoulders a quick massage when she was at her computer. Often volunteering to go into town and pick up something for dinner. However, Mum had always said how caring he was, how he made her feel the centre of his world. 'You've no idea what it's like to have someone to love me after all that time on my own after your dad died.' I only occasionally gave in to the temptation to adjust her understanding of 'all that time' to 'eighteen months, it was, Mum, a year and a half, before you forgot all about Dad and hooked up with Robin'.

I still struggled to believe that Robin was just beating time until he could do a flit with Cath's money too. I hardened my heart. Worst-case scenario, I was pretty sure he'd only have access to a fraction of what she was worth. I tried to convince myself it wasn't my responsibility to stop every middle-aged woman making stupid mistakes.

I stopped trying to puzzle it all out and marched along the corridor, desperate to make sure my little sister was okay. As I pushed open the door to her ward, I saw Jason and Mum clustered around the bed. Unexpectedly, tears sprang to my eyes at the pride in Jason's face and the tenderness in Debs' as she cradled her baby. She looked both exhausted and glowing. A burst of nostalgia filled my chest as I remembered how Graham and I had stroked Megan's shock of dark hair – 'No wonder I had heartburn' – and marvelled at Eddie's long fingers – 'We'll have to get a piano.' All that hope, all that expectation. All that love.

Mum's face took on a defensive look, as it always did when I was around, as though she was braced for criticism. My despair at her living conditions, keeping her food in a padlocked cupboard, walking down the landing with her loo roll at night to the horrible little bathroom with wee on the floor often spilled over into recrimination. To shut me up, she'd say, 'You're right, Rebecca, it was my own stupid fault.' I was never sure she truly believed it.

Today, however, was a day of celebration. Debs handed her little girl to me. 'We've called her Sophia.' Even Jason managed a passable effort at looking pleased to see me. As Sophia started to cry and I handed her back, we did that weird British thing of attempting to appear completely cool about Debs flopping out a milk-engorged boob. It seemed an excruciatingly long time before Sophia managed to latch on, during which we were finding every reason to avert our eyes from Debs' nipple, which resembled an angry red saucer.

'Christ, that looks sore.' I didn't think she'd welcome the knowledge that if she was already suffering like that on day one, she'd rather stick a pin in her eye than feed a baby by day seven.

Debs smiled, the deluded, deranged smile of someone high

on birth hormones. She'd find out for herself that in a few days' time she'd be fantasising about four hours' solid sleep and feel irrationally annoyed if anyone sent her flowers because finding a vase would require an energy that she didn't have.

'She's beautiful. Congratulations.'

Mum patted Debs' foot. 'You make a lovely little family.'

I bristled. I didn't want to hear, 'Lovely stable little family with two parents'. My throat tightened with pining for Eddie and Megan. I was supposed to pick them up after school the day before, but they'd pleaded to go home with Graham so they could practise their snorkelling. In the end, knowing that Debs was being induced today and that she might not want Eddie bouncing around the ward, I'd given in. It hurt that they didn't seem to be missing me. I tried not to imagine the details of their days, garbled out carelessly to Graham rather than winkled out with great effort during stilted phone calls and harvested like treasure.

Mum turned to me. 'It's not too late for you to have another one.'

I felt my mouth clang open. 'That's not very likely as I am in the middle of divorcing my husband.'

Mum nudged me as though I'd made a joke. 'I didn't mean with Graham. You might meet someone else who wants a little one.'

This was why Mum had ended up the way she was. She viewed her whole life through a lens of men.

I didn't want to spoil Debs' day. 'I'm not expecting to hook up with someone else any time soon.'

'You never know what's round the corner.'

I got up to leave before I said something that would have everyone talking about me and saying, 'She always has to spoil everything.'

'I'd better go. I'm supposed to be at work.'

I said my goodbyes and stomped out of the maternity wing

more determined than ever that Robin would return Mum's money so we could all stop thinking that the only possible escape route from our awful lives was trapping a man into rescuing us.

I was going to make my own fate, not rely on someone else.

26

REBECCA

Seven days before Robin's deadline, Cath asked if I would mind taking her mother shopping for something to wear to the wedding. Every time she'd spoken to me for the last few weeks, my heart beat faster, expecting her to tackle me about my demand for money from Robin. But she seemed friendly, almost confiding. 'I've left it a bit late. I didn't dare tempt fate by doing it before Robin's divorce came through. But we've applied for the marriage licence now, so we can relax. I should take her myself, but I'm trying to get everything tied up at work so I can have some time off beforehand. Does that make me a terrible daughter?' she asked.

I made all the right noises, not least because I was delighted to grab every opportunity to be out of the house, away from Robin. Apart from the odd snide comment when Cath wasn't there, he acted as though the conversation had never happened. As the days rolled past, I sneaked into his study whenever possible, hunting for evidence that he'd sold a property to pay me off or applied for a loan. Maybe a month wasn't long enough even for someone like him to gather the money together. With a week left to go and no sign that he was preparing a fat transfer into my bank account, dread and loathing were competing for the upper hand. Maybe he was intending to ignore my threat and laugh it off if I broached the subject with Cath. I alternated between feeling totally powerless and fearing I might lose my temper so completely that he'd be well advised to lock away the kitchen knives.

Shopping with Dolly would provide an entertaining diversion from my increasingly frantic thoughts. She huffed and puffed. 'I don't like taking money from Cath. I've got lots of dresses I could wear, but she would insist on me getting a new frock.' She did a half-laugh. 'I hope Robin isn't turning her head and she's going to be ashamed of me.'

'Dolly, I couldn't imagine anyone being ashamed of you. You are the best.' I pushed down the heavy feeling in my chest that if it all kicked off, I probably wouldn't even get to say goodbye to her, or explain why I'd done what I did.

I helped her out to the car, noticing how slowly she walked since she broke her ankle. She regaled me with memories of her own wedding. 'My uncle Tom could play the ukulele so he jumped on the table and serenaded us with "Can't Help Falling In Love With You", but he got too close to the end, tipped the table up and catapulted the wedding cake into the air.'

I loved Dolly for her stories. She always made me laugh.

'Shall we start at Marks and Spencer?'

I tried to guide Dolly into a navy knee-length dress, but she wasn't having any of it. 'I don't want to be fading into the background. How about this bright pink one?'

My suspicions that she'd look like an exotic bird of paradise were pretty accurate, but despite trailing her around several other stores, I couldn't dissuade her from the parakeet look. Good on her for knowing her own mind. Fingers crossed I still wanted to make an entrance at eighty.

I took her home and hung her dress in the wardrobe

upstairs. As I went to leave, I gave Dolly a hug. She looked so vulnerable sitting there admiring her new shoes and humming along to a tune that, although not obvious to me, was walking her through happy times in her mind. I wished I could disappear out of her life, leave things as they were, avoid destroying the family's happiness to get what I wanted... No, not what I wanted. What was ours. What we needed.

Dolly leaned into me, a combination of musty clothes from a damp wardrobe mixed with Rive Gauche. 'You're a good girl. Thank you for today.'

I held her hand. 'I loved it. I want your energy and humour when I'm your age.'

And then I left, abruptly, before I burst out with the secret that was weighing so heavily on me, that I'd been stalking Cath's house since I'd discovered she was in a relationship with Robin. I'd come up with all sorts of mad schemes for getting close to him ranging from becoming a postwoman to trying to find a job as a cleaner where his business was registered. I'd discovered though that it was a serviced office and Robin only rented a room when he needed one. When I'd asked the young girl on reception if I could make an appointment with Mr Franklin, she'd shaken her head. 'He hasn't been in for a while.' I'd admired the artwork on her nails, talked about Megan and how, at nine, she already loved experimenting with make-up. We had a good laugh about our worst fashion mistakes, then I'd slipped in a request for Robin's personal phone number.

She'd said, 'I can't give that out, but you can leave your contact details with me. Though you'll not be the first woman trying to get hold of his number. Right charmer he is. Think he's taken though. Last time I saw him he was with that woman who runs the recruitment business across the road. Cath Randell? You've probably seen her car – that black Range Rover with the number plate C4 TH?'

Didn't mean anything to me, but I went along with it. 'Oh, I know who you mean. What's her business called again?'

'Randell Recruitment, I think. Not very original.'

And from there, it was just a short hop, skip and a jump to googling Cath's business, learning where she lived and working out that Robin was a regular visitor to the house. But despite walking up and down Hetherington Avenue hundreds of times, even seeing Robin swish in and out in his Audi, I still couldn't come up with a plan of how I could make him return our money.

But Dolly had dropped the opportunity into my lap, through her trust and generosity and I'd taken advantage of her. My heart hurt with the idea that at this late stage of her life, she'd go to her grave a little less confident about humanity, about accepting people at face value. But so would my mum. And she had to be my priority.

That evening, I had a cursory discussion with Cath about how I'd got on with Dolly and I showed her a photo on my phone of the new dress – 'I hope it's not too out there?' to which Cath murmured a disapproving 'She always did like a bit of colour.'

But before I could formulate a polite way of saying, 'Well, you should have taken her then,' Cath stood up.

'I don't know whether you are aware, but Sandy is moving out for a bit, so I was wondering if you would mind taking over some of the admin of the wedding from Robin as you won't have to clean his suite?'

I felt the punch of surprise in my stomach, a rush of dismay that recognises a loss of the hope that I hadn't yet acknowledged even existed. 'Has he gone back to his wife?' I asked.

Her face shut down. 'They're talking, yes.'

For someone who was about to betray everyone, I still had the brass neck to feel the sharp heat of injustice. I knew not to push Cath, but my heart flamed with my own foolishness. As if someone who sneaked into the utility room to wash her pants when everyone was at work was ever going to be a serious proposition for a bloke with his own business and heir to a mansion on the posh side of town.

I walked back down the garden, my legs heavy with the effort of dragging myself forwards, of even thinking that I could go up against people like them, with means and money. I rang Graham. 'Can I talk to the kids?'

'They're on the trampoline at the moment. Can they call you back?'

'No. I want to speak to them now.'

Graham sighed. 'Just a minute.'

I heard shrieks of laughter, Megan's voice, 'I'll be quick. Michelle, don't show Eddie how to flip without me.'

Michelle? Who was that?

'Hi, Mum.' Her voice was a bit flat.

'Hello, love. How are you? I'm missing you! I was wondering whether you wanted to stay here at the weekend?'

'Can you come here for the day?'

I'd never officially agreed that the kids would remain with Graham indefinitely, but I was realising that if term-time was a huge juggle between work and childcare, then the holidays were almost impossible. Megan could amuse herself, but Eddie was a trouble magnet and, at seven, still needed constant supervision. I'd resigned myself to the fact that it wasn't practical for them to be living here while I worked at Cath's and spent several mornings a week over at Dolly's, all the time riddled with guilt that the focus of my day was to keep them quiet and out of mischief. So, little by little, I'd relinquished my insistence on sticking to the schedule I'd agreed with Graham, until my circumstances changed. And that probably relied on Robin refunding Mum two hundred grand and her agreeing to move somewhere big enough for all of us until I could support myself again. It wasn't a top strategy, but it was all I had.

I tried not to sound needy. 'Shall I come on Friday then? I can take a day off so we can go to the beach? Might bring Nan with me. You haven't seen her for a while.'

'Oh. Okay.'

The first rule of having kids should be not to expect them to bolster your ego or show enthusiasm they didn't feel.

I took a deep breath. 'So how have you been?'

We carried on for a few painful minutes while I wondered if Megan was on her iPad while she was talking to me. Without warning, she said, 'Eddie wants to speak to you.'

'Mum! When are you coming to see us? Friday? We're supposed to be going to the zoo with Dad and Michelle.'

I heard Megan hiss, 'Shut up, Eddie, you idiot.'

'Who's Michelle?' I said, taking advantage of Eddie's inability to lie successfully.

'You know, she's that friend...' Eddie faltered. I heard him growl at Megan, 'What?' then a kerfuffle of words between them that I couldn't quite catch.

'Put your dad on, please.'

Megan's tearful voice. 'Now look what you've done, Eddie.'

Graham came to the phone. I could hear him walking away from them. No doubt Michelle was doing a double backflip, while I sat on a settee covered in cat hair, feeling that nothing would be okay again.

'Rebecca, I was going to tell you.'

'When were you going to tell me? Even the biggest dickhead in the world would consider it polite to mention their new girlfriend before introducing her to my kids.'

'Sorry, it's just that Chelle happened to bump into us at the beach...'

My civilised intentions took wings and flapped off. 'Well, you and *Chelle* can go to the zoo on your own on Friday because I'm coming to spend time with my children before they forget what I look like.'

'But they're excited about the zoo. Come on, Rebecca, I should have told you, but don't punish them. You're better than that.'

'I'll drive down on Saturday, ten o'clock. I'm bringing them back here for a few days.' My arms fizzed with a desire to gather them to me, my heart longing for the sound of Eddie tossing about in his sleep, the sight of Megan's hair fanning out on the pillow. I couldn't face any more distracted non-conversations, this one-way love pouring out of me, yet not quite reaching its target.

Graham started to argue, but I stood firm. 'I'm not discussing it. I need to see the children.' I stabbed at my phone, wondering if I was being horribly unfair. On the other hand, if Robin did manage to oust me, this might be my last chance to have them stay overnight for ages.

That thought churned and burned inside me as I lay on the settee, breathing in the chemical smell of bike oil and old paint pots that no amount of fresh air seemed to dispel, intensified by the August heat. The shed door banged. I peered out through a side window, clouded with age, to make out Sandy fetching a ladder. Clearly Chloe had been saving up her repairs for his return. Maybe the builder had slung his hook and Sandy was the mug stepping in to replace a cracked tile.

Before I could stop myself, the upset of my day surged into rage. I stormed out of my hut. 'Sandy! Your mum said you're going back to the wife?'

He looked beaten, weary. And definitely not in the mood for a woman who slept on a sofa bed under a canopy of old nets lodged in the rafters to voice an opinion on how he lived his life. 'We're trying to work some things out.'

Such a blokeish explanation. What things? Money? How to split up without tearing each other apart? Or did he mean they were booking hotel rooms with four-poster beds and fancy massage oils and practising making babies?

It was none of my business.

Unfortunately, I no longer cared if I seemed rude.

'So you're trying to make a go of it?' As I said it, jealousy swelled in my chest. Sandy was a decent and intelligent man, yet Chloe had snapped her fingers and he was back at her beck and call.

Sandy puckered his lips. 'She's sorry about what's happened. Said my wanting kids frightened her, but she's ready now. Anyway, I'm best out of the way of the wedding preparations.' I waited to see if he'd give me a clue about whether Robin had started a counter-attack, but instead he made the schoolboy error of asking, 'How are you doing?'

And that simple question triggered a sweary stream of anger. 'Me? I'm bloody tremendous. My kids are off to the zoo with their dad's new girlfriend, who can bounce on a trampoline without wetting herself, they don't want to come back here, they're flourishing without me. I'm rolling up my socks to stop mice coming in under the door and everyone else is cracking on with life. I, on the other hand, can't imagine a day when I won't wake up in a cold sweat absolutely terrified that I'll end up sleeping under a bridge.'

He stepped towards me, but I backed away. I didn't need sympathy. I needed the man who'd stolen Mum's money to put things right.

And although I should have had my fill of life lessons, I still had space to add, 'Never go near a bloke whose wife is sitting in the wings' to my list. I marched off. 'I hope it works out for you. I really do.' I failed to squash the bitter edge to my voice, which carried an undercurrent of 'I hope it works out with your wife who's probably lining up the plumber and wasp nest man for a quick how's your father right now'.

'Rebecca...'

Honestly, I couldn't be bothered with another person making excuses about why they were doing what they were doing. Anyway, when he realised that I'd inserted myself into all of their lives solely so I could get what was mine, I wouldn't be the only one who felt betrayed.

I opened the door of the pavilion. 'See you around. Good luck.'

27

REBECCA

I begged Mum to come down to pick up the kids with me from my mother-in-law's, but she wouldn't. 'I don't want my nose rubbing in it. She's in her four-bedroomed bungalow and I am stuck in one room. At my age!'

Over time, my anger with Mum putting herself at the mercy of a random bloke had usually outweighed my sympathy with how she'd ended up living. Even now, she was full of stories of how the man who came to check the electrics in her room had said something along the lines of 'How did a good-looking woman like you end up in a place like this?'

'Still life left in me yet. He said if I played my cards right, he'd elope with me to Gretna Green.'

I couldn't raise a smile for her. I still couldn't get past the fact that she'd lost everything my dad had worked for. How I longed for that house that my dad had slogged his guts out to afford. The endless night shifts sitting in his cab outside our local nightclub picking up the drunks who spent half their week's wages on vodka but then became abusive about a ten-quid fare home.

On my good days, I focused on how much pleasure Mum

took in the kids, sitting with Megan doing her sticker books, finding the patience to make a game out of Eddie's spellings.

But today was a bad day, not least because Robin either had to transfer two hundred thousand pounds to me in three days' time, or I'd have to reveal all and pray to the universe that Cath believed my version of events. The last thing I needed was to go down to Graham's and see his mother twittering around 'Chelle' as though her ship had not only come in, but rocked into harbour laden with gold.

'Please come with me, Mum.'

'I can't, love. My nerves aren't very good at the moment. I can't face it.'

I wanted to stand in the hallway of that damp house where all the rooms contained people who almost certainly had hoped for more from life than finding their Cheddar still in the shared fridge and bellow, 'It's not about you! Just step up and support me for a change.'

But there was no point. Mum had chosen her role. She was the woman who'd been unlucky in love – 'First your father dropping dead and then a man who makes off with all my money! I don't know what I've done to deserve it...'

It didn't matter how many times I told her that she didn't 'deserve' anything, it was life, it happened, she had to get on and over it, she never changed her tune. In the end, I swallowed my remarks down. But the fury that Mum had been such an easy target for Robin didn't vanish, nor did the knowledge that for the last decade she'd been working on the till at the same garage, waiting for another man to rescue her instead of figuring out how to rent somewhere better. 'But if I'm on my own, it doesn't really matter where I live, does it?' The only time her voice grew animated was when she had a date with a customer: 'He drives a lovely new Golf.' She'd be full of energy for a few weeks, Brian/Roger/Phil this and Brian/Roger/Phil that, until one day I'd phone and her tone would be flat and all 'Well, it's only to be expected with my luck.'

I gave up on Mum and persuaded Graham to bring the kids to a service station halfway between Conefield and Shoreham-by-Sea. I drove there trying not to cry. If my threat to Robin didn't pay off, I'd probably be homeless in a few days' time. Debs simply wasn't an option – in less than a month, she'd gone from a proud new mum to someone who could barely string a sentence together. Last time I rang, she'd just been to the doctor's for mastitis and sobbed while Sophia wailed in the background. I wanted to be that sister, the one who swooped in and did the night shift while she got some rest. I promised myself that I would be one day, as soon as I had my own life back on track.

'Debs, hang on in there. Get Jason to give her some formula now and again so you can have a break.'

Debs wasn't having any of it and Jason was shouting in the background that she needed to persevere. Nope, Debs wasn't an option.

I tuned in to a golden-oldies radio station and sang at the top of my voice to everything from Abba to the Carpenters. I didn't want Megan and Eddie to take one look at my miserable face and decide that Chelle was so much more fun. The bar wasn't very high though: just about anyone would be better than me, a knackered old harridan nagging about not ruining white socks by running on the grass and using a tiny bit of tooth-paste because 'money doesn't grow on trees'. Thankfully, though, when I got out of the car, both the kids threw them-selves on me. I buried my face in their hair, breathing them in, my mind registering the smell of unfamiliar shampoo and washing powder – the sting of someone else's caring. The rush of love was still there however, my heart relaxing back into its rightful place after days when it ached and bruised at every reminder that they were away from me.

'Mum!' Eddie was squeezing me tightly with Megan fighting to get a look-in.

I glanced at Graham with a mixture of triumph that Chelle hadn't totally won them over and sadness that our life was reduced to handovers among the debris of McDonald's wrappers and crisp packets.

Graham's hair was shaved at the sides and long on top. He looked like a member of a boyband, not someone who'd plunged his family into bankruptcy.

I shuffled the kids into the car before I became that woman causing a scene in public places. Even I couldn't take pleasure in the misery on Graham's face as they hugged him goodbye. Wrenching ourselves away from them on a regular basis over the next decade or so would no doubt prove to be a unique sort of pain guaranteed to pierce any self-protection.

I snatched their bags from him.

'When can I see them again?' he said.

'I'll be in touch.' I couldn't quite stop myself from adding, 'You go and get yourself a nice massage with Chelle.'

Graham threw up his hands. 'You'd like her. Give her a chance.'

I turned round, feeling as though fire was coming out of my eyes. 'Graham, I'm sure she's perfectly nice. But I cannot tell you how much it galls me that you are down at the seaside, cosied up with a new woman, your mother doing all your washing and cooking and you're not even having to work. You have no idea what my life is like, none at all, but what I can say is that I'm not having any little candlelits with a new bloke.' I shoved away an image of Sandy leaning in to kiss me. 'I am killing myself working and, despite that, still sleeping in a shed. So excuse me for not getting out the "congratulations on your new bimbo" banners.'

. . .

I drove home, trying to sound upbeat and cheerful, telling Megan about the stray cat that had taken up residence in the tennis pavilion. 'Even if I shoo her out, she climbs on the water butt outside and gets in through the window.'

Eddie countered with the dog he'd met on the beach. 'She waited for me every day, Mum.'

'And me!' Megan said.

'She liked me best because you wouldn't throw the ball because it had dog spit on it.'

'I'm sure you'll love the cat. She might even come in to sleep on your bed,' I said.

An argument broke out over who was going to have her tonight. Instead of yelling that no one would have her if they didn't stop arguing, I mumbled something about a cat rota. A cat rota for goodness' sake!

I didn't want to be this mother, pulling treats and tricks and trump cards out of a hat. I wanted to sit with them on the settee with popcorn and watch *Harry Potter*, not be stuck in an endless competition with Graham. I longed to 'be', to not feel under pressure to go to the park, the zoo, the pool, otherwise I was losing and Graham and Chelle would spread like ivy over my role in the kids' lives until I had to be content with a few crumbs of contact.

I drew up at Cath's, feeling weary and wretched. Graham and Michelle's glitteringly fun time with the kids meant I'd lost confidence in myself. The reality was even worse than I'd imagined. Everything, from making Megan eat her broccoli, to getting Eddie into bed before eight-thirty, was a battlefield of 'Dad didn't make us.' Given that he was the gold-star prize and I was the nag-bag fun monitor, I was second-guessing myself all the time, terrified of being too heavy-handed in case it led to 'We want to go and live with Dad on a permanent basis.'

I had to make this work.

28

CATH

All weekend, Robin had been bouncing about with so much energy that I teased him about being on drugs. He'd said, 'You're my drug. I'm buzzing at the thought of us having a future together. I can't wait to marry you and to know that you're mine, forever.'

I'd nudged him. 'You sound like you're going to lock me up in an ivory tower.'

'I'd love to be on my own with you for the rest of my days.'

I smothered my suspicion that his current playful mood was the result of Sandy moving out. The unpalatable truth was that I was relieved to have a reprieve from the constant tension in the house and hadn't questioned Sandy's decision to return home to Chloe as thoroughly as I might otherwise have done. I was glad to have escaped a situation where a few glasses of wine and a wrong word from Sandy might have led to a delivery of some home truths I'd have had trouble recanting.

But I didn't have time to dwell on my failings as a parent because my own mother rang on Sunday evening and daughter guilt obliterated it. 'Mum! I've been meaning to phone all week. I gather you had a great day with Rebecca on Tuesday. She showed me a photo of your new dress. Looks lovely. Are you going to get a hat?'

'I'm not trussing myself up like a Christmas turkey. Hats give me a headache.'

In an effort to make Mum feel part of my day, I'd said the wrong thing, though goodness knows what she would have considered the right thing. 'No problem at all, I just meant I didn't want you to be economising or worrying that you were taking advantage of me.'

Mum did a small snort. 'Huh.'

It didn't take me long to work out that Mum had decided that asking me how my wedding arrangements were coming along was not in her remit. Indeed, no conversation seemed to be in her remit and I couldn't muster up the necessary energy to throw bread on the water until I hit upon the subject that would elicit an animated response. We'd done who had what illness and her tomato blight last weekend.

At the risk of unleashing a diatribe about why I didn't eat earlier, I said, 'Mum, if you don't mind, I'm going to go and start dinner. We haven't eaten yet.'

Usually that would trigger a lament about how when my dad was alive, come what may, dinner was on the table for six-thirty. Instead, she said, 'I think I'm losing my marbles.'

I heard the fear in her voice. 'What makes you say that?'

'My watch has disappeared. I've been looking for it all weekend. And I never did find my ring and bracelet.'

I suppressed a groan. The old chestnut of the missing jewellery. 'Mum, I'm pretty sure it will turn up. You've probably put it in a drawer for safekeeping.'

'I've been through everything. It's not here.'

Frankly, it was a miracle that she found anything in all the bags and boxes and papers. 'I'm at work tomorrow morning, but I could get Rebecca to come over and help you look?'

She sniffed. 'I think she might be the problem. I'm sure I left my watch on the dressing table, you know, the one that your dad bought me when—'

'Yes, when you went to Sorrento.' I did not have the bandwidth for hearing yet again how he nipped out to buy it in the evening and produced it at breakfast.

Mum sounded offended, as though I'd stolen her story. 'Anyway, I've gone over and over it in my mind. I took the watch off because I didn't want to catch it when I was trying clothes on. When we got home, she took my dress upstairs for me. I haven't seen it since.'

'Are you sure you haven't put it in the pocket of your dressing gown or something?' Not a single thing made me think that Rebecca was to blame. I was struggling not to lose my temper with my mother. I'd already come close to accusing Rebecca of stealing once. I really didn't want to have to question her again.

'No. I'm telling you, it's not here.'

My Sunday evening watching rubbish telly sailed out of reach. 'I'd better have a look. Shall I come now?'

'But you haven't had any dinner.'

I grabbed a banana and gratefully accepted Robin's offer to drive. Surely Rebecca was too smart to pinch something out of a house where there were very few visitors and the finger would automatically be pointed at her. I'd already marked her card two months earlier. If she had any sense at all – and I was pretty sure she did – she wouldn't risk purloining so much as a ten-pence coin. And my mother's stuff was nowhere near as valuable as some of my bits and pieces.

I asked Robin what he thought. 'I don't trust Rebecca. She's far too comfortable. I've often caught her looking at things in the study. You should check your credit card statements because you always leave everything lying around. It wouldn't be hard for her to get your details.'

'You've never said that before.' It wasn't what I wanted to hear.

'I didn't want to add to your stress. But that's my honest opinion.'

'Let me get this straight. You think if I can't find the jewellery at Mum's, I should sack her? I'm not sure how we could prove it unless we do a raid on the tennis pavilion, which seems a bit over the top.' I leaned back against the headrest. 'She's got nowhere to go with those children.'

Robin patted my thigh. 'The alternative of getting the police involved is much worse. If you present it as a "go quietly and we won't say anything", she'll snatch your hand off.' I sent up a prayer to the universe that it wouldn't come to that and I'd walk into Mum's kitchen and find her watch on the windowsill.

As soon as we arrived at Mum's, she appeared at the door immediately. She looked close to tears. 'So sorry to drag you out in the evening. I think I'm going doolally.'

I could have kissed Robin for his reply. 'Dolly, we're always here for you. It's our pleasure.'

I ran upstairs. Their voices floated up as I pulled out the drawers and looked under the bed in her room. 'I wouldn't have thought it of her. She always seemed such a lovely person.'

'Jealousy can be an awful thing. Perhaps she had a mad moment. Or was so desperate. I wasn't really in favour of Cath inviting her to live there in the first place.'

Mum snapped, 'But it wasn't your house to make that decision, was it?'

I hovered between pride and irritation. Woe betide anyone who criticised me, unless it was Mum herself, in which case it was open season. I wished she could be a bit more pleasant to Robin, though. To be honest, I'd be thrilled if anyone in my family cut him some slack.

I finished turning both bedrooms upside down, tidied up and had a look in the bathroom. Reluctantly, I went downstairs.

'Can't see it anywhere, Mum. But I can't accuse Rebecca when we haven't got any proof.'

Robin leapt in. 'Who else could it be? You'll have to get rid of her. Could you just say that you don't need her any more? Give her a week's notice?'

'I need to think about it.' I still wasn't convinced that the jewellery wouldn't turn up.

Robin frowned. 'Dolly, talk some sense into her.'

I felt the frisson of annoyance that Robin assumed he was the last word in how I ran my own household. The household that, to date, I was funding.

Mum rolled her eyes. 'She hasn't listened to me for years.'

I was too tired to keep a sense of humour about all the little barbs and jibes winging my way. 'I'll ring you tomorrow, Mum. Try not to worry. We'll sort it out.'

I got into the car.

'I know you're looking out for me, but I do run my own business. I don't need anyone to "talk sense" into me. I'm quite capable of making up my own mind.'

'Sure. If you want to keep a thief on the payroll with free rein in your house, that's entirely up to you.'

'You haven't got any evidence of that,' I said.

He snorted with disbelief. If one more person acted as though I was the most gullible person on the planet, I might combust into tiny little particles of wrath.

We didn't say a word all the way home.

29

REBECCA

On Monday morning, I found it almost impossible to open the door to Cath's house, knowing that Robin would have decided by now whether he was going to pay me off the next day. I imagined checking my bank account first thing and doing an immediate runner or the alternative of an unholy showdown.

Cath was late leaving for work, which rattled me even more. I kept waiting for her to storm over to confront me while I was sifting through the piles of shoes that Robin seemed to buy every week. A few pairs of his Moncler trainers could fund a flat for me and the kids for several months. Talk about priorities.

Cath was quite chatty, asking me whether I'd found her mother a bit vague and forgetful the week before. But she also did that thing of standing there a bit too long, as though she was working up to saying something.

Nerves made me jabber on, asking her whether she wanted me to get rid of any of the shoes.

She raised her hands in mock despair. 'I'd be afraid to throw anything out. I don't know which ones he still uses.'

'You could probably get a good price for them on eBay if he's finished with them.'

She said, 'That's a good idea,' in the manner of someone who was far too busy to faff about taking photos of something that might fetch a mere few hundred quid.

I tried to make a joke. 'I'll do it for a commission.'

'I might take you up on that,' she said, but I got the distinct sense that her mind was elsewhere.

Her presence was becoming awkward. Maybe Robin had already told her his version of the truth, putting a spin on it before I barrelled in with mine. I hadn't been able to eat breakfast, my stomach rolling and heaving. I was still clinging to the hope that Robin would have much more to gain by marrying Cath and would do anything to keep the show on the road. I was also trying to let myself off the hook, convince myself he adored her, that she was the real deal for him and he wasn't trying to rip her off. Because otherwise what did that make me? Some kind of accessory to swindling women? I pushed away the guilt that I should tell her what I knew anyway, that I shouldn't let anyone suffer in the way my mum had. I had no idea how to start that conversation and still stand a chance of recovering what Mum was owed. My brain was foggy with what ifs and shoulds as Cath finally wandered off. I couldn't wait for today to be over. Even if Robin did decide to fork out, he'd take it right to the wire and let me stew until tomorrow. Raised voices in the study caught my attention and interrupted the panic that was rising in me.

'If I give her two hundred thousand pounds now, she'll stop blocking the sale, exchange in the next few weeks instead of after Christmas and I'll have a million quid by the end of November, latest,' Robin said.

I tiptoed through the hallway and stood just inside the kitchen door. I couldn't quite hear Cath.

There was a thump as though someone was banging on the desk. 'I know! I know you've already lent me fifty thousand pounds. I gave you shares, remember? If you don't trust me, what's the point of getting married? Shall I get a solicitor to witness an IOU?'

Cath's words rang out louder, high and tight. 'I do trust you, of course I do. It's Moira I'm not sure about. What if she takes the money and still won't leave the house? I've got money in the business, but I still need enough capital to cover the day-to-day running.'

'I'll get my solicitor to draw up a watertight agreement.' His voice dropped. 'I want an end to all this toing and froing so that we can be free to get on with our lives.'

There was a silence, then some murmuring. Cath's voice, placating, soothing.

Then Robin: 'It's so frustrating. I've met the woman I want to spend the rest of my life with and I'm blocked from moving forward.'

My heart was thumping. It couldn't be a coincidence that Robin wanted to borrow two hundred thousand pounds. Part of me leapt with excitement that he was intent on coming up with the money. I allowed myself a brief flirtation with the idea of bursting into Mum's horrible little bedsit and seeing her face light up with joy that she could have her own place again, where she could feel safe and secure.

Dread quickly followed the surge of anticipation. He was going to do to Cath what he'd done to my mother in order to buy my silence. Stupid naïve me. I couldn't let Robin con Cath. I couldn't take – steal – what she'd worked for. That would make me as bad as him. He was a player, an operator, for sure, but I had done my best to fool myself that he loved Cath. With a swirl of understanding that I just couldn't ignore, I realised that, as far as Robin was concerned, love was something he manufactured to manipulate people.

I was reeling from the fact that I thought he'd sell a prop-erty, get a loan against his development, magic money up in the way that rich people seemed to with their contacts and bridging loans.

I slipped out of my hidey-hole and went to check on the children in the pavilion, my heart raw with resignation. They were rolling marbles along the floorboards with complicated rules for winning. I wished I could be the mother they needed, a parent who packed up picnics, invented stories about aliens, made dens with sheets and clothes pegs. Instead, I was barely surviving. My eyes stung as Megan screwed up her face in concentration, the blue marble clearly the one to win. I waved and shouted that I'd make lunch in an hour and not to go near the pool.

I trudged back up the lawn. Would it really be the end of the world if Cath lost two hundred thousand pounds? It was a life-changing sum for my mother. And selfishly, if Mum could afford a house, I was pretty sure that she'd let me move in with Eddie and Megan temporarily. I didn't want to be grabby, but frankly, right now, even if Robin didn't manage to force me out, Mum offering us a place to stay was the only plan I had standing between the fast-approaching autumn and sleeping in a chilly damp shed. But how could I justify letting Robin steal from Cath on my behalf? What if she went to the police? Who was going to believe that I wasn't involved, that I didn't know what Robin was doing? I could find myself in prison.

I paused on the bench under the pergola, breathing in the scent of the buddleia. Slowly, I got to my feet, caught between fighting for what was ours and throwing my future, our future, against the wall like a fragile vase, with no idea where the fragments would land.

When I crept back inside, they were still hissing at each other in the study. I walked upstairs kidding myself that I'd just crack on with the dusting as normal, but every shout, every movement, made my heart hammer.

Eventually, I heard Cath slam out of the room. Her last

words to Robin: 'I'm sick of playing second fiddle to what your ex-wife needs. You either want to prioritise our relationship or you don't.' But her words were saying one thing and her voice another. She sounded as though she was begging, rather than telling him what was what.

I made myself scarce in the bathroom as she went steaming off into her bedroom. I told myself that it was none of my business how they worked out their finances. But I couldn't do it. Weary acceptance weighed me down as I knocked on Cath's door. Without waiting for an answer, I pushed it open. She was lying on the bed but sat up when she realised it was me.

'Sorry to disturb you, but I need to talk to you about something.'

She frowned. 'Now isn't really a good time,' she said, as tears poured down her face.

'It can't wait.' My voice was coming out all urgent.

Cath was waving at me to go, but I shut the door.

'I haven't been completely straight with you.'

I started from the beginning, not leaving anything out, Mum, the visit from Amy, even my taking advantage of Dolly to get into Cath's life. I watched her face pass through astonishment, horror and disbelief before settling on anger.

'I don't know how you dare accuse Robin of this when you've been stealing from my mother. I should go to the police.' Her words were tumbling out all ragged and uneven.

'What are you on about? I've never stolen from anyone, let alone Dolly.' The injustice of trying to help Cath at the expense of my own family flared like a firework in a November sky. I clutched on to the last thread of sanity that was stopping me giving her a good shake.

Cath made some kind of disbelieving snort and that, sadly for her, used up the last crumb of 'lowly cleaner biting her tongue for the mistress of the house'.

'You'd better open your eyes. Comparing notes with his ex-wife would be a good starting point. I bet she could tell you a thing or two.'

Indignation made Cath's face blow up like a puffer fish. But before she could retaliate, Robin appeared in the doorway.

'Don't tell me... she's rolling out that old nonsense about me somehow taking the life savings from her mother?'

Cath's eyes were flicking between us like an umpire at a high-speed tennis match. 'What? You knew about this?'

Robin did that whole voice of reason arriving to counterbalance the madwoman with her mop. 'Cath, love, I knew you were so busy and stressed about the wedding. I didn't want to bother you with Rebecca's, er, how shall I put it... fantastical ideas? I figured you were under enough pressure already.'

I felt that lurch, that panic that she might actually believe him, with his shiny loafers and cufflinks and posh fountain pen that he used to sign all the contracts for their wedding.

I crossed the room. 'You know damn well that you stole two hundred grand from my family.' I turned to Cath. 'You can go and see my mum in her bedsit. She'll tell you the truth.'

Cath's face fell, as though the penny was starting to drop.

But Robin piped up again. 'Cath, she doesn't know what she's saying. She's looking for a way to blackmail me into giving her some cash. Money that her mother and I lost to someone who owned a farmhouse in France we were trying to buy. I didn't take the money; it was the property dealer. I lost out too.'

Cath was battling between what she wanted to believe and what she was hearing.

Robin rattled on. 'I can show you all the correspondence that proves we both invested money and lost it.'

'That's bullshit. You broke my mother's heart by disappearing the day before your wedding and emptying her bank account to boot.'

Robin gestured towards Cath. 'I told you that I didn't think it was a good idea for Rebecca to come and live here. I knew there was something "off" about her from the beginning. I reckon she's been poisoning Sandy against me too.'

Hope marbled Cath's face, that all her doubts, all the things that didn't add up were rooted in me. She rubbed her eyes as though she was trying to clear the fog.

Robin carried on. 'Of course, you don't have to take my word for it. But when that stuff went missing from your mother's house, it was after that shopping trip with Rebecca. How do you explain that?'

I fought back – 'I'm not the only one with a key to Dolly's house' – but I sensed my advantage ebbing away. I could almost see her making up excuses for him, stoking up the outrage that her cleaner, the woman who swept up crumbs, dared to paint herself as the holder of the truth. Except I was. Or at least, I thought I was. Robin was so plausible; he was making me wonder if my mum had told the story as it really happened.

Cath shooed me out. 'Rebecca, would you mind leaving us alone for a few minutes, please?'

The fight all but dropped out of me. I'd gambled on poor odds.

I gave it one last try. 'Stop sticking your head in the sand. I had absolutely nothing to gain by telling you. He was asking you for two hundred thousand to pay me off so I'd keep my mouth shut. I couldn't go through with it. Couldn't stitch you up like that. But you don't have to trust me. That woman from Deal, Amy, will back me up – Robin can explain to you far better than me why she tracked you down.'

Robin started shouting about her being a crazy woman he'd only met briefly once. Cath practically pushed me out of her bedroom.

I ran downstairs and out into the garden. I gathered up the kids, bundling them into the car. 'We're going to see Dolly.'

There was no argument. Eddie loved her dog and Megan loved the Tunnock's Caramel Wafers. With the wedding a little over a fortnight away, I had one last chance to get someone, anyone, to see reason. When we drew up outside Dolly's, Eddie rushed up the path to ring the doorbell, setting Alfie off barking.

There was shuffling and fiddling with the lock and bolt. 'Who is it?'

I shouted through the door. 'Dolly, it's Rebecca. Can I come in a sec?'

She creaked open the door a crack as though the person who had watched her try on everything from a top hat to a peacock feather fascinator was poised to ransack her house.

'Oh, hello, Rebecca.' There was none of her usual energy and joy at seeing me. Soon-to-be son-in-law blood was obviously thicker than water.

Eddie's ability to read the room could easily be balanced on a pinhead. 'Can I play with Alfie? I've drawn him a picture.'

Dolly started to say no, but Eddie was already bending down stroking him and letting him lick his face.

I caught her eye and the desperation that she must have seen there did the trick. 'Would you two like to go through into the back yard and have a caramel wafer – they're in the tin, you know where they are – while I talk to your mum?'

I mouthed thank you as the kids piled through into her little kitchen and out into the garden. She didn't smile.

'Cath will go bonkers if she finds out I've let you in.'

'I'm sorry to put you in this position. Thank you, though, for not making a big fuss in front of the kids. I know you think I've stolen from you, but I really haven't.' I filled her in on my version of Robin.

'Go on with you. You're making him sound like something off James Bond.' She almost laughed until she remembered that she believed I'd pinched her jewellery.

'Even if it's not him, it's certainly not me. You said the only things that have gone are the bits that are worth anything. I can promise you I wouldn't know a curtain ring from a gold ring.'

Dolly couldn't poker face like Cath. She threw her hands up. 'I don't know what to believe. Cath tells me one thing, Robin's bending me earhole about how silly I was to get involved with some woman just walking along the street and you're here telling me that he's the crook. It's like being caught in *Midsomer Murders* trying to work out if it was the butcher, the baker or the blinking candlestick maker.'

Her phone rang.

I could tell it was Cath. 'Yes, yes, she's here. Yes, inside. I'm old but I'm not stupid.'

My heart hurt. Everywhere I went, I caused trouble.

Dolly came off the phone, looking frail and anxious. 'They've just found my watch in the tennis pavilion.' She put her hand to her face and looked as though she was about to cry.

I nodded. 'Of course they have.'

My eyes filled. 'I know you believe me, Dolly. I know you do.'

She wrung her hands. 'She's my daughter, Rebecca. She's all I've got.' Then she seemed to pull herself together, defaulting to Cath's instructions. 'I'm going to have to ask you to go.'

I called Eddie and Megan, who both protested wildly about having to leave the dog. It was all I could do not to start shouting in a way that would have had Dolly's neighbours vaulting the fence to see what was going on. As I shoved them into the car, with Eddie waving madly to Dolly and Alfie, I marvelled at the fact that however low I sank, there was always further to go. It had been bad enough losing our home. My earlier resolution to 'make this work' seemed laughable. Not only had I failed to get Mum's money back, now I couldn't even offer a draughty wooden shack to my kids.

I dialled Graham's number. I couldn't take them down with me.

30

CATH

The rest of the day passed in a blur of doubt and recrimination. Mum rang back to tell me about Rebecca's visit, sounding so hurt and bewildered that by the time Rebecca rolled up to fetch Eddie and Megan's things, I wanted to shake her and bellow about the obscenity of betraying the trust of an eighty-year-old woman.

However, the mother in me took one look at the confusion on her kids' faces, overheard Eddie saying, 'But does that mean we'll never live with you again?' before I reminded myself that good people in difficult circumstances do drastic things. If she'd only admitted it, I might even have been able to forgive her.

She didn't come through the house as she normally would but went round to the side gate.

Robin appeared in the kitchen. 'Good riddance to her. Poking into everything. You should go through your jewellery box and make sure she didn't take anything.'

As I watched the mournful trio trudging down the garden, I wanted to rush out and give her a cheque to put her back on her feet. I remembered only too well squeezing into my mum's house with Sandy and the mortification of not being able to provide for him.

'But what if it wasn't her? What if it really was my mother being forgetful?'

'I love that you choose to think the best of everyone, but you can't argue with the proof of the watch in the tennis pavilion, can you?' He dangled it in front of me.

'Where did you say you found it?'

'It was tucked away under the corner of the tarpaulin.'

'Nothing else there, I suppose? You'd have thought that she'd have had enough nous to hide the evidence.'

Robin shrugged. 'I don't think she's the sharpest tool in the box.'

He pulled me to him. 'Not like you, my darling.'

I couldn't relax into him. I wished I could behave how I did at work when I caught people out. I took the emotion out of the situation, defaulted to the protocols for dealing with whatever they'd done and moved on, with barely a backwards glance. Right now, though, all I could think was that for a few bits of inexpensive jewellery, Rebecca was homeless and the kids would have to go to their dad. I was going soft in my old age.

Robin was made of sterner stuff. 'You can't always be looking over your shoulder. We're getting married in nineteen days. We need to focus on ourselves and what a happy time we're going to have, instead of being distracted by other people's drama.'

Rebecca came to the French windows. 'I'm going to drive these two to meet Graham, then I'll come back and pack the rest of my gear. I'll leave first thing tomorrow.'

I couldn't look her in the eye. Bizarrely, I wanted her to like me even though she'd been thieving in my mother's house. 'Of course. The children can leave in the morning too, if that's better for you.'

Rebecca ignored my offer and rounded on me. 'You know

you're making a terrible mistake, don't you? You don't genuinely believe it was me. I can tell you don't.'

Before I could respond, Robin pushed in front of me, waving my mother's watch. 'How do you explain this in the pavilion, then? It didn't get there by accident, did it?'

The disgust and disdain as Rebecca choked out something between a laugh and a sob made me want to shut the door in her face and pull the curtains. 'I'm not even going to argue. You've both made up your minds.' She walked away, shouting over her shoulder, 'Do yourself a favour and don't marry him. He's the thief, not me.'

Robin snorted. 'You've actually got to feel sorry for her, haven't you? Anyway, I need to get on. I've got a big meeting about the development with another investor this evening. It's all looking quite good.' He went whistling off to the study.

I couldn't tear myself away from the window. Megan struggling with her little wheelie case and her duvet tucked under one arm, Eddie dropping sweatshirts and trainers as he bent down to stroke the cat. And Rebecca. I tucked myself behind the curtain so she couldn't see me, but the sight of her carrying Megan's fluffy tiger and Eddie's football, chivvying them along in that special 'nothing to worry about' voice that mothers use to protect their kids when there is everything to worry about, made me feel small and mean and vindictive. Who knew what I might have been capable of if Sandy and I hadn't had my mother's home to go to?

Her car door slammed and I breathed out. I was about to phone my assistant to see if there was anything urgent when my mobile rang. It was Renee, the woman in charge of the fairy lights and bunting for the wedding. She cleared her throat. 'I'm terribly sorry, but the order has arrived and the lights are pink, not the blue you asked for. I'm desperately trying to get the blue ones on time, but I can't guarantee it.'

Robin would be annoyed because he'd planned every detail

– the lights to match the flowers, to match the bunting. But it was Renee's lucky day. I'd just chucked out a mother and two kids onto the street. I didn't have it in me to fall on the floor over the colour of my fairy lights.

'Send whatever you've got, we'll work around it.'

Renee rang off, oozing relief.

Robin popped his head out of the study. 'Who was that?'

I filled him in.

Within seconds, he was yelling down the phone, 'I don't care what Ms Randell said, I ordered blue lights and that's what I want or I'm cancelling the order!'

I was trying to intervene, my hand up to indicate that he should calm down, when the front door opened. Sandy came into the kitchen.

'Christ, what's got him going?' he asked, jerking his thumb in Robin's direction. Sandy's dismissive tone was the final straw.

'Please don't start. I've had a terrible day and I'm not in the mood for more aggro.'

Sandy flopped down into the armchair. 'I was coming here for some light relief. What's going on?'

To a backdrop of Robin shouting about breach of contract to poor Renee, whose day was probably shaping up to rival mine in its misery, I told him about Rebecca, Robin finding the watch, her leaving with the kids.

I knew he'd be shocked. Originally, we'd all thought of Rebecca as someone who did the drudge we couldn't find the time or will to do. Ultimately though, she'd become not exactly a friend, but certainly someone we'd respected and trusted.

Sandy's reaction was far, far worse than I'd anticipated. A quiet fury. 'You believed his word over hers? It didn't occur to you that he might be the real thief? That he somehow got hold of Grandma's stuff and used it to pin the blame on her. He's the one who jets about on planes, borrows money from you and fills you full of promises. You haven't met any of his family or friends, you've never gone out to Spain to see his "developments". Yet you've sent Rebecca away fully aware she has nowhere to go?'

He was shaking his head as though I was the most despicable person in the world.

'I can't cope with this today, Sandy. I really can't.' Since I'd been with Robin, I'd seen a side to Sandy that made me wonder if the failure of his marriage was all down to Chloe. For the first time, I understood how parents became estranged from their children; I didn't want to be that person. 'Can we talk about this another day?'

Robin was winding up his phone call. 'You either get those lights to me by Tuesday or you'll be hearing from my solicitors by the end of next week.'

Sandy looked incredulous. 'Mum, you're marrying him at the beginning of next month – a bloke who's threatening legal action over fairy lights. I was going to ask if I could come back home. Chloe and I are at a dead end. But I can't live here. Not with him.'

I was so busy steering Sandy into the hallway, away from Robin's ranting, that it took me a moment to register what he'd said about Chloe. 'Oh no, what happened? I thought you were working things out?'

'Still carrying on, isn't she? But, to be honest, I've realised that I don't even like her much, let alone love her. I'd rather be on my own.'

I held my arms out to him, but he backed away as Robin came storming in. 'Idiots! I chose those lights because they matched the hydrangeas on the terrace. Anyway, I gave her a piece of my mind.' I swore Robin put on a 'big man sorting things out' act every time Sandy was around. If only he'd relax and allow Sandy to see the kind and gentle man he really was. He could get angry when something scuppered his plans, but I sympathised with that desire for perfection, as well as his frustration when other people didn't do their jobs properly. 'What brings you here, Sandy?' he asked.

He didn't mean to sound territorial, I was sure. Sandy's antagonism towards him over the last few months had prevented them finding a rhythm in their relationship. I hoped it would develop over time or we were in for a rocky ride indeed.

I jumped in. 'Sandy's reconciliation with Chloe hasn't really worked out, so he's going to take a breather here for a while until he gets himself sorted.' I wasn't quite clear why my stomach was fluttery and panicky or why my tone was so apologetic.

Robin looked at me. 'You're not suggesting he moves back in before the wedding?' Without waiting for my reply, he turned to Sandy. 'That isn't fair on your mum. She's got so much going on. After all this business with Rebecca, I really think you need to consider staying somewhere else until the wedding is over.'

Sandy laughed in his face. 'What? The man who, to my knowledge, hasn't contributed a single penny to anything is now dictating who can stay in my mother's house? The house I grew up in and lived in for years before you came on the scene?'

Robin swivelled round to face me. The anger had left his voice, replaced with a weary resignation. 'Perhaps I'm the one who should leave. Yep, that's what I should do. Why don't I go away for a few days, stay with my mate Simon, down near Chichester, give everyone a chance to calm down before the big day and then we can regroup?'

I touched his arm, but he clomped off upstairs. The noise of wardrobe doors banging and drawers opening filtered into the silence between Sandy and me.

Sandy's shoulders dropped. 'I'm going to my room.'

I reached out to him, but he swerved away and my hand grabbed at air.

Life used to be so simple when I only had Sandy and Mum

to worry about. I'd been naive not to anticipate that I'd be juggling everyone's needs, failing to make anyone happy, least of all myself. I tried to sift through the conflicting information clouding my brain. On the face of it, Rebecca was undoubtedly the thief, but I could tell Mum wasn't convinced and, to be fair, it just didn't feel *right*. But what other explanation was there? There was so much that didn't add up, all these odd things popping up out of the woodwork – that woman from Deal, Amy.

My heart did a little flip of fear when I remembered we weren't even supposed to be going there initially, that the place in Herne Bay had overbooked and upgraded us to its sister hotel in Deal. And then Robin disappearing that night. I reassured myself by casting my mind back to when I'd found him the next day. He'd been so distressed, so concerned I was making a mistake that he'd encouraged me to leave him.

When no one else was sticking their nose in, stirring up my doubts, I felt so loved. At my age, I was unlikely to meet anyone without the baggage of ex-wives and tangled finances. Maybe everyone else – Sandy, Mum, even Jax – just preferred it when I was always available for them rather than enjoying a separate life of my own. Robin and I obviously had a few things to discuss, but I wasn't going to let everyone else spoil my happiness. A few days' break from each other before the big day would settle all of our nerves.

31

REBECCA

Despite assuming that I barely owned anything, it took me ages to pack. Pride made me spend all of Tuesday morning cleaning, so it was after lunch by the time I drew up at Debs'. I'd gambled on not ringing first and turning up when Jason was at work. It would be harder for her to say no to my face than on the phone with Jason doing the big head shake in the background.

Debs was jiggling Sophia at the window. Her face lit up when she saw me, probably delighted at the idea of having someone else to hold the baby for a bit. I walked up the drive focused on a single thought: how did my life unravel at such a speed? One minute, Graham had mentioned that his business ventures were struggling and less than a year later I was an unwelcome guest relying on other people's charity.

Debs came to the door, all smiles. 'Hey! Look who's come to see you, Sophs. It's your Auntie Rebecca.'

I reached out for her and she gurgled, her little fingers closing round my thumb. My envy in that moment of Debs was almost overwhelming. All she had to do was keep her daughter fed and warm and safe for Sophia to look at her as though she was the most incredible human in the world. I couldn't even manage that. I didn't know when I ever would again. I nuzzled into the little fuzz on the top of her head. If I could bottle that smell of warmth and contentment, I could make a fortune and solve all my problems in one go.

'She's gorgeous. She's grown so big!' I stroked her cheek. 'How are you doing?'

Debs showed me in, launching into a litany of complaints about her mastitis, lack of sleep and how Sophia screamed every time Debs put her down. I remembered being that woman, feeling so knackered I could barely open a cereal packet to feed myself. The days wondering whether I'd ever feel normal, smiley, energetic again. I wished I could go back and redo it with a lot more being grateful for what I had. And much more taking notice of what Graham was asking me to sign.

Debs sniffed Sophia's bottom. 'You can't believe how much this baby poos.'

'Would you like me to change her? You can make us a cup of tea.'

I was only delaying asking what I knew would put her in a difficult position.

That soft skin, those chubby legs, that contented gurgling. If I could turn back time.

Debs came through with tea and biscuits. She stuffed a ginger nut in her mouth. 'Still kidding myself that breastfeeding means I can eat as many biscuits as I want.' She smiled at me cradling the baby. 'Look how relaxed she is with you. Anyway, what's going on in the outside world?'

The words were jamming in my throat. I forced them out. 'I've been sacked. The kids have gone back to Graham. I don't want to ask this again, but could I stay, just for a bit?'

Debs' face was a picture. 'Sacked? How did you get sacked?'

'For stealing, which obviously I didn't do. The boyfriend has framed me.'

'What? Why would he do that?'

I hadn't meant to tell her. But my world, my disasters, my grief had become too big to keep inside. I'd failed at everything, in the most basic and important ways. I blurted out the whole sorry story.

Debs squawked in disbelief. 'Are you mad? You tricked your way into the house and tried to blackmail Robin? You were lucky he didn't go to the police and get you arrested!'

'It wasn't blackmail though. He stole from us. Well, from Mum. She could use that money right now, find herself somewhere where she's got her own private bathroom. And I'm not going to lie, if she could put us up for a while too, she'd be doing me a massive favour.'

'I can't be part of any of that. What if he comes after you?'

'He's not a murderer. He's a conman.' I bounced Sophia on my shoulder as she started to whimper at our raised voices.

'You've got no proof of that. Mum and he got caught up in some property scam – he lost money as well.' Debs started folding blankets, picking up squeaky toys, anything to avoid making eye contact with me.

'Maybe he did, but you can't escape the concrete evidence that her money disappeared out of their joint account for a farmhouse in France that he persuaded her to buy and then he was never seen again.'

'I don't know. I'd always understood that the problem was with the owner of the farmhouse. Mum won't talk about it. She says it's water under the bridge.' She dunked a biscuit in her tea and cursed as it fell off into the mug.

Desperation sharpened my frustration that she was so passive about what had happened. 'But it was our dad's money. You know how hard he worked. And then she lost it all on some ooh-la-la dream that never happened.'

'Jason will go crazy if I tell him what you've done.'

'Why does he have to have an opinion?' For once, I wanted someone to take my side.

'Because he's my husband! Sophia's father. I can't do whatever I want and expect him to put up with it.'

'So that means I can't kip on the settee for a few nights while I work out a plan B?'

Debs dropped her eyes and took Sophia from me, snuggling into her to hide her face. 'Rebecca, I wish I could say yes. But Jase and I, we're not getting on that well, lack of sleep, him working and assuming he can loll about watching TV all evening while I try to get Sophia down. He won't agree anyway. His family aren't that close, he's not used to helping out.'

I knew she was between a rock and a hard place and I reminded myself that none of this was her fault, that my failed marriage, my stupid husband, weren't anything to do with her. But I was pleading. 'I've got enough for about three nights at the Travelodge.'

Debs started to cry, which set the baby wailing. 'I've got a bit of cash I can give you.'

She put the baby on her hip and went to fetch her handbag.

Defeat rolled through me like a winter sea.

'It's okay, Debs. I'll manage.'

'Don't go like that.' She tried to grab my arm, but I couldn't be touched.

'I'm not going like anything. I've got to find somewhere while it's still light.' Even to my ears that sounded dramatic, followed by the realisation that it might be dramatic but it was also, sadly, horribly true.

I slammed the door and considered my options. I could sleep in the car, blow my last cash on a hotel, or see if my mother could sneak me into her room without getting evicted for having an overnight guest.

I drove to her house and rang the bell. Someone buzzed me into the dark hallway that stank of bins and weed. I knocked on her door.

'Rebecca!' My mum's face lit up. 'Aren't you at work today?'

It was years since I'd been able to rely on my mother. I couldn't remember the last time I'd gone to her with any hope that she could save me. I didn't have hope now, just a lack of alternatives. The fear in her face as I crumpled on the threshold told me everything I needed to know. This wasn't the way it worked. Her role wasn't to tell me that I'd be okay, we wouldn't give up or give in. Nor was it to join me in making Robin pay for what he'd done. I'd never breathed a word about looking for him – and much less about actually finding him. But I had no choice now.

She retreated to where a kettle stood on a cupboard in the corner, filling it at an awkward angle from the tiny basin. Her panicky words – 'I'll make a cup of tea' – were a poor substitute for 'Whatever's happened, we can get through it and I can be strong for you.'

Mum scuttled out into the corridor. 'I'll just get some milk from the kitchen.'

She came back and handed me a cup of tea. 'Are you okay?' she asked, in a tone that suggested that she could only cope with me spinning her some yarn about sunshine and roses despite the fact that I was sitting on her stool snivelling into my sleeve.

'Not really.' I filled her in on how I'd stalked Robin, inserted myself into his life to try and recover her money.

Her face took on every expression from shock to outrage. Pride at my cunning, gratitude that I'd wanted to get justice for her, even sympathy that I hadn't succeeded, didn't seem to feature.

Mum wasn't one for shouting. She sank down onto the bed, looking at me as though I'd been the one to mess everything up, rather than Robin. 'What did he say when you said who you were?'

'I think you can guess, Mum. Denied any knowledge of it then came up with some measly excuse about you both being ripped off by the property owner.'

Mum looked so stunned. For a moment, I thought she was going to tell me off for getting ideas above my station or some old twaddle. I decided to get it over with; to give her the whole dollop of bad news in one fell swoop; that not only had I failed to tighten the screws on Robin and get him to cough up but I'd also got myself sacked and all of us thrown out.

Mum picked at her sleeve, her mouth turned down. 'Oh dear, Rebecca. I wish you'd spoken to me before rushing in like that. You've always been a hothead, take after your father. You'll never get the better of a man like Robin.'

I clung on to my temper by a thread. It was easy to avoid being a troublemaker if you were so passive, you never attempted to sort anything out. 'You are certain that he took your money though? That you didn't both get scammed by the person selling the house?' It was a bit late to clarify the details now but Mum's horror, not at what Robin had done, but at what I had tried to do, was filling me full of doubt where previously, I'd harboured courage and determination.

'Robin dealt with all that side of things.' She ran her hand through her hair. 'I don't know. I thought he'd gone off with the cash at the time because he vanished the day before the wedding. I'm not sure now. It was so long ago.' She started to cry. 'I loved him so much, I would have done anything for him. I was so happy. After your father never really seeming to notice me, he made me feel so special.'

If there was one thing that would light the touchpaper, it was Mum badmouthing my dad. He wasn't the most romantic husband, but he was solid and hard-working and dependable. And we'd all taken him for granted until we'd been on the receiving end of men who weren't solid and hard-working and dependable.

'I don't think I'll ever meet anyone who makes me feel like Robin did again. I keep going out with these men from the internet, but they're not a patch on him. He had this way with him. I still don't understand why he did what he did.'

I wanted to shake her. If anyone should have realised that a hairy-faced honest Joe knocked the spots off a fake Prince Charming, it should have been my mother. She'd probably be on her deathbed swiping right. Even now, I couldn't say with total certainty that if Robin turned up with a bunch of chrysanthemums he'd nicked out of a graveyard, my mother wouldn't brush over the little matter of the missing two hundred grand and try to persuade us all that he was really a good egg.

To be fair, I hadn't exactly dazzled with my own brilliance as far as men were concerned. Somehow, though, I found letting my husband of eleven years deal with our finances not quite as stupid as Mum allowing a man she had known for a matter of months take control of her entire bank account. But wasn't that human nature? Finding reasons why your own mistakes weren't anywhere near as stupid as other people's.

Mum was shaking, her words coming out in jumpy stutters, as though she couldn't quite connect her thoughts. Eventually she said, 'So what are you going to do now without a job?'

How I would have loved it if for once, she could have given me a hug and said, 'Thank you for trying. I'm sorry it didn't work out.' Instead, there was that tiny hint of blame, that I'd been reckless again.

I snapped. 'I don't know what I'm going to do, Mum. While Graham is watching the sunset in Shoreham-by-Sea with the kids and a new woman, I'm properly homeless. I haven't even got anywhere to sleep tonight. Unless I could crash here?'

Mum shrank back into her chair, hands fluttering. 'You can't stay here. We're not allowed people overnight.'

'Not even for one night? I could get up early and slip out without anyone seeing me.'

My mum's face was a picture. 'I can't, Rebecca. Alan, the one who drinks, is always coming in and out at odd hours. It would be just my luck if you bumped into him and I lost this place.'

I hated having to plead. 'Mum, please. Debs won't have me because she says Jason will lose the plot.'

'Why don't you ring one of your friends?'

'Ali's mum is in hospital at the moment, so the last thing she needs is me kipping on her couch, Liz is on holiday, Fi has got her in-laws staying. And I don't know anyone else well enough that I could ring and say, "I'm homeless" who wouldn't be terrified that they'd be stuck with me forever. I've literally nowhere to go.'

Mum went to her handbag. 'Here. It's all I've got.' She handed me forty-five pounds and a handful of change. 'Why don't you try the youth hostel?'

The reality of what my mother was suggesting seared a pain right through my body. I would never ever be that mother. I couldn't imagine sending Megan off, at any age, to sleep in the car or a hostel or some stranger's spare room.

'Mum, keep your money. I'll work it out.'

I left, with Mum standing helplessly at the door. Hotel bills would soon gobble up my last couple of hundred pounds so I sat in my car, scrolling through my phone and clicking on rooms to rent by the night. Eventually, I found one for £17 in a house not too far away. I booked it and arranged to go straight there.

I parked on the road and riffled through my bags until I cobbled together enough clothes and toiletries to get me through the next few days. I mustered up the last of my energy and rang the bell.

A scrawny bloke, late twenties, in jogging bottoms and a once white T-shirt, opened the door.

'Hi.' He made no move to invite me in.

'Lucas? I'm here about the room?' I wondered if I'd got the right address.

'Oh yeah. You messaged earlier, right?'

I wanted to run away from this man who was frowning at me as though I was trying to trick my way into his house. He stood back and led me into a narrow hallway, then through to a sitting room with a kitchenette in the corner. Apart from a few mugs in the sink and a plate balancing on the armrest of the settee, it wasn't messy, though there was the low-level whiff of a bin that needed emptying. He gestured towards the kettle. 'You can make a cup of tea if you want.'

I nodded. I wasn't quite sure what to make of that luxury offering.

'Your room is upstairs.'

I was still struggling to accept that I was following a stranger with his bum crack poking out of his tracksuit, in a house I'd picked randomly from an accommodation website. He opened the door to a box room with a stack of dumbbells in the corner.

'It's not much, pretty basic really.'

He didn't have a glittering future as an estate agent. Or as a bodybuilder. He probably should try to get his money back on those dumbbells.

I couldn't think of another plan. 'It'll do, thank you. Is the bed clean?'

'Yeah.'

I should have asked questions – how often he rented the room out, how long he'd been doing it for – to establish some connection that would have given me confidence that he was a bit awkward but not a starter-home serial killer.

Instead, he said, 'I don't get the whole seventeen quid. The website takes a cut.'

I wasn't sure why he was telling me. An excuse for washing the sheets every other guest? Expecting me to tuck a fiver under the pillow when I left?

He suddenly seemed uncomfortable in the small space and turned to go. 'The bathroom is next door. I leave for work at eight o'clock, so you'll need to be gone before then unless you decide to stay a second night.'

I hesitated as the true precariousness of my situation penetrated the fog in my brain. I needed a day to phone the council and charities, to see what the options were for someone like me. 'If I stay another night, can I use your Wi-Fi tomorrow?'

He didn't miss a beat. 'Can you pay me cash in hand?'

I rummaged in my bag, counting out the exact money. Living with my kids again felt as though it was slipping further and further away from me.

As soon as he'd gone, I pulled back the duvet and sniffed the sheets. They weren't freshly laundered, but I couldn't see any rogue hairs either. I still lay on top of the bed, staring at the sad little lightbulb with no lampshade.

Please let today be rock bottom.

32

CATH

Over the next couple of days, I swung between doubting what Robin was telling me and the conviction that my upcoming wedding was stressing me out so much I was imagining monsters under the bed. Work had always been my refuge, but on Zoom with CEOs I was supposed to be schmoozing, I was briskly 'take it or leave it' when they argued over terms and conditions. I kept shutting my office door so I could ring Robin, batting away my assistant's reminders that I had calls scheduled in ten minutes. I was so relieved every time he picked up.

'Hey.' That voice. The way he spoke, a mixture of softness and sexiness, made me feel that I could forgive him anything.

'I'm sorry about Sandy. I don't even want to make excuses for him. Please come home. I'll help him rent a flat somewhere after the wedding.'

Robin's tone was gentle, kind. 'It's hard for him. I'd love to get to know him properly. Maybe this is a bit of a test, to see if I'm serious about you, worthy of you, as it were?' He gave a little chuckle.

'Can I just ask one thing? It's been bothering me. Can you

go over how you know that Amy woman who turned up at the house? Rebecca said she'd lent you money and been in a relationship with you?'

Robin sighed. 'For a start, Rebecca's doing a grand job of spreading rumours. She has no idea what she's on about, putting two and two together and making five hundred as far as I can see. But yes, I do know Amy. Or at least, I've met her once. I should have told you about her after we went away to Deal that weekend, but I forgot about it with everything else going on.'

Dread washed over me. I'd never imagined that falling in love again would bring this massive storm swirl of debris with it. I focused on Robin's voice, strong and confident. He wasn't grappling for words or stumbling over his sentences.

'She was sitting on a bench watching the sunrise at the beach when I was doing my marathon hike up and down the coast, trying to get my head straight. We got chatting about life, the universe, how she'd just come out of a long-term relationship, you know how you sometimes do with strangers. I think she felt a connection with me and wanted to see me again.'

'So did you? See her again?' A sting of possessiveness shot through me.

'No, don't be silly. I might have accidentally given her some false hope when I explained that I was planning to marry you but everything had become a bit complicated. I guess she's a bit unhinged and didn't want to leave it there. Invented some kind of romance between us, which I can one hundred per cent assure you bears no relation to reality. She was also fascinated by my property developments. Maybe she deluded herself that she might invest in them or something. Who knows? There are some weird people in the world.'

I relaxed slightly. I could easily imagine a broken-hearted woman attaching herself to Robin, with his skill of finding the right words to make everyone feel special.

'How did she know where I live?'

He grunted. 'That's my fault. I told her all about your business, how amazing you were. I guess she found the address on the internet somewhere.'

For the first time that day, my shoulders came down from around my ears. It was ironic that Robin's kindness had caused such a problem.

I moved on to my next concern. 'Are you still at Simon's?' I tried not to feel worried about what a bloke I'd never met would think about Robin turning up at his door a fortnight before his wedding. I didn't want him telling all Robin's other friends that he gave it a year.

'Yeah. He's really pleased to see me. He can't come to the wedding because he's away on holiday, so it's a good opportunity to kill two birds with one stone – get out of your hair for a few days and catch up with him.'

'When you get back, I'd like to run my speech past you.' I brushed away the disappointment that I'd felt the need to put into words exactly what made Robin such a good match for me, that I still sensed doubt among my friends and family.

'Your speech? I thought you were only going to do a toast?'

'No, we agreed that as you're not having a best man, we'd both say a few words. We talked about it the other night, when we were sitting on the terrace, a couple of days before Mum called to say her jewellery had gone.'

'I don't remember that. It's not very traditional, is it?'

I wondered if my head was so full of conversations I intended to have that I sometimes forgot that I hadn't spoken the words out loud. 'Do we need to be traditional at our age? I'm planning to grow old disgracefully.' I tried to make a joke of it, reminding myself that one of the things that had attracted Robin to me in the first place was that I was such a good public speaker. When we first met at the workshop I was leading, he'd complimented me. 'I've seen so many women, even successful ones, sit back and let men take over their platforms. You really held your own.'

I waited to hear his reaction, hoping I wouldn't be put to the test about how much of a stand I was prepared to make. We had enough to argue about already. Thankfully, I heard the smile in his voice. 'You can do anything you want. I look forward to hearing what you've got to say. I'll probably be back on Saturday morning.'

'Saturday? We've only got two weekends left before the wedding. I was hoping that we could use Friday night to make a list of what still needs doing and make a start first thing on Saturday.'

'Wouldn't it be better to give Sandy the rest of the week to calm down?'

I loved that Robin was being so considerate, but my patience with everyone else was wearing thin. 'It's not about Sandy, it's about us. He's going to have to get used to you being around and accept that my life is moving on. Please come back by Friday.'

'Missing me, are you?'

'Of course I am!' I hated sounding weedy and pathetic, but whenever Robin was out of my sight, all my doubts seemed to feed on Sandy's comments and woodpecker away at my belief in us.

'Okay. I'll see what I can do. I'm pretty snowed under with work and Simon's out all day, so it's easier to concentrate here.'

I opted to put on a brave face. 'I'll have to go to bed with a hot-water bottle then.'

'Lucky hot-water bottle. I'll make it up to you on Saturday. Your penultimate weekend as Ms Randell.'

I knew he was just having a cheeky tease. We'd had the conversation about me not changing my surname several times now. 'I'd better go and make some calls before I give my assistant a heart attack.'

'Oh, I meant to say, I've had to send through the balance for the flowers. They chased me this morning. Seven hundred pounds. I transferred the money to my property company first so that we can put the flowers against tax as an expense for dressing the show homes. Saves us forty per cent, so why not?'

I didn't approve of fiddling taxes like that, but I went along with it. 'Okay, well done. Was that in addition to the two-hundred-pound deposit?'

'Yes. It'll be worth it though. Our own mini Chelsea Flower Show!'

'You'd better show up! I don't want to be left with nine hundred pounds' worth of flowers I don't know what to do with. Have you had any more news on your own house?' I couldn't help comparing this extravagance with the jars of wildflowers and the roses from my mum's garden when I'd married Sandy's dad.

'Yes, it's looking good. The survey only threw up a couple of bits, nothing major, and even Moira seems keen to hurry it all along, now I've called her bluff. She had a terrible meltdown when I told her I was getting married but it seems to have done the trick. Line in the sand and all that.'

I didn't voice my opinion that Robin should have stood his ground a lot sooner. I was just relieved that after I'd refused to lend him the cash at the beginning of the week, he'd had no choice but to tell her he was turning off the money tap. Surprise, surprise, it had been the kick up the backside she'd needed to stop playing games and start finalising their affairs. One hurdle down at least.

By Thursday, I struggled to concentrate on work. Every time I logged into Zoom, I felt rattled and ill-prepared. That morning in particular, I was curt and impatient when a client questioned my fees. 'You're charging a premium?'

'I'm charging the industry standard.'

'Top end though.'

'I provide a top-end service.'

'I bet.' It was the smirk that did it. The smirk that implied that commanding that level of remuneration was nothing to do with talent and everything to do with womanly wiles.

I refused to humour him. 'Do you want to employ him or not?'

'Come on, I was just having a joke. I'll sign the contract today.' His smile faded as though he couldn't believe he'd met yet another woman who wasn't joining in with his 'banter'.

I pressed 'end' and gave the screen my middle finger.

Even for a fat commission, I wasn't going to accommodate a man who assumed that any woman making a successful place-ment needed to lean into the screen with her G-cups on display.

My assistant began to list who'd rung to speak to me. Feeling very *Devil Wears Prada*, I picked up my bag. 'I'll get back to them tomorrow.'

As I pulled into the drive, I wondered if I was getting old. I never used to let these chauvinist pigs get me down, always had some withering yet charming comeback for the old dinosaurs who seemed astonished that there was no successful man in the background driving my business forwards. I could no longer pander to their fragile egos or summon up the will to sit through awards dinners asking them a hundred questions about them-selves when it never occurred to them to ask anything about me.

I was so lucky with Robin. From the very first day we'd met, he'd been magnetic in his desire to understand how I thought, curious about my ideas. Forget oysters, accepting I had some-thing of value to say was my aphrodisiac.

I was so busy reminiscing that it took me a moment to realise Robin's car was in the drive. And Sandy's van was not.

My mood lifted immediately, the stress and irritation of the day rippling off me. I crept in the front door to hear Robin repeating down the phone: 'I'm telling you that the invoice has been paid. I can send you the screenshot. The problem is with your bank not clearing the money for whatever reason. I'll email it through now. You'll have to take it up at your end.'

Thank goodness he was so good at handling all this detail.

I stuck my head round the study door. 'You're here! You told me Saturday. What happened, couldn't keep away from me?'

He leapt up as though he'd been stung. 'I wanted to surprise you and get dinner ready, but, you know, wedding admin got in the way,' he said, sweeping up a load of papers and shoving them in the drawer. 'I couldn't bear to hear you so fed up.' He flicked out his hands. 'This should be the best time of our lives! Why don't we have some champagne while the coast is clear and have a little practice for our wedding night?'

I'd been fantasising about having a glass of wine and a long soak in the bath, but I dug deep for spontaneity. 'You get the champagne. I'm going to have a shower. It's been a difficult day.'

He kissed me long and hard, running his fingers through my hair. 'I'll be right up,' he said. As he left, I realised that he'd dislodged one of my earrings. The back was caught in my hair, but the little diamond starfish was missing. I knelt down on the floor and patted about under the desk, shaking out a couple of loose sheets of paper. The words Cash Express stood out on one of them, a handwritten receipt. Ladies' engagement ring. Twenty-one carat. One diamond. Three hundred and fifty pounds cash.

I stared at it. A pawn shop. Surely not my mother's ring? The ring my dad had saved up for over three years before he judged himself worthy of her. The ring she'd removed when she'd lost weight after his death in case it slipped off. 'I'd never forgive myself. Your dad put away nearly half his wages every week to get that. Most expensive thing I'd ever owned until we got the house.'

Three hundred and fifty quid. For the thing that meant so much to my mother and that I still hadn't been convinced she'd lost.

Where had that receipt come from? Robin was always complaining that Rebecca was poking about in there. My mind was fogging over with the complexities of making sense of it. Surely she'd have thrown away a receipt for something she'd stolen and sold on. Maybe I would have to call the police. I'd get her into terrible trouble. Her poor kids. What if she went to prison? I couldn't just shrug this off, though. I felt sick at the thought that I'd been so cavalier, letting her live in my house to look after Mum. I bet this was the tip of the iceberg. God knows what else was missing that we hadn't yet discovered. I was sifting through the rest of the bits and pieces as Robin appeared at the study door carrying a bottle of champagne and glasses. 'Are you keeping me waiting? I thought you were having a shower?'

'I was, but I lost my earring. Look what I found under the desk.'

I thrust the pawn shop receipt under his nose.

'Oh that, I took an old ring that my mother left me when she died. It was her sister's or something. It had no sentimental value for me, so I used the money to give us a little treat.'

'I thought you were estranged from your mother when she died?' My brain was hopping about, reversing away from the idea that this was the ultimate proof that Rebecca had stolen and sold Mum's things. Relief flooded through me that I wouldn't need to rush to the police station. There was more than one engagement ring with one diamond in the world.

'I was. She forgot to change her will. Her solicitor tracked me down.'

I frowned. I was sure he said that she'd cut him off without a penny. 'Didn't you fall out with your cousin because she'd left everything to her?'

He put his shoulders back and laughed. 'Hey, what's this? Twenty questions on my family background? Champagne's getting warm. Can you save your interrogation for later after I've made the most of my wife-to-be?'

I really wanted to dig deeper, but Robin was hurrying me upstairs. He'd mentioned a few times that I needed to learn to live in the moment. I fancied the idea of myself as a freewheeling, leaping into bed with my lover in the middle of the afternoon sort of woman. Rather than the one who felt a bit panicky about how I'd cope the next day if I went to bed after eleven.

But despite the champagne and Robin's massage of my shoulders – 'You spend way too much time at a desk' – I couldn't get into the mood. A low-level thrum of alarm was forcing its way through. His eagerness to change the subject had unnerved me. A pawn shop? Weren't pawn shops for people in debt, who couldn't pay their bills? Why wouldn't he go to a jeweller and get a proper valuation rather than walking away with a stash of notes? I made an effort to concentrate on Robin's caresses, but I kept thinking about when we were in Deal and Robin paid for the hotel room in cash. When I'd remarked on it, he'd said he'd sold a piece of machinery and the buyer had turned up with a bunch of twenties. 'Suits me. I don't have to put it through the books.'

As he kissed my neck, I told myself that there wasn't a single woman alive who didn't harbour a few doubts about whether she was doing the right thing as she approached her wedding day. After two decades without having to accommodate a husband's idiosyncrasies, it was no wonder that so many things seemed odd. I couldn't expect a fifty-three-year-old man to share my exact attitudes to money. There'd be plenty of time to hear about his peculiar family. From what I'd learnt so far, it was amazing that he'd become such a kind and generous person given how cold-hearted his mother had been. I didn't want to wish my life away, but part of me couldn't wait to escape on honeymoon.

Away from everyone who seemed to begrudge us our happiness, fuelling the doubts that kept clouding my mind.

33

REBECCA

When Lucas said, 'You might want to give the bathroom a few minutes before going in there,' he clearly meant a few centuries. After a bruising time the day before exploring my limited options now I'd declared myself officially homeless, it lit the last tiny spark of anger to channel my upset into useful action.

I marched out of Lucas's, not even bothering to clean my teeth after seeing his toenail clippings on the basin. My mind flitted between my own predicament and the growing sensation that I couldn't allow Cath to twirl into the glass atrium of the registry office, all giddy with hope for the future and commit herself to someone who harmed everyone he came into contact with.

As I started the car, I tried to take an objective view. Maybe Robin really did love her. Even thinking those words made me want to give myself a good slap. Men like that were all about themselves.

There were sixteen days left to the wedding. I was going to have to pull something pretty stunning out of the bag to force Cath to mothball her happy ending. I googled an address and squinted at how much petrol I had left. Just enough for a day at the seaside.

I crossed my fingers that Amy wouldn't remember me, as well as half-hoping that she wouldn't be at home anyway so I could say I'd done all I could without actually having to do all I could.

No such luck. She greeted me as though she was slightly afraid of what I might do next. I rushed out with 'I'm sorry I wasn't very helpful last time we met. Is there any chance I could talk to you now? It's about Robin.'

I loved that life sometimes delivered people who were much more forgiving than me. She waved me through to the sitting room. 'Did he send you?'

'Absolutely not. I'm here because you're the only one who can stop Cath making a terrible mistake.'

Her face relaxed. 'I thought you might be covering for him when I came to the house. I wrote a letter to Cath after that, but I've never heard from her.'

I frowned. 'I've never seen any letter there from you. Not that I would necessarily.' I didn't want her to start thinking I was always snooping about, even though I most definitely was.

I poured out my story with the caveats of 'Mum doesn't seem too sure of the facts...'

Amy rested her chin on her hand. 'Robin proposed to me about three years ago. We'd been together for about two. We kept setting a date, but there was always some reason why it couldn't happen. Initially, it was because his divorce was slow to come through.'

'His divorce? But he's only just got divorced. Like in the last couple of months.'

'No, he showed me his divorce order. At least two years ago.'

'From Moira Franklin?'

'Yes.'

I felt like I was trying to complete a jigsaw of a Norwegian fjord where half the pieces had been swapped for a picture of a unicorn.

'But I swear I saw a certificate very recently, the absolute thingy?'

Amy breathed out heavily. 'Maybe he remarried her? Nothing would surprise me. That whole divorce dragging on was a sideshow for all the other millions of excuses he came up with for not marrying me – he was needed in Spain otherwise his biggest project would fail; investment funding had mysteriously been withdrawn and he was in a "pinch point" money-wise; his uncle – his last remaining relative – was on his last legs and he wouldn't be able to look himself in the face if he didn't care for him; he wanted to sell the marital home so he could start again with a clean slate... I've lost count of the amount of times we looked around for venues. I even sent out a save-the-date card once.'

'What happened?'

'I was thirty-five when we started dating. I'd almost given up hope of finding a partner. I couldn't believe that I'd finally met this wonderful man who wanted to have babies with me.'

She did a little snort of disbelief. 'He promised me that we'd start trying as soon as we were married, but, of course, that date kept getting pushed back. I should have left him, but I kept thinking that it would take me ages to meet someone else and that I'd be too old to have a family by the time that happened anyway. So—' Her voice trembled and she cleared her throat. 'So I hung on in there.'

She swiped at the tears that forced their way out, despite her best efforts. 'I was happy to have a small registry office wedding, but Robin is all about showing off to other people. It's not enough for him to be winning, someone has to lose.' Amy threw her head back in frustration. 'I'm thirteen years younger than him. He was so proud of that, saw it as proof of his virility to brag about to all and sundry. He wouldn't hear of having a tiny ceremony, whereas I just wanted to make it happen as quickly as possible so I could concentrate on getting pregnant.'

Her voice broke completely. 'First of all, I added money onto my mortgage so he could get his project finished in Spain and we could hurry things along. Then because he had a bad credit rating after a property development went bust a few years earlier, I took out a credit card in my name but gave it to him. He said he paid it off every month by direct debit. Then a few weeks ago, on a Saturday when he said he was in London working, a statement arrived showing that he'd only paid off the minimum amount and was ten thousand pounds in debt – mainly cash withdrawals. I called and gave him an ultimatum, told him that I wanted my money back or the wedding was off. He acted all hurt and devastated and said as soon as he finished his very urgent business he'd come straight over.'

She blew her nose. 'He turned up about seven that evening, full of apologies, saying that he hadn't wanted to worry me, but there was a "snafu" in cash flow so he'd used the credit card to draw money to pay suppliers – "I had to, Amy, because I knew how important it was to get the project done and dusted so we can get married."

'I'm so stupid, so utterly stupid, I fell for it. He stayed the night and somehow he talked me round. Sounds pathetic, but he was so convincing, full of plans for our future. He even suggested giving the baby a Spanish name. I was blinded by the thing I wanted most.'

Her face crumpled with the loss of her dream. She was trying to pretend that it didn't matter, that she was silly to have wanted it in the first place. But I understood her. The death of the future you took for granted, especially when with hindsight, you should have noticed huge red flags whipping up a hurricane, was a particularly nasty type of pain, laced with anger about your own ability to lie to yourself.

I got up and pulled her into a hug. Her sadness at not having children plugged right into my despair about not being able to provide for mine. Soon we were sitting there wailing and snotty, clinging to each other in the wreckage of our lives. Eventually, Amy fetched two mugs of tea and some chocolate biscuits – 'If ever there was a day for chocolate, I think today is it.'

Over tea, she told me how Robin left to finish his urgent work in London early on the Sunday morning: 'I've got a meeting with a guy who's come over to discuss increasing his role on the Spanish project'.

'Of course, I questioned why he had to do that on a Sunday – but apparently he'd cancelled dinner with him the night before so he could come home to me. "I couldn't leave you in that sort of state, could I?" I felt grateful, relieved even, took it as proof that he was committed to me. But then my friend Em popped in that morning.'

Amy took a bite of biscuit and carried on. 'Em had been at the Italianate Glasshouse in Ramsgate the day before and spotted Robin. Em's a work colleague and she'd only met him once when he picked me up from our studio. She wasn't sure it was him until she heard Cath say his name. She took this photo.' She pulled out her phone and showed me a picture of Cath and Robin holding hands and leaning in towards each other.

'How did she bring up that little nugget in conversation?' That was a good friend indeed. I wasn't certain whether I'd have the balls to turn up at a mate's house and start waving about pictures of the husband-to-be canoodling with another woman.

Amy gave a sharp laugh. 'Her husband went off with her best friend, so she's got a low tolerance for that kind of thing.'

'Did you recognise Cath?'

'No, I had no idea who she was. It was an absolute punch in the gut.'

I could barely stand to witness the pain on her face but I needed to get a handle on the whole story. 'How did you find out where Cath lived then? Surely Robin didn't tell you?'

'It turned out to be ridiculously simple. Em and I did a bit of digging on Google, found a group photo of them both at a conference where she was giving a workshop. Once I'd found that, it was quite easy to track her down from the Companies House website.'

'So then you came steaming straight along the motorway to Surrey to be met with the obstructive housekeeper, who wanted you out of there as soon as possible.' I winced at the memory. 'I'm so sorry. But threatening to stop him marrying Cath was the only leverage I had to get my mother's money back. I'm desperate – I'll bore you with that story another time, but Mum and I really need that cash. I couldn't let you mess it all up by alerting Cath.' Understanding darkened Amy's face. I felt a flash of shame, as though she was contemplating my obvious self-interest. I pushed on. 'Did you ever confront Robin?'

'Yes, but you can imagine what a cock-and-bull excuse he came up with: about her being a colleague who'd just lost her mother. She was supposed to be at the dinner on the Saturday night, but when he cancelled it to see me, he suggested that she came with him to get some sea air in Deal. Apparently, she was so distressed that he tried to cheer her up by taking her to the tea garden and in the photo he was merely comforting her. I longed to believe it, but I knew. Even gullible old me couldn't deny that the day after the picture was taken and he'd spent the night with me, he'd rushed off the next morning to his supposed "meeting". He'd promised to phone me later on, but his mobile was switched off and I didn't hear anything for a couple of days. Can you imagine? I'd had a huge row with the man I wanted to marry over a ten-thousand-pound debt, then he'd been photographed all over another woman and disappeared. I couldn't lie to myself any more.'

Although it was tempting to say, 'No shit, Sherlock,' I had some sympathy for her. When Graham was busy sticking the house up as a guarantee for his burger business, I'd chosen to ignore the nagging feeling in my stomach that he wasn't telling me the whole story. Far easier to shut my eyes and hope that if I didn't see it, it would somehow fix itself.

Much to my delight, Amy decided this wasn't a day for calorie counting and came back with some Victoria sponge. With every sugary hit, my thoughts drew closer to revenge. 'Have you managed to get him to pay off the money he owes on the credit card?'

Amy avoided my eye. 'No, because it was in my name. Credit card companies don't care about marital disputes. Don't ask me about the loan I gave him for the business because I think you know what the answer will be.'

'What an utter bastard. Do you think he's marrying Cath with the intention of divorcing her at some point to get half of her money?'

Amy sighed. 'I don't know. Robin is so persuasive and credible. I know my story sounds like something out of one of those sensationalist magazines where a rich pensioner marries a twenty-year-old waiter in some far-flung country and is astonished when it turns out that he was only interested in her money, but Robin has that way of making you feel that you are the most unique person, not just in the room, but in the whole world. He remembers details about everyone, logs it all away to charm initially, then exploit later.'

I nodded. 'I know what you mean. When I first started working for Cath, I'd sometimes forget what he'd done because he was so nice, much friendlier than Cath, brought me little pastries when he popped down to the baker's – "We can't have you wasting away."'

Amy lifted her hair off her neck. 'In the end, though, that charismatic attention to detail was his undoing. The reason Em recognised him when she saw him at the Italianate Glasshouse was because when he met her at our studio, he'd recalled everything I'd said about her in passing. That she was a single mum, even that her son's name was Nathan, which I'd probably only mentioned once. He'd really stuck in her mind.'

I made a mental note that if I was ever ready to dip a toe into the dating water again, I'd go for one of those surly but salt-of-the-earth types who only had eyes for me. And right behind that thought was Sandy... No. No men. Just a big lolloping dog to keep me company. I'd still have to deal with shit, but at least I could bag it and bin it.

Amy drummed her fingers on the arm of the chair. 'Even if he does love Cath, he was still here, having sex with me barely six weeks ago. That's not going to end well for her, is it?'

'But they're getting married in a fortnight's time.'

Amy stood up. 'We'd better not mess around then.'

34

REBECCA

For the first time in ages, I felt high on energy, giggly and giddy, as though Amy and I were setting off on some gun-toting expedition in the Wild West rather than targeting a posh area of London to have a frank and meaningful with Robin's ex-wife – the one he'd apparently managed to divorce twice in a three-year period.

We got quite hysterical as we drove into Fulham in the late afternoon, coming up with outlandish ideas of what we might find at 29 Sartre Street. 'I reckon we'll find rooms of wedding dresses that have never been worn.'

Amy laughed. 'I could take them back to my studio and set up an offshoot styling brides. Or perhaps we'll find fifty-five women called Moira Franklin living in Robin's cult.'

'Maybe he's fathered twenty-five children,' I said. Then immediately I wished I could rip my tongue out. 'Amy, sorry. I got carried away with trying to be funny.'

'Don't worry. Can you imagine what it would be like to have a child with him?' But sadness mottled her face and the air went out of the frenetic hilarity in the car.

'Is that it?' I asked as we stopped outside a house, the sort where chauffeurs, basement gyms and deliveries of white lilies were the norm. I craned my neck and stared at the entrance. 'There are two bells by the door. That probably means it's divided into flats.' This was the point where my idea of a flat and the one in front of me were poles apart.

There was a big For Sale sign attached to the wrought-iron railings. 'Well, at least he was being truthful about trying to sell it,' Amy said, her face flashing with hope, as though there was still an explanation that would mean Robin hadn't conned her completely, that he was still intending to reimburse her, even if he wasn't going to marry her.

I couldn't be too judgemental. I'd been the same gullible idiot, believing that cheeseburgers and fried onions were going to make us millionaires. All I'd had my heart set on was a reliable car that meant I wouldn't have to do a dance to the MOT gods every year. Times that by a thousand if what you longed for was a baby. I could see how your brain might find hundreds of reasons to refuse house room to any doubts that stood in your way.

We parked up the road. Amy poured pound after pound into the meter. I shuffled about, feeling like the biggest freeloader on earth, the woman who drank tap water in a pub but double vodkas if someone else was at the bar. 'I'm sorry. I don't have anywhere to live at the moment, so I'm a bit tight for money.'

She frowned, then half-smiled, as though 'nowhere to live' meant I didn't really like my little flat or I was waiting to complete on a new house and lodging with family until then. 'Where are you staying then?'

'The past two nights, in the spare room of some bloke who left toenails on the sink.'

As we walked, I explained a bit more, treading a fine line between not making her feel obliged to give me a bed for the night and backing her into a corner so that not offering me the settee would be downright heartless.

When we reached the house, she asked, 'How do you manage to stay so positive?'

'Hate is keeping me alive.' I smiled as her eyebrows shot into her hairline and said, 'Right. Let's knock on this door then.'

I couldn't help feeling that Amy was more likely to get a result. A scarf that brought out the blue of her eyes. Wide-legged trousers with those fancy trainers that on me would have looked like I was about to shimmy up a rope in a school gym but on her were like an advert about how to dress down a work outfit for a casual dinner.

Amy turned to me. 'What if she doesn't know anything about Cath? What if they're not actually divorced? What if she goes mad and calls the police?'

I didn't know whether it was bravado, anger or feeling that I didn't have much further to fall, but I marched up the steps to the front door and studied the names on the bells. I rang the one that said Franklin. A distant chime echoed somewhere inside the building, the sort of noise that I associated with summoning servants.

Amy hung back behind me. We waited. I couldn't hear any movement. I felt that odd flat sensation of being geared up for a fight and the opportunity slipping away. I stepped back to see if there was any sign of life.

'There's no one here.' I moved to peer inside, as though some evidence of Robin's double-dealing would be sitting on a table by the window. But as I was debating whether Amy would draw the line at giving me a leg-up, the intercom crackled. Amy bent towards it and gave her name, but there was no reply, just a buzzing, then it went dead. We stood looking at each other. 'What happened? Shall we ring again? There's obviously someone in.'

While we debated, the entrance door opened and an elderly

woman stood there, leaning on a stick, her knotted fingers
dotted with fancy rings that didn't look as though they'd slip off
over her knuckles any time soon.

'Sorry about that. The intercom is playing up. Can I help
you?'

Amy stepped forward. 'So sorry to disturb you. I was
looking for Moira Franklin?'

The woman tucked a long strand of white hair behind her
ear, her lined face dithering between suspicion and welcome.
'I'm Moira Franklin.'

Amy was far more tactful than me. 'Oh. I'm not sure if I'm
in the right place. I was after the Moira who's married to Robin
Franklin?' – whereas I was all agog thinking it was a turn-up for
the books that the smarmy old toad had a wife who was at least
twenty-five years his senior.

A shadow darkened her face. 'There isn't a Moira Franklin
married to Robin here.'

I gathered myself. 'Do you know a Robin Franklin?' I pulled
out my phone and scrolled through my photos. 'This man?' I
asked, thrusting my mobile towards her.

'I can't see without my glasses.'

I could sense the door about to close in our faces. I nearly
put my hand on her arm, but it occurred to me there might be a
panic button just inside. 'Please, this is really important.'

'Is he in trouble?' There was a catch in her voice, something
between resignation and defiance. But definitely not shock, not
'I've no idea why someone with Eddie and Megan tattooed on
their forearm is standing on my steps asking about Robin'.

Then it came to me. It was the eyes. Although Moira's were
hooded with age, the blue of them faded, her eyebrows sparse,
she had the same direct gaze as Robin.

'Are you his mother?'

A deep haze of sadness passed over her features. 'I haven't
seen him for years.'

'I promise we're not here to make trouble, but can we ask you a few questions?' I said.

Amy wheeled out her most refined voice and those words that rich people relate to about not wanting to 'cause distress' and 'how grateful' we'd be. I wondered if I'd ever be able to learn this language that meant people trusted you, when all she'd done was say exactly the same thing as me but in some posh code that I didn't seem to have the hang of. It did the trick.

Eventually, Moira led us through one of the two doors in the entrance hall and up a beautiful staircase. Despite her uneven shuffle, she was elegant in a way that I'd never be able to mimic. Some people could wear cardigans and skirts and even old woman's sensible shoes and still blend in at the Ritz.

We sat in what she called the drawing room as Amy explained that there'd been a 'little misunderstanding' about money with Robin. I couldn't help myself. It wasn't the best way to go about squiggling information out of her, but my mother's two hundred grand was a long way from a 'little misunderstanding'. I let out a snort.

'Has he stolen from you?' Moira asked.

I came to appreciate that part of Amy's job as a stylist was suggesting alternative realities. As she gently told Moira the bare bones of her story, the extra mortgage, the credit card debt, I could quite imagine her saying, 'The pale blue is a lovely colour on you but something even more striking might be better.' While I admired Amy's tact in delivering bad news, I couldn't help feeling that the real implications of Robin's behaviour were being buried under the avalanche of her good manners.

'What Amy's trying to say is that Robin stole a lot of money from her and my mother and pretended he was going to marry them both. In a fortnight, my boss is expecting to marry him because he's supposedly divorced a "Moira Franklin". He's been borrowing a ton of cash from her while he waits for this house to be sold and he can pay her back.'

The old lady brought her hand to her mouth. 'He will never get a penny from this house. I'm selling it to pay for a flat in a care home complex. I can't do the stairs any more' – she indicated her stick – 'but whatever is left over is going to my daughter.'

Amy said, 'I thought Robin was an only child.'

Moira twisted a ring round her finger. 'He's the youngest of two.'

I felt bad putting this classy old lady through the wringer. Telling us the truth would take its toll, risking the judgement of two strangers not being able to separate Robin's behaviour from her qualities as a mother. Even though I was a mother myself and fully aware that bringing up children was far from an exact science, it took me a few minutes to rein in the whole 'wow, your parenting took a wrong turn, and guess what, I'm allowing myself a smug moment'.

Once she started though, Moira couldn't stop. 'My husband was a charmer. He was in the army, away a lot. Just like Robin, full of tall tales, with a good excuse for why he'd been unfaithful, master of the big gestures to make amends, promising it wouldn't happen again. He was a bully to the kids, full of sunshine and fun one day, then spiteful, cold and critical the next. My dad encouraged me to leave him back when divorce was shameful. "Moira, it's a simple choice. Save yourself or let him take the three of you down with him." I didn't know anyone else who was divorced. I was frightened of being ostracised. But I did it for my kids.'

She pulled a handkerchief out of her sleeve and dabbed her eyes.

'It was too late for Robin. His father had already infected him with that odd restlessness that meant he could never be satisfied. They needed everyone to adore them, to admire them, to see them as somehow superior, the best, the bravest, the richest.'

Amy was all, 'Don't upset yourself, I'm sure you did your best.' I both envied her for her kindness and wanted to hustle her out of the room before she killed the conversation. I was firmly in the mode of striking while the iron was hot and gathering every little detail into the armoury of weapons I intended to turn on Robin.

'Why did you fall out with him?'

She did what any mother would do. Paused for that split second to overcome the love that refused to die, that need to forgive ingrained from the first day children stand with chocolate round their mouths and outright lie about not going near the biscuit tin. But she got there. She dug into the place in her heart where she had accepted she couldn't go back, that she could never risk that level of vulnerability again, where she'd learnt to save herself.

'He pretended to help me out with my dad, who had dementia. Robin was adamant that we shouldn't put him in a home, that we could look after him in his own house with some help. Carers popped in throughout the day and one stayed overnight. I thought Robin was amazing, visiting several times a week and singing with him – Dad loved all the old songs. It felt as though after all the years of drama, of Robin never quite finding his niche, starting businesses, relationships, hobbies, you name it, and losing interest after the initial thrill, that he was proving that he was an honourable man. I thought he'd found a purpose.'

Moira stopped, closing her eyes for a second. She leaned her chin on her hand. When she looked up again, her eyes were watery, but she ploughed on. 'Dad kept grumbling about stuff going missing. We blamed his dementia. But he had a pocket watch that my mother gave him the Christmas before she died. Even when he didn't know my name or how to put his socks on, he kissed that watch every night and said, "Love you, Penelope, sleep tight." Of course, I didn't want to believe it was Robin. I wished on every star it would be one of the carers. I wouldn't even have gone to the police; I'd have just been so grateful to get it back.'

I never intended to feel sorry for this woman. I wanted to stay furious that the little boy she brought into the world had grown into a horrible man who'd marched through all of our lives, taking everything he fancied and never had to pay the price.

But I could tell she was a decent person.

Amy was all hand-patting and 'Can I get you a glass of water?' To be fair, I was also worrying that we were causing Moira so much stress she might fall apart, but my need to know won out. 'So was it Robin?'

Moira seemed to be looking over my shoulder, as though she was replaying scenes in her head from long ago. 'Lorna, my daughter, was always on Robin's case. She thought he was a total waste of space, a user, the sort of man who never did anything without wondering what was in it for him. I thought she was too harsh, possibly even part of the problem, putting him down so he lost confidence in himself. Behind my back, because she knew I would never agree to it, she asked the carers what they thought had happened. Two of the three were too scared to say anything, but the third woman, who had a real soft spot for my dad, said she'd returned unexpectedly to fetch her umbrella one day and overheard Robin asking my dad where his will was. On another occasion, she'd caught him going through Dad's wallet and he'd muttered something about sending his driving licence back to the DVLA as he wasn't safe to drive any more.'

Amy said, 'None of that proves that he took the watch.'

Moira managed a tiny, resigned smile. 'No. It doesn't. But after pleading poverty for months, even asking me to pay his petrol, he was suddenly turning up in designer shirts, waltzing in with bottles of champagne saying he'd pulled off a fantastic deal at work.' She massaged the knuckles of her right hand. 'The thing that really gave him away though was how he kept dropping little snippets into the conversation designed to make me mistrust the carers. He's the master of undermining people.'

She did a delicate little sniff. 'In the end, I couldn't ignore what the carer told Lorna. She begged me never to have any contact with him again. She told me to cut them both out of my will, to leave everything to charity if it meant that I would stop giving Robin any more chances. She kept saying, "Let him go, Mum. He's not going to change." So I did. I gave up on him. I haven't seen him in over ten years.'

'But I overheard my boss say he'd come into the house a few weeks ago? She waited outside while he supposedly went in to persuade his wife to agree on a financial settlement.' She'd been very definite when she was on the phone to Jax.

Moira frowned. 'He'd only be able to get into the communal entrance hall. Lorna made me change the lock to our front door years ago. When was this?'

'Beginning of July maybe?'

Her face sagged. 'I've got a timeshare in a hotel in Dorset then. I've gone every year for the last forty years. He knew I wouldn't be here.'

There was a pause while we all considered the scenario of Cath lurking in the street outside while Robin skulked about in the foyer.

Moira's high cheekbones quivered as she gave in to sobs that were surprisingly loud considering her genteel manner. She grasped Amy's hand. 'I'm glad you didn't have children with him. No good would have come of it.'

Although she was probably right, Amy wasn't quite ready to embrace those good tidings. I ended up scooting off to grab some kitchen roll to mop her up as well. Even in these circumstances,

I obviously hadn't fulfilled Moira's dainty handkerchief vision of life and she pointed me in the direction of her downstairs cloakroom to find the 'tiss-yous'.

By the time we said our goodbyes, we were all exhausted. As we walked to Amy's car, my voice sounded as though I was slurring. 'Will you come and see Cath with me?'

Thankfully, she agreed immediately. 'No time to waste. We should go tomorrow.'

'We'll have to go to her office if you don't want to see Robin,' I said.

'Sure. Let's get it over with first thing in the morning. Shall I pick you up?'

'I've left my car at yours, remember?' My heart sank at the thought of sleeping in it.

'Oh, I'd forgotten that.' She gasped. 'You haven't got anywhere to stay, have you?'

'No, but I'll work something out.' I'd have to kip in the car. I couldn't wait for Liz to get back from holiday so I could beg a settee for a few nights without worrying about accidentally leaning on the horn at three in the morning or waking up to find a face pressed on the window. Not to mention creeping out in the dark if I needed a wee before dawn.

'Would you like my spare room for tonight? I won't be offended if you don't feel comfortable staying in a stranger's house,' Amy said.

I was still wearing the pride I couldn't afford like a badge, so I replied with a restrained, 'That would be fab, thank you,' when really, I wanted to explode with gratitude that I wouldn't be spending all night checking the wing mirrors for masked men with crowbars.

I hated what the fear of being homeless was making me become. I ate too much at dinner, stayed too long in the shower taking full advantage of Amy's 'Help yourself to shampoo and towels and anything else you need.' I considered stealing one of her loo rolls but gave myself a talking-to. I even had the cheek to be disappointed when we finished the first bottle of wine and, despite some indiscreet eyeing of the rack in the corner of the kitchen, Amy sensibly said, 'We should go to bed, so we can get to Cath's office for 9.30.'

My mind whirred around the best way to convince Cath a) of my stealing innocence and b) of Robin's stealing guilt. Hot on the heels of that came the question of how I'd ever have my kids living with me again. The waiting list for a council flat was well over two years and I wasn't a priority. And underneath all those concerns swirled the realisation that despite my original inten- tion to worry about my own family rather than Cath's, I couldn't live with myself if I let Robin bulldoze through their world as he had ours.

Tomorrow would be a day to remember, whichever way it went.

35

CATH

I leaned over the banister to see how Sandy was getting on with the new greenery displays in reception. Although he'd been working in landscape gardening and plant maintenance for years, part of me still thought of him as that ten-year-old goal-keeper who fluffed four saves in a row before falling face down in the mud and bursting into tears. He was so confident, fixing a new trellis to the walls, moving pots around until he was satisfied. I craned my neck to see who he'd stopped to greet with great enthusiasm.

From my viewpoint, I could make out the back of someone with short brown hair and a taller blonde woman. Sandy flung his arms around the smaller of the two and shook hands with the other one. They chatted for a bit and then Sandy gestured upstairs. As the women turned, I recognised Rebecca and all the pride at witnessing my son totally in control of his craft shrivelled away as I prepared myself for confrontation. Maybe that was her lawyer, though I'd never had a contract with Rebecca. My mind was racing through the criteria for unfair dismissal and, simultaneously, flicking through my contacts for legal help I could call on.

As Rebecca and her companion made their way towards the lift, I ran down the stairs, reaching them before the doors opened. 'Rebecca, hello. What brings you here?' I left off the 'You've got a cheek turning up here,' but it was burning in my throat.

Unusually for Rebecca, she was apologetic rather than quietly defiant. 'Yes, sorry to butt in when you're at work, but I – we – really need to talk to you.'

'We? This is—?'

The other woman was very polished, slick. 'I'm Amy. I'd like to add my apologies for disturbing you at the office, but it's rather important that I speak to you.'

I probably failed to sound sincere. 'I don't want to be rude but I haven't really got time for this. I'm trying to tie up loose ends before I finish work next week.'

Rebecca threw her hands up in frustration. 'Cath, you have to listen to what Amy has to say.' That was the Rebecca I recognised. Straight-talking, direct and unflinching in a way that made me feel bizarrely intimidated given that she'd been lucky that I hadn't called the police on her and I was standing in the reception of a business I owned.

I smothered my instinctive reaction of 'I'm not sure I need life lessons from the person whose existence is a thousand times more chaotic than mine'. The urgency in her voice pierced my arrogant belief that nothing Rebecca had to say to me was critical. 'I've got fifteen minutes before my next meeting.'

'We'll be out of your hair before then,' Amy said. 'Is there a quiet corner where we could have a quick chat?'

She reminded me of a school nurse used to calming down hormonal teenagers.

I showed them into the meeting room next to reception. Rebecca sat down and, after looking at me for permission, Amy followed. I stayed standing. 'What can I do for you?' That well-used phrase actually meant the opposite: 'How soon can I get rid of you?'

Amy took a breath and said, 'I've been in a relationship with Robin for the last few years. We were supposed to get married, but he was struggling to finalise his divorce from Moira.'

I'd often wondered how I would react to bad news. I suspected that initially I would go into problem-solving mode, quickly clicking into next steps, doing what I could to mitigate the immediate disaster. But it was as though the words were rushing over me, sweeping away the future I thought was mine, snagging and grabbing at the dreams and hopes and desires that had made me so vulnerable. I stood blinking, trying to pull this new world, this sphere of deceit, into some kind of focus. I had the sensation of being caught in a crowd of strangers, whirling around, while I searched frantically for the people I came with so I could find my way safely home.

Amy seemed to wind down, as though the spiel she'd been determined to deliver was not only playing havoc with my reality, but hers as well. She said it twice – 'Moira is his mother. Not his wife. There is no wife.'

I put my hands on my hips. 'No. I saw the solicitor's letters, the divorce papers, everything. He went into the house in London. I was there. They were negotiating their settlement.'

But for everything I used to refute her claims, to cling on to the notion that bad things like this didn't happen to good people like me, Amy had a counter-argument. She offered to compare diaries to prove that when Robin wasn't with me, he was with her.

'How do I know you're not conning me, rather than Robin?'

Pity didn't so much flash across her face as drench it. My gut told me she was kind and honest. She didn't want to tell me more than I needed to know. She was hesitating, working out how to lay the truth onto a soft fleece and dull its impact.

'Just say it.' Everything in me was hollow and dazed.

'We'd had a row because he'd run up a huge debt on my credit card and I'd given him an ultimatum. He needed to come and calm me down, but I think he'd planned a weekend away with you and ended up combining the two? Did he bring you to Ramsgate, or somewhere near? My friend saw you at the Italianate Glasshouse.'

'We stayed in Deal.' Despite my searching for another, far more palatable explanation, everything was falling into place: the last-minute swap from Herne Bay, his insistence on going to Ramsgate rather than strolling round Deal, why he wouldn't sit on the beachfront where we could be seen. The row over my drinking. The whole thing engineered to give him a reason to walk out and spend the night with Amy.

Then I felt it. The strength of betrayal. The white-hot heat of being played for an idiot. Of fretting away in my hotel room, my imagination running riot while he was gallivanting with this woman in front of me.

I sat down. 'I'm supposed to be getting married two weeks tomorrow.'

'Have you lent him money?' Amy asked.

It was too late to save myself from any humiliation. 'I've paid everything for the wedding because he's waiting to sell the London house.'

An undercurrent of 'Are you going to tell the poor deluded fool, or shall I?' passed between Rebecca and Amy.

I screwed up my eyes. 'Presumably that's the house where you've just visited his mother?'

Slowly, I sieved my way through the shares I'd bought in his company, the bills I'd paid. With every new thought, new revelation, I felt the ground I'd walked on with such certainty, such confidence, crack and crumble. I didn't cry. I held on, so numb that I wondered if I'd ever have another emotion – good or bad – again.

How life taught us the things we refused to learn ourselves.

The number of times I'd sat smugly judgemental, marvelling at how my female friends allowed their men to have a say in how they dressed, what they spent, when and where they went, positive I'd never be that woman. But, in the end, I was no better than anyone else. Worse actually, because I'd let Robin take priority over Mum and Sandy. I'd stuck my head in the sand and built a castle around it rather than heed any of the warning signs. What did that say about me? Was I desperate for a man? Stupid? Or was he so incredibly clever at manipulating me? I didn't have the answer to that.

However, I wasn't as frozen as I thought. The unmistakable sense of shame at how I had treated Rebecca scorched through my body, the image of her trying not to cry as she left with her children ripped at my conscience. I lifted my chin. 'I'm sorry I thought you'd stolen from my mum and that I didn't believe you when you were trying to protect me.'

She grinned and in her typical forthright manner said, 'Apology accepted.'

There were amends to be made. But first I was going to stage a fightback.

36

REBECCA

I'd always found Cath intimidating, a woman with a proper handbag packed with proper things – lipsticks, spare tights, nail file – instead of the debris I kept in mine – old hairbands, the odd hairy mint, random napkins that I picked up in case of a snot/sick emergency. But in the wake of the Robin disaster, she'd shed that veneer of someone who delivered conversation in efficient chunks as though wasting words was for losers. Seeing her on the back foot made her so much more likeable.

It was a measure of my mean little spirit that I took great joy in witnessing the slinging out of Robin. I did, however, recognise in Cath that same defeat that I'd felt when my marriage failed. Amy and I sat in the garden, our conversation stilted, unsure about whether we should even be there, observing this very private unravelling of Cath's life. She hadn't wanted to confront him on her own though, so here we were, glimpsing Robin passing the landing window with his arms full, then trailing through the kitchen with holdalls, dangling ties and shirtsleeves. The sound of Cath screaming at him to hurry up and get out, her voice full of tears that she hadn't yet given in to, made me wince. Anger was holding her together for the moment, but bone-crushing pain couldn't be far behind.

Amy took the initiative and went into the kitchen to see if Cath was all right. I still felt a bit more 'staff' rather than 'confidant' and wasn't sure that Cath would need me as an onlooker, so I hovered awkwardly on the patio.

Eventually, Amy re-emerged with her arm round Cath's shoulders and guided her to the table.

'Has he gone?' I asked, just as Robin appeared at the French windows and stormed over to us.

'I'm going now,' he said, throwing his keys on the table. He was the picture of total bemusement. 'You'll regret not believing me over these sad women whose lives are so empty that they have to cause trouble in someone else's. I loved you, Cath. I do love you.'

Robin was the ultimate showman. He delivered this intimate declaration with no embarrassment about Amy and me all agog a couple of feet away.

Cath tensed beside me, a connection between them that she was battling to break. Hats off to her that she pulled calm and strong words from somewhere. 'I won't regret anything, Robin, not even that I wanted to believe the best of you despite all the many opportunities I had to see the truth. I am capable of love, of honesty, of being a trustworthy human being. I also know you are not.' She waved her hand around our little circle. 'And these women know it too. And although you'll think you've won in some perverse and sorry little way, I genuinely have people who love me, and you, I don't think do.' She stalled, as though she didn't have enough air to finish what needed to be said.

Amy stood up. 'I second everything Cath says. Now get out.' I nearly let a nervous giggle escape but managed to bite my cheeks and squash it back down. Amy glanced over at Cath for permission and took a step forward.

Robin scowled. 'You're the bouncer now, are you? Far cry

from showing women how to put on a scarf so they don't look so fat.'

Oddly, it was that arrogance, the act of putting down decent women instead of falling on the floor and apologising that finished me off.

'Oh fuck off, Robin. Your mother won't even acknowledge your existence because your behaviour is so disgusting.'

'Leave my mother out of this.' He still had the gall to snap at me.

'Why? What are you going to do if I don't? Swindle me out of my millions?'

With one accord we all moved towards him, although I wasn't quite sure what we intended. I had no problem getting physical, but Cath and Amy were a bit too manicured to be manhandling Robin out the door. Happily, with one last sneer, he turned on his heels and stalked out.

We all sat in a moment's silence as the front door banged.

Cath was working so hard to look like she could see the funny side. I didn't want to patronise her and she was so scarily clever that I wasn't sure that I could add much value. I was grovelling about trying to find the right way to say, 'You don't have to put on a brave face, this stuff is really awful and you're going to feel like a total idiot, but you're not the dickhead, he is. You were just a woman trying to catch a break, which made you forgive a few things that you should have examined a bit more thoroughly.'

Thankfully, Amy pulled it all together in an elegant bouquet of words.

She reached out and squeezed Cath's hand. 'There's no disgrace in wanting to find love, Cath. We can make endless compromises and justify all manner of things when we love someone. And Robin is probably the most charming man I've ever met.' Her voice wobbled. 'While Robin was choosing bridal bunting with you, I was fantasising about what our son or daughter would look like. I hoped they'd have the same magnetism as Robin.' Her gaze rested on the fairy lights and triangles strung throughout the trees. 'I was no better than you. I interpreted all the delays to marrying me as good fortune that he wanted to do things in the right order, a sign of his commitment. I didn't question all the occasions he was supposedly "in Spain", all the times he went up to London to try to talk some sense into "Moira".'

Cath looked up sharply. 'Do you think he wasn't in Spain then? What about the property development he's doing out there?'

Amy's face scrunched then softened. 'After I got the credit card bill, I went on Companies House to check out the company. It was dissolved five years ago.'

'You're not getting muddled up with a previous one, are you? When I invested, he gave me actual shares. He was confident that I'd make a good profit in the end and...' Cath's voice petered out. 'He probably printed the share certificates off the internet, didn't he?' She pinched the bridge of her nose. 'What a mug. Honestly, if someone else was telling me this story of handing over fifty grand to someone they'd only just met...' Despite her attempts to make light of it, her eyes filled. She swiped at the tears running down her face, leapt to her feet and shot off up the garden.

I hovered between envy that she had fifty grand to spare and awe that she sounded quite philosophical about it. I was sure that at some point, she'd say that thing that rich people said, 'It's only money. No one's died.' I'd have to watch out that I didn't become one of those people who started every conversation with a chippy 'It's all right for you.'

Cath reappeared with a couple of bottles of champagne and said, 'I'd got four crates in for the wedding and this feels like a great time to make a start.'

I couldn't fault her style and I certainly felt obliged to help out.

We sat there for several hours, doggedly making inroads into the booze, while Amy and Cath raked over the details of their time with Robin until I felt I'd missed out on a pivotal bonding experience.

We'd got to the stage of the evening where Amy had lost the air of someone who never left her gloves on a train or tripped up a step. She suggested a swim in the pool. Given that a few hours earlier I'd been feeling as though Cath was about to say, 'Put that champagne down and go and find the bleach', it still felt a bit odd to throw off my clothes and take a dip in my bra and pants, which were nowhere near as classy as Amy and Cath's. Although I knew I'd have the fear big time the next morning, my champagne brain was daring and defiant. That came to an abrupt halt when Sandy triggered the floodlights, stopped dead and said, 'What on earth is going on?'

Cath scrambled up the steps, grabbed her towel and ran towards him, while Amy and I scuttled off to the tennis pavilion.

We dried ourselves and got dressed, hovering on the edge of the sort of funereal hilarity that develops when you just can't cry any more.

Amy pulled herself together before I did. 'I can't drive home. I've had too much to drink.'

I started laughing. 'And I haven't got a home to go to.' But somewhere in the midst of my side-splitting banter, my heart began aching for Eddie and Megan and I sank down onto the settee, one step away from the beer tears that I always made the mistake of thinking alcohol would ward off.

Amy was patting my hand and suggesting I have a lie-down. 'I'm sure Cath won't mind if you have a little sleep here tonight.'

Before we got any further, Sandy appeared at the door of

the pavilion. 'Mum's gone to bed. She's rather worse for wear. Am I right that the wedding's off?'

Amy sounded surprisingly coherent given that she'd drunk as much as me. I had to keep one eye closed to focus. She filled him in, graciously tolerating me skipping ahead with the things that, in my opinion, showcased Robin's guilt.

Sandy was muttering obscenities about Robin as though we were two delicate damsels who'd fall on the floor if he turned up the volume. He beckoned to us. 'Right, neither of you is in a fit state to go anywhere tonight, so I suggest you stay here. The beds are made up in the spare rooms.'

I hadn't expected to be ''promoted to one of the fancy bedrooms in the main house. ''S'all right. I'll just sleep in here.'

Sandy looked at me with exasperation and amusement. 'I'd be worried you'd wander out and fall in the pool.' He pulled me to my feet, staggering backwards as I swayed.

Amy was more of a practised lush than I'd given her credit for. Despite her not holding back on the fizz, unlike me, she managed to exit the pavilion without getting tangled in table legs, tennis racquets and – embarrassingly – Sandy. I steadied myself by grabbing his belt, which led to a joke about me only having to ask if I wanted to see him naked. That sounded like something I could enjoy, but, luckily, my brain was too slow to formulate the words to say that out loud.

He steered us up the stairs, sorting out bedrooms and finding toothbrushes for us. Even through my champagne-addled fug, I was impressed. Graham couldn't find a loaf of bread in the freezer without a diagram.

I was just stripping off my T-shirt when there was a knock on the door. 'Hang on a minute.' I leapt under the duvet and pulled it up to my neck.

'I've brought you a glass of water,' Sandy said, putting it down on the side table. 'I'm not sure it's worth having this conversation now because you'll probably have forgotten by the morning, but I wanted to say thank you for stopping Mum making an awful mistake. I wondered why you'd come to her office earlier.' He grinned. 'Lovely as it always is to see you, though.'

'I don't deserve thanks.' The booze was making my head cloudy and heavy. I forced myself to concentrate. One thought was thrumming around my brain: I couldn't let Sandy think I was better than I was. 'I wanted to get my mum's money back. Robin stole off her too. I nearly didn't tell your mum what had been going on. I'm sorry. So sorry. I almost let her marry him. It was the only bargaining power I had, threatening to tell Cath what I knew and putting a big old spoke in Robin's wheel. She could have lost loads more money.' My eyes were filling with tears as the alcohol ripped the lid off my failure to make Robin pay, coupled with my regret that I'd been prepared to throw Cath under a bus to achieve justice for Mum and a bit of respite for me.

Sandy patted my shoulder. 'I know, Mum told me. But even she acknowledged that she didn't want to listen to anyone. When you confronted her, she didn't believe you, did she? She was dead set on marrying Robin. You were in such a difficult situation. I've seen how hard you're trying to hold it all together for your kids. It's easy to take the high moral ground when you've got plenty of options. And anyway, you're nicer than you think – you drew the line at letting Robin steal from Mum to pay you.' He smiled. 'Better late than never.'

'Don't be nice to me. Really don't.' But it was too late. I couldn't stop the tears leaking down my face.

Sandy plonked down onto the bed. 'Hey. Get some sleep. We'll talk about it all in the morning.'

I sniffed. 'Will she get any of the money back that she's lent him?'

'Maybe the police will be able to do something. If I can persuade her to make a statement. I think she's pretty mortified at being taken for such a ride, to be honest.' Sandy paused. 'Also, I'm sorry she jumped to the conclusion that you were the one who stole Grandma's jewellery. I never believed it for a second if it's any consolation.'

'It is. Thank you.' I leaned back on the pillows, reaching for the box of posh tissues on the bedside table. 'What's happening with you and Chloe?' I wasn't so drunk that I couldn't imagine how nice it would be to kiss Sandy, though even I could see that my snotty face wasn't the best offer he'd had all week. All year even.

He stood up. 'That's a story for tomorrow. Goodnight.'

'Goodnight, unless you wanted to stay up and chat for a bit?' In that moment, the longing to cuddle up with someone, not for sex – though that definitely held some appeal – but to share the warmth of another human, to not feel so alone, was nearly my undoing.

Sandy saved me from myself. 'It's bedtime. I'll bring you a cup of tea before I leave for work.'

There was enough firmness and promise in his voice that I stayed where I was. Thirty-six and I still needed other people to make the good decisions for me.

37

REBECCA

Six weeks ago, at the beginning of September, when Cath had turned into the driveway of a huge house in the avenue parallel to her street, I'd forgotten myself for a moment and sworn in surprise. 'When you said he was looking for someone to house-sit, I didn't think I'd be moving into a mansion. It'll take me all my time to find Megan and Eddie at teatime.'

I couldn't say any more because of the lump in my throat, the relief that I could finally stop lying awake hour after hour worrying about both the immediate need to find somewhere to live and the long-term necessity of becoming stable enough to have joint custody of the kids. Right there in double-glazed, double-garaged glory was my breathing space, my chance to get myself back on my feet.

'Do you like the look of it?' Cath had asked, as though I had choices, as though one glimpse of a garish paint colour or in-your-face wallpaper and I'd be turning it down. I chose to think that she was just being polite, or doing that thing of pretending to ask a question but actually fishing for a big grateful reaction. She was going to get the reward she was after if that was the case.

I'd patted my chest and tried to steady my breathing, as silent sobs suffocated me. I finally got the words out. 'It looks amazing. I can't believe that he's paying me to live here while he's in America.'

'I told him what a brilliant housekeeper you are and how lovely Eddie and Megan are.'

'Thank you. Thank you very much.'

Cath had directed her gaze to the steering wheel. 'It's me who should thank you. If it hadn't been for you, I would have ended up in a right pickle.'

Although I'd gone along with Cath's thanks and her insistence on finding accommodation for me, I was weighed down with a burden of guilt, unable to shake off the idea that I didn't really deserve her help. I kept trying to talk about it but she brushed me off. I didn't know whether it was out of embarrassment at being sucked in by a fraudster or that she'd doubted my trustworthiness. But I did know that before I could properly accept that she'd found me somewhere to live for at least a year, negotiated what felt like a fortune in salary and was still paying me to look after Dolly, I couldn't keep glossing over it.

I leaned back against the head rest. 'Cath, I have to apologise for not coming clean with you much earlier. You've been very generous but I'm really ashamed of how selfish I was. I suppose, if I'm honest, I was so fixated on organising a new home that I took the easy way out and told myself you'd be all right whatever happened.' I hesitated. I had to get it out into the open. 'Because you had money.' It felt so shallow saying it aloud.

Cath raised her hands. 'Don't even think like that. I had loads of opportunity to work it out for myself – literally everyone was stacking up the warning triangles – Jax, Sandy, Dan – and I chose to ignore them all. It wasn't up to you to stop me making a huge mistake.'

'But I had targeted your house so I could get close to Robin.

Abused your trust really.' My whole body was cringing with the effort of not backing away from what I needed to say. I didn't expect her to understand completely but I needed her to know that I wasn't that person, that circumstances had trapped me into behaving in a way I wouldn't normally.

A burst of sadness washed over Cath's face. 'I don't have the energy to be angry about that when what Robin did was so much worse. I never thought I'd say this but it was a good job you did winkle your way into my house. Otherwise I'd be married now and he'd probably be in the running for half of everything I own in a few years' time.'

She twisted round to face me. 'I still have my own guilt about accusing you of stealing. I'm truly sorry about that.'

My turn to wave a dismissive hand. 'Water under the bridge. Robin was the expert at smoke and mirrors.'

Her face relaxed and she hopped out of the car. 'Come on. Let's go and look at your new home. A fresh start for you all.'

I really hoped it would be. We'd already agreed that I shouldn't go back as Cath's cleaner. She'd sold it to me as feeling that it was better for us both to move on. 'To be honest, I'd rather have someone new who doesn't know all the history and with housesitting and looking after Mum, you've already got enough on your hands.' I was slightly insulted, but also thankful to dodge the awkwardness that our relationship had now crossed into different territory. It would be hard to go back to 'which duvet cover would you like me to put on the spare bed and can you buy some more limescale remover?' when we'd shared such an intimate insight into each other's lives.

Part of my disappointment about not being reinstated had less to do with the job and far more to do with bumping into Sandy on a regular basis – him apologising for dirtying a shower I'd cleaned, the banter between us as he trailed mud over a floor I'd just mopped, the occasional coffee break with him. I'd cheered up when I discovered he'd won the contract to do the garden at my new pad while Cath's client was abroad. He'd grinned when he told me. 'I'm going to be there twice a week. Do you think you'll be able to make me a cup of tea?'

He'd been so kind to me the morning after the champagne/bra and knickers swimming debacle by telling me that I'd been funny and 'sweet' rather than the drunken idiot leching all over him that was probably far nearer the truth. Every time he came near me, I wanted to breathe him in, that combination of masculinity and gentleness that made me forget about teapots and milk jugs and focus far more on what he would look like with his shirt off. But fear of making a fool of myself, of losing Sandy as an ally and friend, a steady anchor in the stormy sea of my chaotic life, made me stand-offish. I couldn't risk trouble, couldn't destabilise the solid base I hoped to give Megan and Eddie while I figured out what came next.

Mainly I managed it, though I still had an indecent interest in what was happening with his wife. I'd find myself asking leading questions about what he'd been up to at the weekend, if he was planning any holidays. It was like sprinkling fish food on a pond and waiting for a rare koi carp to surface bearing the definitive piece of knowledge that would either kill my hope stone dead or, far more riskily, turbocharge it into an ill-advised move.

My first priority, however, was to make sure my kids knew I was a mother they could rely on totally. On the day that Graham had driven them up to the house, I'd been a bag of nerves, as though I needed to be more than their imperfect mother who loved them, sometimes grumpily, sometimes distractedly, often so completely it was hard to know where I finished and they began. The thought of folding them into me, my fingertips recognising every part of them, as familiar as my own face, made my heart feel airy and light.

The reality, of course, was something in between. Eddie ran up and down the garden, racing Megan until she got bored, then timing himself until he was so worn out, he'd cried. Megan was more subdued, waiting till Eddie had gone to sleep to snuggle up next to me on the settee. She wangled hot chocolate out of me, but paid me back in diamonds when she held my hand and said, 'I missed you every day when we were at Dad's.' I managed not to spoil the moment by grilling her about how she'd got on with Chelle.

Over the month and a half that we'd been living there, we'd slowly settled into a routine and the one weekend in two when they'd go off to their dad's – as Cath had said – began to be less traumatic. I even appreciated time on my own. Despite all the bargains I'd made about loving every single minute with Eddie and Megan if 'I could just get them back', I hadn't factored in that I would still get tired and stressed, so I was sometimes glad to flop in front of the television without anyone wanting anything.

There was no denying that weekends dragged without them though, which made Sandy's gardening visits on a Saturday a beacon of excitement that I wouldn't have admitted to anyone. I hared around getting all my chores out of the way so I could faff about making myself presentable in case Sandy turned up. With any luck, he'd think that was the real me, rather than the staggering, belt-grabbing boozy woman who'd asked him to – wink, wink – stay up and chat for a bit. The memory of that was still enough to make me blush every time I saw him.

One gloomy weekend in November I got up to the sort of rain that made me feel like spring was five years away. I was staring out of the window wondering whether Netflix would blow up through overuse when I spotted Sandy done up like an astronaut in his wet-weather gear carrying the ladder to the rear of the house. God knows what was so urgent that he had to risk being swept to his death in a torrential downpour. I crept upstairs to spy on him but came face-to-face with him at the top of his ladder in the first bedroom I went into. He knocked on the window and gestured to me to open it.

'Sorry, should have said I was coming. The owner texted me ages ago about clearing the gutters, but I forgot all about it until now. Thought I'd better get on with it in case all this rain caused a leak or flood somewhere.'

I was practically dangling out of the window so I could hear him. He was leaning in sideways to avoid the torrent of water hammering down from the gutter. It was the closest we'd been to each other since that night by the pool. I was slightly higher than he was. With the rain sweeping his hair off his face, my whole focus was drawn to his eyes. For one mad moment, I was tempted to hang out an extra couple of inches and kiss him.

He clambered a bit further up the ladder, saying, 'If you've got time, I'll love you forever if you make me a cup of tea and bring me a towel when I've finished. An hour or so?'

I tried not to be that woman. The one who heard what she wanted to hear. But, of course, I nipped into my bedroom, had a quick squirt of deodorant and dug out the perfume Debs had given me for my birthday. I then panicked that I'd be exuding the giveaway smell of hope and desperation. I rubbed at my neck with a towel and scooted back downstairs, lighter on my feet despite the stern words I was having with myself.

I spent the next hour peering out from behind curtains to check he was still up the ladder and hadn't decided to stash his tools and disappear. By the time he finally rang the bell, shrugging out of his waterproofs and shaking on the doorstep like a wet dog, I was exhausted with nerves and on the verge of being short-tempered and irritable.

'On your own today?' he asked.

'Yes, the kids are with Graham. I'm loving the peace and quiet, to be honest.' I didn't want to sound like a sad loner-loser.

'I won't stay long.'

'I didn't mean that. Even antisocial old me can stand company in the time it takes to drink a cup of tea.' Honestly, if this was the extent of my friend-making, let alone my flirting skills, I'd better stock up on jigsaws.

Sandy ruffled his hair, flicking about little droplets of water. 'Do you mind staying in this big house on your own?'

'No. Oddly enough, after not having a house at all, I've decided not to mind having five bedrooms and three bathrooms.'

'Sorry. Stupid question.' He blushed, proper all over radiating heat red.

He looked so mortified that I laughed. 'Don't be silly. I'd have probably said the same if I hadn't understood what it looks like to run out of options. I've got Robin to thank for throwing me a lifeline.'

'What do you mean? He stole all your family's money.'

'True. But, because of that, I stopped your mum falling into the same trap and then she sent the karma right back round to me and found me this place.'

Sandy shivered. I scrabbled about for something I could do to make him stay. 'Shall I get you a blanket?'

'No, it's fine, I'll just sit over here by the radiator.'

My turn to blush. 'The heating's not on.' Even though I was living rent-free, I was terrified of how much the heating might cost and ran it on a strict hour in the morning, hour in the evening basis, piling on jumpers in between.

Luckily, Sandy had enough nous not to question why I was sitting in a cold kitchen on a rainy winter day. 'A blanket would be great, thanks.'

I ran upstairs and pulled the duvet off Megan's bed.

Sandy made himself at home on the big settee in the corner of the kitchen, stretching his arms behind his head and pretending to go to sleep. 'I could get quite comfortable here.'

'Do you want some toast?' I had a sudden memory of Cath mentioning that his ex-wife could make an 'exquisite' beef bourguignon. Pah. That was a common old beef stew with mushrooms. I'd raise him a bacon sandwich with brown sauce and show him what he'd been missing.

Giving myself something to do seemed to right me. It was easier to chat when I wasn't looking at him. I handed him the toastie with a flourish. 'There you go.'

He took a bite and rolled his eyes back in mock delight. 'That is good. I'll come here again.'

'I might invite you again. Though, strictly speaking, you invited yourself.'

The air hummed with that sense of leading towards something, of one conversation about bacon sandwiches and a different one on a whole other level bubbling along below it. It felt like an adult version of Grandmother's Footsteps, with both of us taking it in turns to tiptoe towards Grandma, ready to turn into a statue at any moment and act as though nothing was happening.

All too soon, Sandy was standing up and making noises about getting home before he took up any more of my time and I stood there like an idiot, wanting to hang on to him, to stop him leaving. I plastered a smile on my face and walked him to the door, passing his boots, asking myself if I'd imagined that spark between us. But I couldn't think what to say or do that would leave me with a grain of dignity if I was reading it all wrong.

We dithered at the door with both of us going, 'Have a nice weekend' and the classic from Sandy, 'I might need to pop in next week to cut back the wisteria. It does benefit from a good winter prune.'

I felt like a teenager whose friends had been whispering that the guy she fancied kept looking over at her, only to watch him ask another girl to dance. I did a last wave and shut the door, loneliness drifting in where laughter and warmth had been a few minutes earlier.

I marched over to the sink and banged about washing up. I

wiped the table down with more elbow grease than was necessary and switched the telly on, flicking through the channels until I landed on *Grease*. I wasn't sure I was in the mood for someone else's romance succeeding against all odds, but singing 'Greased Lightnin'' paired with the dance moves seemed to offer a slim possibility of avoiding total despair.

I was in full flow with the pointing action when there was a knock on the window. I snapped my hand back to my side. Sandy was doubled up laughing. I stomped to the door, gearing myself up for instructions about not forgetting to put the olive trees into the sunroom if it looked like frost.

He leaned against the door jamb. 'Well, that was a sight for sore eyes.'

I sifted through for my least offensive retort. 'Shut up.' Embarrassment made me abrupt. 'Did you forget something?'

He directed his gaze to the floor. 'You?'

I narrowed my eyes, flicking through all the various ways I could misunderstand one simple word.

He looked up again. 'Sorry to interrupt the John Travolta moves but—' He screwed up his face. 'Oh sod it. I'm just going to say it.'

I stood there waiting for a few moments and then said, 'Do you want to come back in before you catch pneumonia?'

He stepped in, right up close to me. Shyness was crippling me. I dropped my head down and he moved in until my forehead was resting on his chest. 'Rebecca. I'm thinking that there's a little bit of something going on between us.'

As always, I had to spoil the moment. 'A little bit? Is that all?'

He pulled me right into him until I had to look up and meet his eyes. 'Well, I wasn't sure how you'd react to a great big declaration. I'm keeping it manageable here.' But he was smiling. And then he wasn't smiling because we were kissing and my heart was filling with sunshine totally at odds with the rain outside.

I should have had more faith that good times would come again.

38

REBECCA

I'd never understood before what it was like to have time rather than every moment being a rearguard action to avoid the wheels coming off. So instead of approaching Christmas on a count-down to exploding with stress, I was ahead of the game. I had a proper budget for presents. No Graham squeaking in at the last minute having blown a hundred quid on 'an extra little some-thing for the kids'. Nothing that would require batteries we didn't have and someone to put it all together on Christmas morning while the children got bored and wandered off. I genuinely hoped that the kids wouldn't miss him too much. Now I wasn't so strung out about where I was going to live, I could see that he was a good dad, despite being a shabby husband. Over time, that had made our discussions more civil, if not friendly.

A couple of weeks before Christmas, Sandy had asked if I'd like to join him, Dolly and Cath with the kids for Christmas Day.

'Did your mum suggest that?' I was still looking for evidence that Cath was sending all the vibes up into the universe that her son would not end up with her ex-cleaner. I'd only bumped into her a couple of times since I'd moved out when I'd been over at Dolly's. She'd seemed genuinely pleased to see me, though neither of us had mentioned Sandy.

Sandy pulled me into a hug. 'She did. Stop looking for problems where there aren't any. She's happy if I'm happy.'

I hadn't expected to get invited to Cath's, so I'd already told Debs to come over with Jase and the baby. I'd been ungrateful when we'd stayed with her earlier in the year and it was a chance to build some bridges. Megan and Eddie loved Sophia, so I was hopeful that would help defuse the whole hideousness of the first Christmas without Graham. Debs had leapt at the chance. 'I was wondering how I was going to cook with Sophia refusing to be put down.' She'd paused. 'You'll have to invite Mum. We can't leave her on her own.'

'Of course. I was going to,' I'd said, immediately feeling annoyed that my sister didn't credit me with the kindness to include Mum automatically. I wasn't such a hopeless daughter.

When I told Sandy that I had arranged for my own family to spend the day with us, he threw his hands in the air in mock despair. 'So you'll be partying here while Dolly watches every musical going, Mum pretends she's not looking at work emails and I'm getting slowly sloshed on the mulled wine?'

'We can spend New Year's Eve together. Get over it. It's just one day.' And, to be honest, I was a bit relieved not to have to sit at Cath's table watching my own Ps and Qs, let alone making sure Eddie didn't sneeze into the potatoes or Megan knock over one of her crystal glasses. I would have loved spending Christmas with Dolly though. Even if I wasn't exactly what Cath had in mind for Sandy, Dolly was over the moon. 'Precisely what he needs. Someone without all them la-di-dah ways, down to earth, not afraid to eat a KitKat without a blinking lecture about how chocolate causes an insulin spike.'

I had to laugh that my value to Dolly was my ability to scarf down a chocolate bar without a second thought.

She carried on. 'That wife of his couldn't have a custard cream because it upset her stomach, wouldn't eat after five o'clock because she was doing a two and eight.'

Dolly was confusing her cockney rhyming slang with what I'd heard about Chloe's strict 16–8 fasting, but I didn't correct her.

On one of my visits to keep on top of the tins of hot dog sausages, the collection of money-off vouchers – 'Dolly, when do you think you're going to need fifty pence off a box of tampons?' – and have a general clean, Dolly started reminiscing. 'I miss them Christmases we had when I was young. We invited all the cousins and kids and neighbours and any old Tom, Dick and Harry that didn't have a place to go. My mum was brilliant at making a little bit of anything go a long way. We'd all get up and do charades and sing and the little ones would end up kipping under the table.' She looked at me. 'Such a pity we can't all spend it together. Seems a nonsense, you being in one house with your family while we're in Cath's big old place, just the three of us.'

I'd always been a soft touch. The words burbled out before I'd engaged my brain. 'Perhaps you'd all like to come to me? It will be my sister and her family and my mum as well.'

Dolly clapped her hands as though I'd rustled up a brilliant idea all on my own, while I had an overwhelming desire to back-pedal and say, 'No, no, that will be so stressful and I really don't want Cath thinking that because my roast potatoes never go crispy that means that I'm a rubbish partner for her son.'

However, the idea gave Dolly so much pleasure that it was almost contagious. She immediately trotted off to dig out her *Christmas with Val Doonican* CD and told me to look in the guest-room wardrobe – 'I bought some snow globes in the January sale at that funny little gift shop behind the station. You can have them.' That translated as getting rid of her own clutter and transferring it to my house, but there was an outside chance

Megan might like them, so I dug through all her bargains to find four snow globes. 'Only £1.49 each, reduced from £10!'

To my surprise, and also to my horror, Cath welcomed the invitation with what Dolly described as 'gusto'. So instead of rocking up to the big day with my simple schedule of 'turkey in the oven, get Mum to lay the table, make sure the Queen's speech is on record', I had to add in 'prat about with make-up and try on everything in my wardrobe before discarding it as too common, too casual, too cleanerish'. In the end, I decided that no one was going to dictate how I dressed and put my jeans on. Mum filled me with confidence by saying, 'Are you getting changed?' just as they arrived.

Thankfully, Dolly was so overexcited at being able to instruct Alexa to play any song she liked – 'Alexa, play – Cath, who's that bloke, Michael someone,' that we got distracted by a new Christmas game of 'Guess which song Dolly wants'. Sandy lowered the tone by asking Alexa to play 'Fairytale of New York' and cemented himself in Eddie's affection forever by singing all the rude words.

While I shook the roast potatoes, which apparently only needed a quality oven to crisp up beautifully, Debs chatted to me, fed Sophia and whispered questions about Sandy. 'You've fallen on your feet there. Don't suppose you'll have to cram onto my settee again.'

Since where I was going to live had dominated everyone's thoughts for so long, I couldn't blame her for assuming that I'd seen a meal ticket and snatched it up. I let the season of good-will wrap itself around me and restricted myself to saying, 'He's a really lovely man.'

Debs said, 'I can see that. He adores you, doesn't he?' so I let her off.

She disappeared to change Sophia and Cath wafted in, all glamorous trousers and flowing sleeves. 'How are you? You look so at home here. Is it all working out well?'

My need to impress the mother of the man I really liked made me so awkward and tongue-tied. I took refuge in talking about how the kids were settling down into a better routine and how I was finally managing to save some money. 'It's been lovely to be able to give Mum a break from where she lives. She feels like a queen when she's staying here with her own bathroom.' I found myself prattling on about any old rubbish, to avoid dealing with the tricky subject of Sandy, hanging uncomfortably between us. Finally, I ground to a halt. 'That was a bit of a longwinded answer. I love it here, thank you. And I'm glad you've all come today.'

As I said it – against a backdrop of Eddie repeating the worst parts of 'Fairytale of New York' at the top of his voice – I realised that I was. It was good to be part of a noisy, chaotic family. There was nowhere else I'd rather be than in that kitchen, right then, with Dolly and my mum shouting, 'Play John Denver! Play Dean Martin! Play Bing Crosby!'

Her cool soft hands squeezed my arm. 'Sandy's really happy with you.'

I so did not want to get into this conversation. I made a show of stirring the gravy. 'I'm glad to hear that.'

'What I'm trying to say is, I'm so pleased he's found you.'

I turned to look at her. 'Do you mean that?'

'I do. I really do.' And, for the first time, I saw, mother to mother, that although I probably only ticked a few of her original boxes on the checklist of 'Qualities I require in the perfect partner for my son', she'd realised that all the things that make us happy distil down into just a few. Maybe my bar was very low, but if my kids were fine and I could get out of bed without having to struggle through a big black cloud of worry, I'd choose that over a fancy holiday or a flash car any day.

As the afternoon wore on and the kids moved off to watch the television, the conversation inevitably turned to Robin. The steady flow of wine led to Mum and Cath competing for who'd been taken for the biggest fool. Cath admitted that when she contacted a lot of the wedding day suppliers, Robin had been adding twenty or thirty per cent onto their prices and making a profit. 'Some of them he hadn't even paid at all. No doubt he's laughing all the way to a hammock in Antigua by now.'

But Mum wasn't going to be outdone. 'I met Robin on a dating website and after it all went wrong, I discovered he'd paid his new subscription on my credit card.'

I couldn't help it. I burst out laughing. The cheek of the man. I almost admired him for his gall. Thankfully the Sauvignon Blanc meant that Mum was seeing the funny side of everything and didn't take offence. She was bonding in the most unlikely way with Cath, who was the friendliest I'd ever seen her. Cath said, 'Who knows whether he was really intending to marry me? Maybe he was preparing to do a moonlight flit again.' She sounded as though she was trying to make light of it, but her words were sore and raw.

Mum reached out and squeezed her hand. 'You keep reminding yourself what a good person you are. How lucky you are that you're not rotten to the core like him.' They nodded at each other intently, understanding passing between them with that surge of comfort that comes from the painful privilege of recognising the exact ache in the other person's heart.

Sandy kept glancing at me conspiratorially. Knowing that we were managing our mothers together filled me with inexplicable warmth. Debs and Jase were eyeing the proceedings as though they'd landed slap-bang in the middle of the set of *East-Enders*, while Dolly took every opportunity to say, 'I'll drink to him ending up in prison' and necking back another glass of Baileys.

At some point, Cath turned to Mum as though they'd been best friends for years and said, 'I wouldn't put it past him to be on dating websites now.'

It didn't take long for Mum to insist that Cath look on the

most popular websites to see if he was on there. The rest of us lost interest as they hunched over Cath's phone. I started doing that Christmas thing of 'Who'd like a chocolate? A mince pie?' even though we were so full from lunch we were barely capable of waddling through to the sitting room.

Suddenly both Mum and Cath shouted out, 'There he is!'

Cath read his profile out loud. '"Me: Sincere, charming, solvent, educated. Work hard all week so I can spend weekends planning trips away with you. Not interested in playing games, just connecting with someone who wants to enjoy life and live in the moment."' She smacked her palm on the table. 'Solvent! Solvent on my money! Enjoying life on the cash I gave him for shares that didn't even exist!'

Mum carried on, '"You: Honest, straightforward, career-minded, adventurous." I suppose career-minded means he's looking for someone rich. I can't bear the thought of him pulling the same stunt on someone else.' She murmured the rest, finishing with: '"Don't be lonely, come and have fun with me!"'

'In the New Year, we're going to the police,' Cath said. It was the right thing to do, but I dreaded all the joy going out of today with Mum spending the rest of the evening putting forward the flimsiest excuses about why that wasn't going to happen.

But before I knew it, her hand shot out to grab Cath's. 'Shake on it. It's a deal.'

I raised my eyebrows at Sandy. The water that Mum had always insisted was under the bridge was about to swirl back. The question that remained was who it would knock off their feet and who would swim away unscathed.

Right there, right then, I was not going to bet on the outcome.

39

KRISTA

This year I didn't care that my sister was sporting a Victorian locket that – what do you know? – her perfect 'hubs' happened to pick up at a little antiques fair. I could just about raise a smile at Mum leaning in and whispering, 'Your turn will come, darling. Mr Right is out there somewhere for you.' I didn't even mind that, yet again, I would be spending New Year in a roomful of couples, cringing at the awkward pause at midnight when I'd hover on the sidelines as everyone kissed their other halves. My friends almost seemed embarrassed to hug their husbands because it underlined that this was the fourth time in a row I'd shown up without a man in tow since my marriage had blown up on a bonfire of his affairs.

But, this year, I was hugging my own little secret to me, not ready to share with the world yet, not prepared for their scrutiny.

I knew he was something special from the first time I met him. Gentlemanly. 'I think it's better if we have a coffee during the day. It must be quite intimidating meeting a stranger when it's dark.'

He'd pulled my chair out, been charming and polite to the waitress – 'no rush, we're quite happy here', ascertained whether or not I was pressed for time: 'I don't want to keep you, but I could sit here and listen to you all day.'

We'd swapped war stories about our marriages. I'd been very careful to be clear that I'd moved on, that John's infidelity had done me a favour. 'I could have wasted many more years of my life on him.'

He wasn't quite baggage-free – 'I'm getting there. The divorce is through, just the house sale to complete now, but that should be any time soon and then I'm footloose and fancy-free.' He'd laughed and dropped his eyes, almost shyly. 'I do miss being part of a couple though. I love travelling, but I find the joy has gone out of it slightly, you know, simple things, not being able to hold out a glass of wine and say, "Try this", not sharing a sunset or a stunning mountain range with someone else.'

After John thinking he was the consummate romantic if he suppressed a belch after dinner, I couldn't help but feel a glimmer of excitement that I might finally have found a man who combined a career as a go-getting property developer (I had visions of telling my friends that we were off to Marbella for a long weekend) with an appreciation of nature and the small but important things in life. Every time I thought about next year, my mind delivered a picture of us sitting in a beachfront restaurant, the sun dropping towards the horizon, this handsome man reaching for my hand and doing that thing he did so well: making me feel like I was the woman he'd been waiting for.

It had been a long time coming, a difficult search, but incredibly, my mother had actually been spot on. Mr Right was indeed out there. It had only been three months, but as soon as all the festivities were over, he was going to move in to my home. I'd present my friends and family with a fait accompli because I didn't want all their words of warning taking the edge off my joy. Yes, it was fast, but there comes a certain point in life when you have to trust your own judgement. Robin was the perfect match for me and I didn't see any point in wasting a single minute.

Happy New Year at last.

A LETTER FROM KERRY

Dear Reader,

I want to say a huge thank you for choosing to read *The Woman in My Home*. If you did enjoy it, and want to keep up to date with all my latest releases, just sign up at the following link. Your email address will never be shared and you can unsubscribe at any time.

www.bookouture.com/kerry-fisher

This story was partially inspired by an article I read in a newspaper about a woman who thought she'd found love and after more than a decade realised she'd just found a conman. The thing that struck me most was that she was intelligent, successful and confident, yet she'd made endless excuses for the increasingly manipulative behaviour of the man she loved. It set me thinking about the times friends I've loved have been involved with men I haven't trusted. When I was younger, I would voice this (and cannot recall that ending well, ever). Now I'm older, I've learnt that no one can be told unless they're ready to hear – and I also understand that we all have different lines in the sand as to what is unacceptable. But it still fascinates me that people seem to adore partners who are deeply unpopular with everyone else.

Alongside that, I'm interested in how adult children react to their parents finding new partners. It's such a complicated dynamic, with some children heaving a sigh of relief that they don't have to carry the total responsibility for parental happiness, while others feel ousted from a family unit that – in their view – didn't need anyone else. And, of course, every emotion in between.

At some point in the plotting process, I became taken with the idea of a cleaner observing other people's lives as a dispassionate outsider, as well as the unequal balance of knowledge. A client might know very little about the cleaner's life, but every bin, every desk, every bedroom tells a story. Cleaners have an intimate knowledge of the house's inhabitants, in a way that even close friends don't. I was only half-joking when I wrote in this book that a reality TV programme where a psychologist analyses what cleaners discover about their clients would be compelling. Who knows what they'd make of the heap of unmatched socks residing in a basket on my landing?

Ultimately, however, I was drawn back to the idea of families – the bonds that bind, bend and sometimes break. As always, I enjoy exploring the intricacies of motherhood – when my children were little, I naively believed that they would get to eighteen and I could more or less stop worrying... rather disappointed that this has not proved to be the case! This time, I also wanted to examine the tricky stage when a child starts to become the parent and has to tread the complex line between supporting an elderly relative versus causing resentment by interfering in how they live their lives.

I'll finish by saying – again – that one of the biggest privileges of my job is receiving messages from people who've enjoyed my books. I don't know whether lockdown has prompted more introspection, but I've had so many messages over the last year in which readers have shared their own very personal stories sparked by something they've seen in one of my novels. That's a very generous act of trust. Thank you.

I hope you loved *The Woman in My Home* and would be

very grateful if you could write a review if you did. I'd love to know what you think, and it makes a real difference in helping new readers to discover one of my books for the first time.

I love hearing from my readers – you can get in touch on my Facebook page, through Twitter, or my website. Whenever I hear from readers, I am reminded why I love my job – your messages never fail to brighten my day.

Thank you so much for reading,

Kerry Fisher

www.kerryfisherauthor.com

facebook.com/kerryfisherauthor
twitter.com/KerryFSwayne

ACKNOWLEDGEMENTS

Whenever I come to the final (glorious) stages of completing a novel, I always think about naïve me, gaily writing my first (and deservedly unpublished) book and expecting it to be snapped up immediately. I had no understanding back then of the crucial role of an editor, but ten novels later, I certainly do now.

This book, in particular, required a lot of clever input from my editor, Jenny Geras. I love working with her, on both a personal and professional level. She has a wonderful ability to pinpoint what's needed but then trusts me to get on with it – I have total faith in her judgement and that's a rare and special thing.

I'm also privileged to have the whole of the Bookouture team working their magic to make the finished product the best it can possibly be, including (but I'm sure, not limited to) the editorial manager, copy editor, proofreader and cover designer. Special thanks to Alexandra Holmes for her world-class grammatical knowledge – I do love a person who has a definitive rule for every rogue apostrophe or hyphen! Thanks also to the wonderful publicity team – Kim, Noelle, Sarah and Jess. I will never be able to fathom how you cover so much ground.

I am, as usual, hugely grateful to Clare Wallace, super-agent, calming influence, wise guru on all things publishing (life too, actually) and all-round top human.

But I couldn't finish my acknowledgements without saying a massive thank you to all my readers – you are the best cheer-leaders. And also to everyone who chips in on my Facebook page, offering their expertise on the many random questions that could easily trip me up in a book but would take me days to pin down on Google. I appreciate it enormously.

Finally, my family for keeping things in perspective. I don't think I was ever going to start believing I was a legend in my own lunchtime, but the astonished tone in which my kids deliver the information that a friend's mum has read one of my books 'and really liked it' makes me laugh every time. You're the best.

Printed in Great Britain
by Amazon